BEACON STREET GIRLS

This book belongs to:

VERITAS AMICITIA GAUDIUM
truth friendship fun!

Be sure to read all of our books:

BSG Special Adventure Books:

Coming soon:

BEACON STREET GIRLS

Crush Alert

BY
ANNIE BRYANT

ALADDIN MIX
NEW YORK   LONDON   TORONTO   SYDNEY

A special thanks to Aliza Rosen

ALADDIN MIX
Simon & Schuster Children's Publishing Division
1230 Avenue of the Americas, New York, NY 10020
Designed by Dina Barsky
The text of this book was set in Palatino Linotype.
Manufactured in the United States of America
4 6 8 10 9 7 5 3
Library of Congress Control Number 2008936277
ISBN-13: 978-1-4169-6437-7
ISBN-10: 1-4169-6437-1

Who's Who

BSG

Katani Summers
a.k.a. Kgirl . . . Katani has a strong fashion sense and business savvy. She is stylish, loyal & cool.

Avery Madden
Avery is passionate about all sports and animal rights. She is energetic, optimistic & outspoken.

Charlotte Ramsey
A self-acknowledged "klutz" and an aspiring writer, Charlotte is all too familiar with being the new kid in town. She is intelligent, worldly & curious.

Isabel Martinez
Her ambition is to be an artist. She was the last to join the Beacon Street Girls. She is artistic, sensitive & kind.

Maeve Kaplan-Taylor
Maeve wants to be a movie star. Bubbly and upbeat, she wears her heart on her sleeve. She is entertaining, friendly & fun.

Ms. Razzberry Pink
The stylishly pink proprietor of the "Think Pink" boutique is chic, gracious & charming.

Marty
The adopted best dog friend of the Beacon Street Girls is feisty, cuddly & suave.

Happy Lucky Thingy and alter ego Mad Nasty Thingy
Marty's favorite chew toy, it is known to reveal its alter ego when shaken too roughly. He is most often happy.

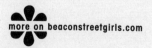

more on beaconstreetgirls.com

Part One
The Big Crush

1

Dream Date Dilemma

I think Mondays are just horrible!" Maeve pronounced with a dramatic flourish as she munched on her tuna salad sandwich and glanced around the table at her friends. The Beacon Street Girls, otherwise known as the BSG, sat in the cafeteria together as they did every day at Abigail Adams Junior High. Chaotic sounds of kids laughing, talking, and eating filled the lunchroom, mixing with smells of pizza, hamburgers, and French fries.

"Don't worry, Maeve. Lots of people hate Mondays," Charlotte chimed in as she popped a potato chip into her mouth. "Even me, and I love school!"

Charlotte gave a little shiver as she thought about how she'd snuggled down in her covers this morning after the alarm went off. She would have liked to stay there the entire day, reading, scratching Marty (the official BSG mascot) under his chin, and drinking hot chocolate.

But her dad had come in, urging her to "rise and meet the day." He wasn't a Monday morning person, either, but when it came time for them both to get going he would sometimes sing Charlotte out of bed in a loud, off-key, operatic voice. Today had been one of those mornings.

"I love Mondays . . . especially this Monday!" Avery exclaimed. "We're having a pickup soccer game after school today."

"In February?" Isabel asked.

"Hello! Haven't you noticed the warm spell we've been having?"

"Ahh." Maeve let out another dramatic sigh and stared at her soggy sandwich. "Well, in *my* very personal opinion, Mondays are the worst! Starting with those pop quizzes Ms. O'Reilly gives us in social studies. I mean, really, who can face a pop quiz at eight o'clock in the morning?"

Katani shook her head, her gold hoop earrings swinging from her ears. "Maeve, did you stay up late watching reality TV again last night?"

Maeve gasped. "I had to find out what happened to Chad and Lara!" She shook her red curls in disgust. "Besides, how can I learn how to become a great actor if I don't watch great actors?"

Avery hooted, "Maeve! Get real. Chad and Lara aren't actors! They're just paid show-offs."

Maeve giggled. "You're right, Ave. But Chad is sooo cute."

Isabel took a bite out of her apple and chewed thoughtfully. A strand of dark hair fell into her eyes and she flipped it aside. "Seriously, I'm not a big fan of pop quizzes either, but I think I like Mondays too. I'm always more inspired at the beginning of the week. That's when I'm most creative and I do my best artwork. I'm all relaxed from the weekend, and I feel pumped for a new challenge."

Maeve leaned forward on her elbows, her eyes sparkling with mischief. "Okay, guys. Enough about Mondays. Let's discuss something much more interesting. Like Fridays. Like *this* Friday in particular—*hello*, everybody—the Valentine's Day Dance! I just can't wait!"

All of a sudden, her hands flew to her chest. Maeve, the "great" actor, was off and running. "I mean, it will be just like that old black-and-white movie where the girl goes to the dance and meets the prince in disguise. He falls in love with her and she has no idea that he's royalty. It's with this English actor named Sir Laurence Olivier. Doesn't that name sound lovely?" Her eyes danced as she waved her sandwich with excitement.

"Loverly," mouthed Avery at the other BSG.

"Well, I agree with Maeve. The dance is going to be totally *maravilloso!*" Isabel said, beaming at her friends. "I can't wait. I came in early this morning with the decorating committee to hang up the posters we designed last week." Isabel's artistic skills were famous at AAJH, so it was no surprise to her friends that she'd been asked to help make posters.

"So," a determined Maeve continued. "Has anyone thought about who they'd like to go to this *marvelous* dance with?"

There was silence at the table. "Ms. Ramsey," Maeve said, staring pointedly and holding a fake microphone under Charlotte's nose. "Inquiring minds want to know:

What *are* your thoughts about a certain dreamy, popular, handsome boy with the initials NM?"

A rush of pink flooded Charlotte's cheeks as her friends exploded into giggles. "Nick's just a friend," she mumbled, secretly wanting to throttle Maeve.

Undaunted, Maeve folded her arms, raised her eyebrows, and smiled coolly. "Next! How about our dear friend Katani? Who should she go to the dance with?" Putting her finger to her cheek, Maeve turned to face her sophisticated friend.

"That's easy," Isabel chimed in, wiping her mouth with a napkin. "Reggie. Ever since he gave her that rose at the science fair, that boy's been talking to the Kgirl every chance he gets. It's like he's in L-O-V-E," she spelled.

"He is not," Katani protested, but fought back a smile while struggling to keep her famous Kgirl cool. Reggie, aka Math Boy, was cute. In fact, he was downright adorable, especially since he had given up the geek look for preppy. And just last week he had left a funny card taped to her locker.

"Talking doesn't mean we're in love or anything, but the boy does have style now." Katani brushed an imaginary piece of lint from her black shirt—a shirt she'd bought at the used-clothing store, ruffled the collar, and voilà: her creation looked fresh off the New York runways!

"Better watch out, Katani," warned Charlotte. "The romance queen, here"—she nodded at Maeve—"is pelting everyone with love arrows!"

On cue, Maeve shot an imaginary arrow at Isabel.

"Ladies and gentlemen, this lovely lady here might already have a date to the dance!"

Isabel wadded her lunch bag into a ball and looked around the table at her friends. "Really? With who?" she asked, feigning innocence.

"Kevin Connors," the other BSG chimed. Kevin was Isabel's *special* friend—a rather sensitive artist type who had also just happened to be one of AAJH's all-star athletes. The two of them had been hanging out ever since Kevin stuck by Isabel when the Queens of Mean were spreading untrue rumors about her a couple months before.

Isabel permitted herself a tiny smile but refused to comment. She was going to love every minute of the dance whether Kevin went with her or not, just because she would be there with her friends. But it *was* fun to imagine whom each of the BSG might go with. She turned the spotlight back on Maeve. "Okay, Ms. Entertainment Reporter for AAJH. Now it's your turn. Spill! Who's your dream date?"

Maeve bit her lip, looked around to make sure no one was in earshot, and confessed. "Dillon . . . of course. He's the cutest guy in school."

Katani groaned and threw her hands up in the air. "Girlfriend, you think half the boys at Abigail Adams Junior High are the cutest."

"Yes, that's true," said the aspiring movie star, flipping her hair over her shoulder. "But Dillon is the cutest of the cute!"

"Maeve, you're one of a kind," Katani pronounced, the rest of the BSG nodding in agreement.

Maeve slurped the last drop of her strawberry milk, then leaned forward to ask the one BSG who had been flicking peas into a milk carton goal for the whole conversation what her plans were. "Okay, Ave. Fess up. Who will have the honor of escorting you to the Valentine's Day Dance?"

Avery shrugged as she sent a pea flying across the room at Billy Trentini. "I dunno," she answered while ducking the piece of Fig Newton Billy sent back at her. "I just want to do what I always do . . ."

"And," chorused the BSG, "see what comes up!"

Avery gave her friends her signature thumbs-up. They knew she was the kind of girl who liked to go with the flow.

Maeve shook her head. "Avery, but this is different! It's the Valentine's Day Dance! You'll be, like, the *only* girl in this school who doesn't care who she goes with."

"No big deal." Avery shrugged, popping a piece of cookie in her mouth. "Besides, I won't be the only girl without a date."

When her friends continued to look at her skeptically, she leaned back in her chair and stretched her arms above her head. "Seriously," she said, gesturing toward a table of boys who were all watching to see how many Fig Newtons Billy Trentini could cram in his mouth, "if you think any of *them* are going to ask a girl to the dance, you are craaazy!"

Maeve grimaced as she saw Billy's face swell up like a squirrel's. "I guess you've got a point."

"Well, promise me that you're at least going to dance?" Katani teased.

Everyone laughed, including Avery. Her "creative" dance moves were legendary!

Suddenly a long arm encircled Avery's neck in a gentle choke hold. Before she knew it, five knuckles dug into her head.

"Hey!" Avery yelped, wiggling away to see to see Dillon grinning behind her. "I figured it was you, doofus!"

When Avery wasn't hanging with the BSG, they could usually find her chilling with Dillon and his posse—the Trentini twins, Henry Yurt, and occasionally Nick Montoya. Avery and Dillon liked the same things: the Red Sox, soccer, basketball, baseball. Avery thought it was too hilarious that many girls at school (including Maeve) were totally crushing on the dude. And to make things even funnier, Dillon hardly ever noticed girls in the hallway drooling over him.

"What? You don't like my special super noogies?" he asked as he pushed back a shock of blond hair.

He is so cute, Maeve thought, almost choking on her potato chips while Avery playfully slugged Dillon on the shoulder.

"Whoa!" he joked as he rubbed his arm. "Weight-lift much?"

"Hey, dude, you deserved it."

Then Avery crossed her arms and announced, "It's nothing compared to how you're going to feel at the game today. I'm going to wipe the field with my new goal kick. I practiced all weekend with my brother, Scott."

"I'll believe it when I see it," Dillon retorted, but he looked a little uncertain—Avery could be a fierce competitor.

Maeve anxiously chewed her bottom lip. Dillon was so dreamy! He used to think she was dreamy too, but she'd made a huge mistake when she lied to her parents and friends to sneak off to a basketball game with Dillon and his dad back in the fall. Things had sort of chilled since then.

But now, for some reason every time she saw Dillon's beautiful smile and gorgeous blue eyes, her heart did a frantic tap dance. *I just know we're destined to be together, and it's up to me to make it happen!*

Maeve tried to edge her way into the conversation, but Dillon kept goofing around with Avery. She couldn't believe how Avery managed to be good buddies with just about every guy in the seventh grade. *Doesn't that girl even notice when a boy is cute? What would Elle Woods from* Legally Blonde *do in this situation?* Maeve wondered. *Hmmm . . . take control!* came the answer.

Maeve inhaled, smoothed down her riotous curls, and put on her best movie-star smile. "Hey, Dillon."

He turned around and gave her a friendly smile back. "What's up, Maeve?"

Katani, Isabel, and Charlotte watched the usually confident Maeve turn three shades of pink and giggle. All the boys liked Maeve. There was something about her sparkly personality that made the day seem a little brighter for everyone.

But Dillon just shrugged and turned back to Avery. "Dude, did you finish your math homework?"

Avery raised her eyebrows. "Oh, yeah. I actually made it to school ten minutes early this morning and managed to finish the last problem. What about you?"

Dillon looked surprised, like he was sure Avery hadn't finished either. The two of them often commiserated on what a waste of time homework was.

Maeve was getting frantic. Was *this* what Dillon wanted to talk about? Math homework? Her mind quickly tried to think of something to say to him—to make him look her way. Well, if it was math homework he wanted, then math homework he would get.

Finally she let out a high-pitched laugh that sounded like she had been sucking on a helium balloon. "I'm terrible at math. I mean, I'm barely scraping by with a C. I would love to have someone tutor me."

"Um, Earth to Maeve. You already have a tutor," Avery reminded her. "Remember Matt? The 'charming college guy' you couldn't stop talking about, like, two weeks ago?"

Maeve could have killed Avery for embarrassing her like that in front of dreamy Dillon . . . the boy she adored! Instead, Maeve just blinked and stared at Avery. "Of course I remember Matt! I meant . . . you know . . . I need another tutor. Someone who is taking the same class, you know." Maeve stumbled awkwardly over her words. "'Cause . . . like . . . I need a lot of help."

"Gee, I could use a tutor too, Maeve. Can I have your guy's number?" Dillon asked.

"Umm, sure," she answered. With a sinking heart she watched him turn back to Avery. She barely heard Katani reassuring her that she was *not* actually that terrible in math.

As Maeve rested her chin in one hand, she tried to

quiet the uncomfortable thoughts swirling around in her head. Maybe she had read Dillon wrong. But boys were funny: Sometimes they ignored you if they liked you. Didn't they? *Didn't they?*

Just then, Riley, leader of the AAJH jam band Mustard Monkey, passed by the BSG's table. Every day he walked by them at least once during lunchtime. His eyes immediately locked on Maeve as he approached. Riley opened his mouth as if to say something, but changed his mind at the last minute. He made a U-turn. Charlotte and Isabel looked at the rocker boy curiously as he hurried away. "Strange," Isabel mouthed to Charlotte.

"Dillon," Charlotte whispered back. She and Isabel suspected that Riley had a serious crush on Maeve but was just too insecure to talk to her in front of other guys.

Meanwhile, Maeve was getting more and more concerned that however Dillon might have felt in the past, he definitely didn't like her anymore. *I can't believe this. I really can't believe this,* Maeve wanted to shout. *Dillon's having this whole long conversation with Avery, right at the lunch table, and he's barely even said two sentences to me.* She swallowed the lump in her throat and tilted her face up toward the ceiling so the tears wouldn't spill over.

Isabel whispered to Maeve. "Are you okay? Why are you staring at the ceiling?"

Maeve's face reddened. "I . . . I have something in my eye."

Isabel saw immediately through her friend's words. Those were definitely tears brimming in Maeve's eyes. *Oh no.* Isabel stared, suddenly realizing that her romantic friend was most likely crushing on someone who wasn't crushing back.

As soon as lunch was over, Maeve raced off to the library. Inside, she made a beeline for her favorite swivel chair. For some reason, twirling around in a circle always helped her think more clearly. She took out her laptop and began to type.

Notes to Self:
1. Buy adorable dress I saw at Think Pink.
2. Ask Mom and Dad for a bigger allowance so I can buy the adorable dress at Think Pink.
3. FIND A WAY TO MAKE DILLON LIKE ME AGAIN!
4. Buy more guinea pig food.
5. Rename guinea pigs. Maybe Chocolate and Chip????
6. Practice my new monologue for acting class.
7. Study harder for pre-algebra. Pull C up to a B!!!!
8. TEACH AVERY TO BE UN-CLUELESS!
9. Ask Katani to style my hair in an Audrey Hepburn French twist.
10. Practice new acceptance speech for the Oscar I'm def going to win someday.

Abigail Adams Junior High

Valentine's Day Dance!
Hoppin' Music by DJ Fantastic

Refreshments

**Friday,
February 13th
7-9 p.m.
in the gymnasium**

CHAPTER

2

Headline News

A
wesome poster," Charlotte complimented Isabel. "It looks like we're going to have a fabulous heart convention."

"If I ever need someone to draw a heart, I know who to ask!" Chelsea Briggs grinned. The poster Isabel had designed for the Valentine's Day Dance was pinned to a bulletin board outside *The Sentinel*'s office, right over a reminder about that day's newspaper meeting. As usual, Charlotte, Isabel, and Chelsea were the first to arrive. Eighth-grade editor-in-chief extraordinaire Jennifer Robinson was already in the office, but she didn't count. The BSG had a theory that she slept there.

"Did I go overboard on the heart thing?" Isabel asked.

"Of course not! It *is* the season of love, after all," Charlotte teased.

Chelsea shrugged and shook her head. "Not for me!"

"Come on, Chels." Charlotte put a hand on her arm.

"There's got to be somebody you'd like to go to the dance with."

"I don't like anyone right now," said Chelsea. "Really." She used to be shy and quiet, absolutely sure that no one liked her because she was overweight. But ever since the class's adventure trip to Lake Rescue, Chelsea had gotten pretty fit and confident.

"Isn't there someone you think is even a tiny bit cute?" Isabel urged. "I mean, I do kind of like Kevin. We have so much to talk about since we both want to be artists when we grow up. I showed that poster to Kevin while I was working on it, and I swear we talked for two hours about the perfect shade of pink for the background!"

"Umm, okay . . . well, Nick is kind of cute," Chelsea blurted out. "He's got nice hair and a great smile. You're a lucky girl, Charlotte!"

It was no secret Nick Montoya had a crush on Charlotte. Sometimes it seemed she was the only one who didn't see it.

Nick Montoya was the cutest boy Charlotte had ever met, but thinking about him that way made her feel embarrassed. "We really don't have to have dates to go to the dance. After all, we're only in seventh grade. Avery doesn't want to go with anyone."

"What about . . . Chase Finley?" Isabel asked innocently.

"What?" Chelsea yelped. "No way! Sure, he's *dreamy* Kevin's friend, but talk about obnoxious!" The girls lost it laughing. Chase Finley was like everybody's annoying brother, plus he could be really mean.

Jennifer stomped over to the door and flung it open. "Hello. This is a newspaper office, not gossip time. You're late."

Charlotte began to apologize to "the Queen of the Paper," and Chelsea stepped back, leaning against the bulletin board with one shoulder.

Suddenly, it seemed like the whole wall was falling over! Chelsea twisted and reached behind her to push the bulletin board back up against the wall, but it was too late. Everything went pink, and with a huge crash, Chelsea was on the floor.

"Chels! Oh, my gosh, are you okay?!" A very worried Isabel plucked the pink thing—the Valentine's Day Dance poster—off of Chelsea's face. The bulletin board was on the floor, cracked down the middle. About a million pink and green announcements fluttered over Chelsea. *Is it time to die of total embarrassment?* a shaken Chelsea thought, also thinking that just might be preferable to getting up.

"You okay?" a concerned voice asked.

Chelsea opened her eyes slowly.

There was a boy standing over her. A boy she had never seen before. His cropped blond hair, tan face, and light green eyes were right off the pages of a surfer magazine. Were birds singing somewhere nearby? Was the sun shining down? Chelsea blinked. No, she was still on the floor in the Abigail Adams Junior High hallway, and the lights were all fluorescent. But the boy's face was still there, and the worry in his eyes made her heart flutter.

"That thing smashed right on top of you!" he said.

Charlotte quickly grabbed Chelsea's hand to help

her up. "Chels? Don't worry; we'll get this cleaned up." She was usually the one to cause a major commotion, so she knew how horribly embarrassed Chelsea must feel.

"I can't believe they let you kids out of elementary school," Jennifer groaned, and started picking up thumb-tacks.

The boy continued to stare into Chelsea's eyes as she staggered to her feet.

"Oh," she mumbled as she started to feel an ache in the back of her skull.

"Where's the nurse's office?" the boy asked.

"I . . . I'm okay," Chelsea managed to stammer. Her head felt like it was going to split in two, but she held steady. There was no way she'd let this boy escort her to the nurse. That would be beyond humiliating.

Jennifer held a couple of thumbtacks out to Charlotte. "Make yourself useful and put these somewhere?" Then she turned to the new boy. "Can I help you?"

"Well, I was looking for the newspaper meeting. . . ." He glanced at Chelsea again, with that same look of concern. Chelsea, meanwhile, wished she could crawl back under the bulletin board.

Jennifer smiled widely. "You're in the right place! I'm the editor in chief and I'm always looking for fresh perspectives on my newspaper staff. Do you have experience?"

"Sure, I covered everything at my old school. Sports, drama, art—you name it. . . ." He looked at Chelsea again. "Are you sure you're okay?"

"I'm Chelsea," she stammered. *What an idiot! He didn't*

even ask my name. And why can't I stop nodding? I feel like a bobblehead.

"Cool name," the boy said. "I'm Trevor."

"Well, Trevor," Jennifer interrupted smoothly and opened the door to the office. "Why don't you sit in on our meeting and we'll find a job for you?"

Trevor gestured for Chelsea to go in first. Charlotte gave her a reassuring smile as she entered the room with Nick, who'd just come running down the hallway with a couple of other seventh graders.

Soon, the whole newspaper staff was assembled in the room, chattering and laughing about the bulletin board and the dance. Long writing desks with computers for the reporters lined the room. Nick and Charlotte sat together at one; Chelsea sat next to them, watching Trevor talk to Jennifer.

Finally, Jennifer rapped her desk with a pencil, surveying the room. Charlotte squelched her annoyance at Jennifer's prima donna air. *This is just practice for when I have to deal with a real editor,* she reminded herself.

"Okay, everyone, I'd like to introduce you to a new student who may be joining our staff—Trevor Miller, from Santa Monica, California. Now, everyone come up with at least three ideas for this month's issue. Think *love* and *romance*, people!"

There was a flutter of activity as students pulled out notepads and pencils so they could begin the process of brainstorming possible news topics. Chelsea couldn't write. Her head throbbed, and she couldn't keep her eyes off Trevor. He was just . . . so cool. How could he be comfortable in a room full of strangers? Where did he get that confidence? She fought to pay attention to the meeting, but it was basically impossible.

Jennifer rapped her pencil again. "Earth to Chelsea! Give me one idea."

Chelsea stared at her blank paper.

"Look," Nick said, coming to her rescue. "I'm tired of doing the same old stories. I want to write something really newsworthy."

"Give us an example, Mr. Montoya."

Nick leaned forward. "Something real. Like an article about the unhealthy food the cafeteria dishes out each day."

"What's that got to do with love?" a kid at the other end of the table teased.

"Unless you're in looooove with French fries!" the student next to him called out.

"That's not a bad idea, actually," Jennifer responded. "But let's make it more general. Something about what the students at Abigail Adams love. We need a title. . . ."

Chelsea wasn't listening. She couldn't concentrate. Trevor was twirling his beach blond hair around one finger, and he looked so focused. His shirt was pale yellow, the color of sunshine, and it seemed like sunlight sparkled in the air all around him.

"Love is in the air!" Chelsea blurted, then put one hand over her mouth. *Was that out loud?*

"Perfect." Jennifer stood up. "Nick, you write the article. Chelsea, take the pictures. Talk to people at school; get short interviews about what they love. Could be a favorite pet, class, person, outfit—whatever. You can even do favorite foods, if you want. Get some shots of couples, too. It will go along great with a story about the Valentine's Day Dance. Charlotte, you'll cover that event."

Charlotte didn't want to write about the dance. She didn't even want to think about the dance! Whenever she did, Nick's face floated into her mind and her stomach filled with butterflies. But when she tried to raise her hand to tell Jennifer she would like to work together with Nick and Chelsea on their article, her elbow hit a big bowl of barbecue potato chips one of the eighth graders had brought to share.

It must be something in the air or klutziness is catching today, an embarrassed Charlotte thought as she watched bright orange crumbs scatter all over her notes and Nick's white shirt. He'd taken the brunt of the disaster. Charlotte bowed her head into one hand so she wouldn't have to look at a barbecue-chip-covered Nick.

"I always wanted an orange shirt," Nick whispered as he brushed chip dust off his clothing. Charlotte peered nervously through her fingers. But good-natured Nick was just sweeping chips back into the bowl and smiling.

Jennifer threw up her hands. "What is it with everyone today? You guys need to get it together and stop acting like you're still in grade school. Why don't you all just e-mail me any new ideas from home. I'll post the assignments by the door tomorrow."

"On what? The bulletin board's busted!" shouted the French fry–loving troublemaker.

"That's your assignment, Adam. Fix it!"

With that, Jennifer dragged Trevor over to her computer.

She's probably going to tie him down with enough assignments for the rest of his life, thought an annoyed Chelsea.

"I'll walk you home," Nick said to Charlotte as she got up to leave with Isabel. "I want to ask you something."

"Wait!" a frantic Chelsea grabbed Nick's arm. She'd just noticed how Trevor's blond hair curled adorably around the nape of his neck. *I've got to stall until Jennifer's done talking to him!* "Nick, we've got to plan out our article."

"I'll meet you outside in a few," Charlotte promised as Isabel led her out the door.

"Chelsea, can't the article wait for later?" Nick sounded exasperated.

Chelsea bit her lip. "Sorry, I mean, I'm just nervous about the whole approach to this thing."

"All you have to do is take pictures!" Nick leaned out the door where Charlotte had disappeared. "You're great at taking pictures."

"Just a minute," she stalled. "I know, but what pictures? Do we want candid or staged? Should we set them up like yearbook stills, or are you going to interview for captions?" Chelsea knew she was rambling, but she couldn't help it. If only she could take a picture of Trevor right now! Chelsea framed the shot in her head. He was leaning on Jennifer's desk with his beautiful hair shading his eyes. The light was a little low, but if she adjusted the lens filters . . .

"Chelsea? We can figure this all out tomorrow or

something. I've got to go." Nick looked down the hall again.

"No! Wait. Ummm . . . let's practice. What do you love?" Chelsea pretended to hold up a camera, but knew just as soon as she asked that this was the wrong question. Nick's cheeks got all red and he seemed to be perspiring way too much for February.

CHAPTER
3

The Crush Trap

As the wind gusted, an anxious Maeve stood by the front steps of the school waiting for Avery. Maybe the soccer game would be cancelled and the group could head off to Montoya's for hot chocolate.

Maeve warmed herself with that hopeful thought. But as she looked around, she noticed that all the snow had melted into chilly mud puddles and the sun was shining stronger than ever. That was probably enough for the boys (and Avery) to head out to the soccer field.

Maeve couldn't imagine why anyone would choose to run around for an hour on mushy dead grass, especially when it was still cold enough for her to wear her soft pink sheepskin boots. Her discount pair looked exactly like the brand name. Katani had even helped decorate the pink fur with sparkles.

But why didn't her cool boots get Dillon's attention? Everyone in school loved them! And Riley told her just this morning they were rad. Maeve gazed down at the sparkles. *How can I get Dillon to notice me?* If only she could be a little bit like Avery. Avery had no trouble fitting in with boys. Probably because all she ever seemed to talk about was sports.

Maeve grinned and wriggled her toes. Of course! Why hadn't she thought of it before? She knew how to get Dillon to look at her! It was so easy. She would show him that she was a complete sports girl. *After all, I'm an actress.* She threw her shoulders back and lifted her chin. "If it's a soccer girl he wants, a soccer girl he'll get!"

A passing ninth grader gave Maeve a strange look. She flashed him her best Academy Award acceptance smile and watched the last buses thunder away from the curb, spewing out smelly fumes.

"Miss the bus, movie star?" Joline Kaminsky jibed as she sauntered past with her partner in crime, Anna McMasters. *Wonderful,* Maeve thought. *The Queens of Mean.*

"She's waiting for her limousine," said Anna. "Oh, wait! She's too poor to afford one. Now that Maddie Von Krupcake dropped her, she has to travel like the rest of us."

"Ah, excuse me, double trouble," Maeve retorted. "I dropped Maddie for being a boring phony! You know all about phony, right?" Maeve knew Anna was jealous that Maeve had starred in a sort of movie and had gone to Hollywood with the über-rich Von Krupcakes. Charlotte always told her to ignore Queens of Mean comments, but sometimes Maeve couldn't help herself. Anna was just *so* annoying.

"I know you'll enjoy your long walk home," Anna

said, and smirked as she tossed a yellow and blue soccer ball into the air and caught it behind her back.

"Show off," Maeve whispered almost loud enough for them to hear. *Looks like the game's on, after all. . . . Maybe I should go watch Dillon play.* This thought easily morphed into a fantasy. After the game, Dillon would ask her to the Valentine's Day Dance. They'd dance just like Fred Astaire and Ginger Rogers, her favorite ballroom-dancing actors from the old black-and-white movies she loved so much. Dillon would twirl her around the floor as she flitted about in a floor-length gown that rustled lightly as she spun across the dance floor. Maeve could see it now—Dillon's arms holding her close as they swayed to the sounds of an orchestra, his face looking down at her with stars in his eyes.

"Hey, Maeve. What's up?" said a familiar voice next to her. She turned with a gasp.

"Riley! Hey. Sorry I didn't see you there."

Riley stood there without saying anything, chewing on the inside of his cheek. *Why does Riley look so uncomfortable?* Maeve wondered. Was that sweat sprouting on his forehead? It wasn't even warm outside!

After an awkward moment of silence, she finally asked, "What have you been up to lately?"

Riley hitched his backpack higher on his shoulders and grinned. "Uh . . . nothing much. Mustard Monkey has been practicing like crazy. We have a gig at a bar mitzvah in a couple of weeks."

Maeve stopped twirling the strand of hair and looked up at him. "Really? That's so cool! You guys are totally taking off. It's just like that movie I saw last year about the garage band struggling to become famous—they're always performing in grungy nightclubs and stuff for, like, basically no money, and then one day they're discovered by a famous music producer and the next thing you know, they're huge rock stars!"

Immediately, she noticed Riley's tense muscles relax. That was the great thing about Riley. He could act all jumpy and nervous with her one second, but when she talked about music, it always seemed to help him chill. Especially when he talked about *his* music and Mustard Monkey.

Maeve liked that Riley was totally committed to his music. It was inspiring. Maybe she and Riley could go to New York and be struggling performers together when they grew up. It would be so nice to have a friend in a big city like New York, she thought.

"Well I've written a couple of new songs we're going to try out."

Maeve leaned toward him, really getting into the conversation. "That's fantastic! You know, I've always thought I should take voice lessons. If I'm going to be a movie star one day, I definitely should improve my singing voice. I mean, if I could act, dance, and sing, I'd totally be a triple threat."

"I doubt you even need singing lessons," Riley said. "Your voice is so pretty already."

Maeve smiled. "That's so sweet, Riley. I . . ." Maeve's head snapped around, swishing Riley's face with her red curls. Charlotte and Isabel were flying down the steps, laughing.

Maeve dashed up to sweep her friends into a group hug. Riley stood at the bottom of the stairs, swinging his guitar case, alone and forgotten. He waited for a few awkward minutes, then walked away, shoulders slumping.

"Maeve, the newspaper meeting was such a disaster," Charlotte confessed. Her face flushed just thinking about her latest klutz moment and Chelsea's bulletin board incident.

Isabel filled Maeve in on the latest events while Charlotte watched the door, hoping for Nick to appear.

"So why are you still here, Maeve?" Isabel asked after she'd finished describing the gorgeous new boy Trevor.

Charlotte wrinkled her forehead. "Yeah. You're always the first one of us to run out of here as soon as the bell rings."

Maeve rolled her eyes and hoped her face wasn't turning pink with embarrassment. "Oh, I was just hanging around, waiting for you two to show up. I just didn't feel like walking home yet. I can't face my five tons of homework."

"Well, I was going to wait for Nick. He wanted to ask me something," Charlotte added.

Maeve sighed. "That's so romantic! Walking home from school with your future husband. You guys are, like, one of the great love stories of all time."

"Ha-ha, very funny." Charlotte rummaged inside her crocheted purse and found a stick of gum, which she popped into Maeve's smiling mouth. "Maybe that will help you lose your love obsession."

"Obsession? What obsession?" Maeve joked in between slurpy chews.

Isabel pressed her lips together, her eyes dancing. "Now, Maeve," she teased, "I'm sure Dillon will appreciate the sweet aroma of Tru Blu gum over that gross tuna fish sandwich you had for lunch."

"Do you think?" she said wistfully.

"Oh, Maeve," Charlotte replied, ruffling her friend's mass of curls. "No one is as wrapped up in romance as you."

"That's for sure," Isabel agreed.

The sound of the huge metal doors opening made them look up toward the school entrance. Betsy Fitzgerald walked down the school steps, a very serious expression on her face. Her hair caught up in a neat ponytail, she walked briskly as if late for an important appointment.

"What's up, Betsy?" Maeve asked, stopping the serious girl in her tracks. "You look kind of stressed."

Maeve hated to see anyone unhappy, especially when love was in the air. Charlotte was seconds away from having a date, and her own plan to snare Dillon was flawless! She didn't want anyone to be that serious.

Betsy shook her head. "Oh, it's nothing, really. I'm just thinking about ideas for the Valentine's Day Dance decorating committee." Maeve tried not to look at Isabel and Charlotte. She knew they were thinking the same thing. *Is there a committee at school that super overachiever Betsy isn't on?*

Oblivious to her reaction, Betsy just plowed on. "It's so important that the dance turns out well. I mean, I'm the head of the committee, and everything is resting on my shoulders, you know." Betsy so loved impressing an audience with her accomplishments.

Isabel, who was also on the committee, nodded with sympathy. "We'll get it done, don't worry. This dance will be the event of the year!"

"Forget about committees!" Maeve struck a pose and held out her imaginary microphone. "Has anyone asked you to the dance yet?"

Betsy's face brightened. "Yes. I'm going with Henry."

"The Yurtmeister?" the three other girls exclaimed in shock. The BSG were totally blown away. Why on earth would Betsy want to go to the Valentine's Day Dance with the seventh-grade class clown? Then again, Henry Yurt *was* the class president.

Betsy straightened her collar and explained. "Henry is really sweet when he isn't trying to make everybody laugh. Besides—"

"But, Betsy," Maeve interrupted. "I thought Henry was gaga over Anna." Charlotte nudged Maeve as Betsy's face darkened.

"Anna made fun of Henry last week, so he doesn't like her anymore."

"Whoa!" Maeve couldn't believe it. Henry Yurt had been crazy about Anna since the beginning of school, even though she towered over him. Now he was going to the dance with Betsy? *Romance is so unpredictable*, a suddenly shaken Maeve thought.

"And, after all," Betsy continued, "somebody who wins the class presidency has a lot going for him. I respect that kind of ambition." She hitched her backpack higher on her shoulder. "Well, I've gotta run. Mrs. Rodriguez gave me permission to write a five-page extra-credit essay on William Shakespeare. See you all later."

The BSG watched Betsy glide down the sidewalk, her backpack weighted down with textbooks.

"That girl is going to own the world before she's eighteen," Isabel said with a mixture of horror and respect.

Maeve's face paled. "Five pages! She doesn't even *need* the extra credit." Maeve had to work so hard just to get average grades. People like Betsy had it so easy—earning good grades as smoothly as collecting seashells off the beach.

Charlotte shrugged and glanced at her watch. Was Nick still in the newspaper office talking to Chelsea? What could they possibly be talking about all this time? Charlotte tried unsuccessfully to squash something very shaky gnawing at the pit of her stomach.

"So Betsy's going with Yurt!" Maeve exclaimed. "And not one of the BSG has someone to go to the Valentine's Day Dance with."

"I wonder if Kevin will ask me?" Isabel pondered.

Charlotte forced a smile. "It's only Monday! Don't worry, Isabel. We can just go together. I mean, lots of kids won't have dates. We'll have more fun that way."

Isabel's face brightened. "Oh, I know. If no one asks us to the dance, it's no big deal. We'll have fun, just us girls!"

Maeve crossed her arms and frowned. "Speak for yourself. I'm going to get Dillon to ask me or die trying!"

Charlotte stared at the door to the school, willing it to open and let Nick out. "Maeve, you are going a little crazy about all this date stuff. It's just too much pressure." But suddenly she felt a tiny bit hypocritical. Wasn't she going a little crazy, too, waiting for a certain boy with dreamy eyes to walk through the door?

"Trust me, if Dillon doesn't ask you to the dance, you will survive." Isabel danced around Maeve. "Besides, you can always ask him. This isn't the olden days, you know."

Maeve put her hands on her hips. "Well, I know, but I don't want to ask him. Where's the romance in that?"

Charlotte looked at her watch again. Marty was waiting for his walk. But where was Nick? *Oops, here I go again. I shouldn't get myself all worked up waiting for him. I should just go.* Charlotte turned to her friends and announced, "It's getting late. Marty's going to go crazy if I don't get home soon."

Charlotte looked at the door one last time and smiled at the other girls, struggling to keep her voice light. "I guess Nick decided to stay later." *Maybe he'll ask to walk me home again tomorrow,* she thought regretfully.

"Okay," said Isabel. "Are you coming, Maeve?"

Maeve shifted from one foot to the other. "Uh . . . not right now. I'm going to wait for Avery."

"But she's going to play soccer this afternoon," Charlotte pointed out.

Maeve shrugged her shoulders. "I know. I . . . I thought I'd tag along and check out the game . . . maybe even play."

Charlotte stared. "Wait a minute. Did I just hear you correctly?"

Isabel placed her hand on Maeve's forehead. "She doesn't have a fever . . . so she can't be delirious. Maybe she's been taken over by some alien life-form."

Maeve pouted. "*Very* funny. But I'll have you both know that I think soccer is a really cool sport. And as an actress it's important I explore new things in order to become a well-rounded dramatic artist."

Isabel and Charlotte stared at each other in disbelief, and then both of them burst out laughing. Maeve hated sports. Why on earth would the future actress want to spend a Monday afternoon in the middle of winter chasing after a soccer ball when she could be home trying on outfits and dancing to her favorite music?

"Uh . . . okay . . . whatever you say, Maeve," Isabel said teasingly. "Have fun . . . with Dillon!" She ran off before Maeve could grab her sweater.

A Pretty Pink Poodle

At the bottom of Charlotte's hill, Isabel spotted a familiar pink figure with magenta hair strolling down the sidewalk, a matching pink pooch beside her.

"Ms. Razzberry Pink!" Isabel waved to the owner of the BSG's favorite store, Think Pink.

"Isabel, Charlotte!" Ms. Pink waved one hand. Her wrist jangled with rose-colored bracelets, and a constellation of pink jewels on her belt matched her dog's collar. "I thought I'd take advantage of the lovely weather and get La Fanny some exercise. We've been busy!"

"What's the occasion?" Charlotte asked, reaching over to pat the pink poodle.

"Only the most wonderful holiday of the whole year!" Ms. Pink threw her arms up with joy, and La Fanny started barking. The poodle had a dainty voice, and even daintier features. Charlotte wished Marty were there. The little dude had fallen head over heels for Ms. Pink's pooch the first day they'd met at the park.

"Of course, how could we forget Valentine's Day?" Isabel laughed.

"That's right! You must come by and see Think Pink! I have candy hearts, paper hearts, giant fuzzy hearts, and tiny heart beads! Not to mention the heart wallpaper and heart balloons."

"I'd love to see!" Isabel said. "Want to come, Char?"

"I would, but I have to walk Marty. Can you wait for us, Ms. Pink?"

"Ah, I'm so sorry, Charlotte! Maybe a different day, today . . . oh, there he is!" Ms. Pink waved to a young man with a rottweiler on a leash. "That's my new boyfriend, Zak. He said he'd meet us here for a stroll. Doesn't he have the most adorable dog?"

Charlotte wouldn't call the brown-and-black bundle of pure muscle marching toward them "adorable." "Scary" and "intimidating" were much better adjectives. But the dog was looking at La Fanny with a big doggy smile and drooling. That was sort of cute, Charlotte had to admit. *Maybe it's a good thing Marty's not here,* Charlotte thought as she waved good-bye to Ms. Razzberry Pink and La Fanny. *He might get jealous.*

4

Love Is in the Air

C hels, I really have to go," Nick repeated.

Chelsea blocked the doorway, struggling to keep Nick's attention in a way that wasn't totally obvious she was *really* waiting for Trevor. "Maybe we should interview kids arriving at school. How's this: 'What do you have in your locker that you couldn't live without? Your skateboard? What do you looove most about skateboarding'?"

"Aren't the questions my job?"

"I'm just giving you some ideas!" Chelsea frowned. What was up with Nick today?

He paced in the doorway, accidentally knocking Chelsea's camera hand aside.

"Ah . . . sorry, Chels. . . . This is a big help . . . but how about we meet before school one day this week?" he said impatiently.

Chelsea stepped back, hands at her sides. She'd never seen Nick really annoyed before.

"Look," he said, holding up his palms and backing out

the door, "I'm sorry, but now is just not a good time. Okay? Call or IM, and I promise we'll figure this out." With that, Nick bolted through the door.

Chelsea stood there, one foot in and one foot out the door, wondering how long she could go on pretending the speckled linoleum tiles on the floor were the most fascinating thing in the universe.

Finally, Jennifer swept past, with a look that said *out of my way*, and Trevor was standing there, right in front of Chelsea. His lopsided grin sent her eyes scrambling for somewhere else to stare before she started drooling on the oh-so-interesting floor. "So you're the photographer?" Trevor asked.

Please don't notice how heavy I am. Chelsea clasped her hands in front of her and forced herself to smile back. But she had to concentrate on breathing in and out. *I guess that's what people mean when they say someone takes their breath away,* she thought. "Yes. You're Trevor, right?"

"Yeah."

"I'm Chelsea."

Trevor cracked a smile. "Uh . . . yeah. You told me that before."

"Oh . . . yeah."

They stood staring at each other for a long awkward moment. It was so quiet, Chelsea could hear the ticking of the clock on the wall all the way in the back of the newspaper office.

Finally, Trevor shoved his hands in his pockets. "My dad bought me a digital camera last year. I have some books on photography too. Dad lets me use his Photoshop software to manipulate the images and stuff like that."

Chelsea smiled for real this time. "Really? My digital camera is such a dinosaur. I'd love to get a new one. I've been saving my allowance, and my parents are going to split the cost with me."

Before Chelsea knew it, she and Trevor were talking about cameras and photography and how they both loved the same type of ice cream: cookie dough. And, to her amazement, she didn't see any sign that Trevor was weirded out talking to a girl who was heavy and someone he hardly knew. It seemed like magic, until Avery came charging down the hall. "Hey, Trevor!"

"What's up, A-Train?"

"Not much, T-Dawg!" Avery greeted him, effortlessly bumping fists in a complicated way that it looked like she had practiced for months. But Chelsea knew Avery had just met Trevor today, along with everyone else.

Chelsea wanted to ask Trevor a million questions about his old school and Photoshop and whether he liked black-and-white or sepia photos better, but she was just a fly on the wall now that Avery was there. Why did that girl have such an easy time talking to guys? Chelsea wished she knew Avery's secret.

"Hey, Chelsea," Avery said. "Want to take pictures of the ultimate soccer game? Trevor, you should totally come play! It'll rock!"

"Um, it's February," Chelsea stated.

"Yeah, and that means it could snow again any day! This is our only chance! The team has to take advantage of a February thaw," she explained.

"Sounds cool." Trevor ran his hands through his blond hair. It stood up in little tufts all over his head. Even with his hair all messy Chelsea thought he looked adorable. *Thump thump.* Chelsea almost jumped. *Oh, my gosh! Can Trevor hear my heartbeat?*

If Trevor was going, she had to go too. Even if he never looked at her. "Okay, but I have to get my camera and stuff from my locker," Chelsea mumbled.

"Catch you later?" Trevor turned the full force of his dazzling smile on Chelsea.

She nodded as her knees actually began to shake.

Missing You

"Is she here?" Nick demanded, rushing down the steps toward Maeve.

Maeve stared at him in confusion. "Who?"

"Charlotte." Nick's eyes darted about.

Maeve shook her head with a smile. "No. Sorry. She left already. Try calling her at home."

Nick shook his head. "Can't. Gotta help out in the bakery this afternoon. I guess I'll talk to her at school tomorrow. Later."

"See ya." Maeve waved, watching him lope down the sidewalk. Nick and Charlotte's puppy love always made her heart flutter. If only Dillon felt the same way about her. Her lips tightened. Well, later this afternoon, Dillon would see she was the perfect girl for him.

Five minutes later, Avery and Trevor emerged from the school, laughing and shoving each other as if they'd been buddies for years. *How does that girl do it?* Maeve asked herself as she shook her head. *I mean, she doesn't even want to have a date for the dance, and she's already, like, best buds with that cute new boy.* He wasn't as cute as Dillon, though! Not even close.

Maeve danced halfway up the steps to Avery. "What took you so long? I thought you'd never get out here. I'm *freezing.*"

"I had to find Trevor," Avery said. "He was hanging in the newspaper office with Chelsea. I wouldn't want anyone to miss an AAJH pickup winter soccer game." She turned to the blondhaired boy. "Trevor, this is one of my best friends, Maeve."

"What's up? You coming?" he said, his eyes crinkling at the corners.

Maeve smiled and shrugged. "I wouldn't miss the game for the world!"

Avery grinned. "That's cool. You should round up some more fans. But you gotta cheer for my team, okay?"

Maeve shook her head. "No, Avery. I don't want to watch. I want to *play.*"

Avery looked at Maeve as if she were crazy. "You're not serious."

Maeve put her hands on her hips and tapped one pink boot. "Of course, I'm serious! I've played soccer before. You know that!"

"In those clothes?" Avery asked.

"Of course. I have to look my best for our team's triumphant victory! Let's go!" Maeve grabbed Avery's arm and marched out back to the soggy, gloppy field.

Field of Dreams

"Uh . . . Maeve . . . what are you doing here?" Dillon asked as Maeve performed her best dramatic entrance onto the soccer field, avoiding puddles and a few clumps of brown snow.

She gave him her brightest smile and tried to hide her disappointment that Dillon didn't look thrilled to see her. "I'm here to play, of course."

Dillon glanced at Avery, who looked concerned.

"Play what?" Dillon asked.

Maeve stuck out her lip. Dillon's face was so gorgeous, even when he was being a pain! "Soccer, silly. This game is the event of the week. After the *Valentine's Day Dance*, that is." Maeve dropped the hint with as much emphasis as she could, but it went right over his head.

"Do you even know the rules?" Dillon asked.

"Maeve," Avery took over. "Our soccer games can be kind of intense. People get knocked around all the time. Maybe you should just, you know, watch for a little while?" she said in a worried tone. Avery hated to see people get hurt. She was kind of a softie that way.

"No way!" Maeve said. "I'm here to play, and I'm ready!"

She stomped one foot and cringed as her soft pink boots sent up a shower of gross mud. It went all over the sparkly fur and splattered her favorite pair of jeans! Maeve took a deep breath. *Compose yourself. An actress must always maintain composure!*

"You?" Maeve turned to see Anna kick her blue and yellow soccer ball as hard as she could. Maeve jumped out of the way, and Avery went running after the ball, yelling, "Use your *head*, Maeve!"

My head! Maeve thought, horrified. *I have to sacrifice my hair to that ball of flying mud?*

"I'm a captain and I pick first," Anna announced. "Trevor, you're with me."

Avery passed the ball as gently as she could to Maeve. It came to a stop between her boots. "Okay, Maeve, you're on my team."

"What a waste of a perfectly good pick," Joline whispered from the sidelines.

That's when Maeve noticed Chelsea was there, toting her camera.

Maeve gave her a movie star smile, but she was starting to worry. Was she in way over her pink boots?

"I can play! Watch this!" Maeve picked up the ball and tried to twirl it on one finger. It actually worked for a second, but no one seemed to care.

"Maeve, you can't touch the ball with your hands," Avery whispered.

"I know that," she shushed.

"I get Dillon," Anna announced.

In the end, both Trentini twins, Henry Yurt, and two random guys from Maeve's math class wound up on her side. The other team was all Anna's eighth-grade soccer friends, plus Trevor and Dillon.

Maeve wasn't entirely sure when the game began. It was like a tornado swept in, whipped her up in a chaotic whirlwind, then spun away laughing, only to come back for more.

"You're on defense, Maeve! Go back, *back*!" Avery shouted.

"Here, take the ball away from me." Dillon practically passed it to Maeve, earning a furious glare from Anna. "Stop trying to be nice," she growled at Dillon as she swiped in and stole the ball before Maeve could even swing back her leg.

Was Dillon trying to make me look like a total loser? Maeve ducked as Anna sent the ball sailing over her head, straight into the goal.

The goalie, Henry Yurt, threw up his hands. "You're supposed to stop it!"

"Here, try offense," Avery suggested. "Just follow me, but not too close! I'll pass it to you."

Maeve managed to snag the easy pass, and Dillon low-fived Avery behind Anna's back. "Nice pass, Ave!" Dillon whispered, and they both laughed.

Was this really happening? Her future husband was laughing with her best friend! And they weren't even on the same team!

An eighth-grade girl came barreling down the field just as Maeve felt her toes cramping inside her boots. The soles kept slipping and sliding in the muck of partially thawed grass. Maeve didn't dare look down. She knew her perfect pink boots were perfectly ruined!

With a grunt, she kicked the ball back toward Avery. Only Avery wasn't there anymore.

"Thanks, Maeve!" Anna laughed, and Maeve heard Chelsea's camera shutter snap. This was bad. She couldn't believe Chelsea was actually documenting her misery.

Every muscle in Maeve's body throbbed with pain. What made her think she could play soccer with the best players in school? She must have been suffering from temporary insanity! She felt the tears brimming up behind her lids when Joline whistled from the sidelines.

"Halftime!" Avery shouted, and trotted up to Maeve. "You could sit out for a while, if you want."

"No! I'm fine!" Maeve snapped, dusting off her jeans as best she could. Her legs pricked from the heat of running and the cold of the air at the same time. A chilly breeze blew across the sweat building up beneath her hair, and Maeve shivered. Avery was smart to wear sweatpants and a ponytail, she admitted.

Maeve thought halftime meant at least ten minutes of rest and refreshments, but after just two seconds of slurping water from colorful bottles, her whole team was back out on the field.

Dillon stood in the opposite goal now, looking cuter than ever with his hair all slicked back and his goalie shirt sleeves rolled up. "You okay, Maeve?" he called.

She couldn't tell if he was teasing or serious. *Composure*, Maeve reminded herself, and pranced into position. "Are you kidding? I'm better than ever!"

In reality, she wanted to die. She absolutely wanted to die. Whatever had she been thinking? Actresses could take on personalities, but not skills. She couldn't just become a star soccer player because she wanted to. But there was no way she would quit now. Maeve Kaplan-Taylor was going to show the world she didn't give up.

"Are we winning?" Maeve asked when she had a

chance to stop and breathe for a second. Avery had stuck close through the second half, and now Billy Trentini was backing up for a corner kick. Before today, Maeve had had no idea you kicked anything from corners in soccer.

"We're tied," Avery said. "Look, if the ball comes to you, tap it back to me. I'll run it up the side, and you get in front of the goal—got it?"

Avery made some sort of signal with her hands. Maeve didn't understand, but she'd do anything to get this nightmare over with.

"Okay," she said, and looked at her fingernails. The pink polish was chipped and dirty, and so were her nails. *Oh well, I'll just pick a new color tonight . . . maybe magenta?*

"Maeve!" Henry Yurt shouted.

The ball was arcing straight toward her! Maeve backed up, but the ball hit her flat in the chest. "Ouch!" she yelped as the muddy missile hit the ground in front of her.

"To me!" Avery yelled.

Maeve tapped it back, and watched her sporty friend weave in and out, dancing effortlessly past Anna, Trevor, and an older girl. Maeve trotted up the center, watching with growing jealousy. Maeve could memorize a complicated dance move in a few minutes, but no way could she dodge so many angry, shouting faces and kicking feet!

Suddenly, she was right in front of the goal, face-to-face with Dillon.

He grinned, and gave a two-finger wave. *Is he grinning at Avery or me?* Maeve didn't have time to figure it out.

"MAEVE!" Avery screamed.

Suddenly, the ball was right there, bouncing across the mud. *This is it!* Maeve glowed inside. *I'll make a goal, and Dillon will lift me up on his shoulders!* It didn't matter that he was on the other team; Maeve knew he had to be cheering for her. She'd show him what she was made of, then he'd ask her to the dance!

Maeve stared at that ball as hard as she could. Timing was everything, in dance and in soccer. She swung back her leg . . . and timed it perfectly. One dirty pink boot hit the ball, but the other . . . went slipping, sliding, and then flying up into the air! Maeve hadn't noticed the giant puddle directly in front of her feet.

As she fell, Maeve watched Dillon double over as the ball sailed past his head into the goal. He could have stopped it, but he didn't. He was laughing too hard. Everyone was laughing! Even Avery. Maeve could hear her trying to hide her familiar high-pitched giggle. Flashes from Chelsea's camera topped off the greatest public humiliation of the century.

Maeve could feel mud clinging to her hair, dripping down her nose, and oozing between her fingers. Anna and Joline were beside themselves whooping and hollering. As her team began to surround her, it didn't even matter that people were actually cheering, too. Her dream crush was laughing. That's all the late, great MKT could concentrate on. That and the disgusting feel of icky, oozy mud. Even the new boy, Trevor, was laughing so hard he could barely stand.

But Avery was the worst, kneeling in the puddle beside her, holding back great gasps of laughter.

"I . . . I'm sorry, Maeve, but that was the . . . the BEST goal . . . I have EVER seen!" Avery held out a hand, but Maeve ignored it.

"We won! That flip move totally saved the day!" Avery flopped down in the mud too, and splashed around a little. "See? It's not so bad to get dirty sometimes! Hey, can I coach you? You could be really good! But you'll have to ditch the boots."

Maeve turned away and slowly, painfully got to her feet. "You're crazy! I don't want any more of your kind of coaching, Avery Madden."

Just then, Dillon walked up. "Nice job, Maeve. No one EVER gets it past me when I'm in goal. That was quite the move. And that face plant? Awesome!" He reached out to high-five her.

Composure, she thought, trying to ignore a large drop of mud trailing down her cheek.

"Thanks," Maeve said. "I planned it all along." And she high-fived him right back.

Then she dashed away from the field, to walk home— alone . . . covered in mud . . . with tears running down her face.

Notes to Self:
1. Try to forgive Avery the Traitor.
   Future movie stars must be gracious
   and kind.
2. Stay away from soccer. Forever.
3. Make Dillon fall hopelessly in love

with *MOI*!!!! A goal is a goal,
after aall.
4. Convince my dad to have an Audrey
   Hepburn Film Festival.
5. Stay away from soccer. FOR
   ETERNITY.
6. Check out the new sales at Think
   Pink!
7. Learn the new line dance I saw on
   YouTube and teach it to the BSG—but
   maybe not Avery.
8. Practice acceptance speech for the
   Tony Award I plan on winning after
   earning my Oscar. And don't invite
   Avery!

CHAPTER

5

One Sad Little Dude

Charlotte closed the front door behind her and climbed the winding front stairway to the second-floor apartment she shared with her dad. Where was Marty? Usually the little dude was waiting right there at the foot of the stairs, barking and wagging his stumpy tail with excitement—as if he hadn't seen her in a month.

"Marty?" she called out. But there was no pitter patter of little dog feet. *Where is that little dude?* Charlotte went to check the kitchen. When Marty chowed down on his dog food, the house could fall down around him and he'd never even notice.

"Marty!" she shouted, but when she entered the sunny kitchen, there was no Marty. She glanced over at the answering machine to see if there were any messages. Maybe Nick had tried to call when he FINALLY got through with whatever he was doing with Chelsea. She sighed when she saw the red zero blinking on the answering machine screen.

She grabbed an oatmeal cookie from the cookie jar and went back into the living room. Surely the little dude would come running for an oatmeal cookie treat!

"Marty!" she yelled out again.

Okay. Maybe he was in her dad's bedroom. *Oh, no.* Charlotte hoped he wasn't chewing on her dad's bedroom slippers again. The last time her dad left his slippers out, Marty chewed a huge hole in the left toe. Mr. Ramsey hadn't been happy. "Those slippers have been around the world . . . twice," he complained loudly to a cowed Marty.

"Marty," Charlotte called in a singsong voice. Mr. Marté always came for her baby-dog voice. Except this time . . . he didn't.

"Marty!" she cried louder, her voice growing unsteady. This wasn't like him at all. Charlotte hunted frantically through the rest of the house, until there was only one more place to look: her dad's office.

She pushed the door open and rushed inside. Then she saw it . . . a little furry foot poking out from under her father's desk. She fell to her knees. "Marty? What's wrong, little puppy?"

Marty stared at her with sad eyes, barely able to lift his fuzzy head. His tail weakly thumped against the floor.

Charlotte scooped him up into her arms and held him close. "Oh Marty, poor baby. Are you sick?"

Heart thumping, Charlotte raced back down the stairs to their landlady's apartment and pounded on her door. "Miss Pierce! Miss Pierce! Something's wrong with Marty!"

Thankfully, the door opened right away and Charlotte's

landlady stood in the entrance. "What's wrong, Charlotte? Are you all right?"

Charlotte tried to steady her breathing as she looked up at Miss Pierce. She cradled Marty's face next to her shoulder. His warm body trembled in her arms as if he were standing in a freezer. "Marty's sick, and I don't know what to do." Tears sprang to her eyes, and her words came out in a rush.

Miss Pierce motioned Charlotte inside. "Come in, Charlotte dear. Let me see him."

Miss Pierce took the dog from Charlotte and settled him on the living room sofa. He huddled on the cushions and whined.

"Charlotte," she said as she looked up, "I agree with you. Marty is not acting like a well puppy. You'd better ask your dad to take him to the vet as soon as he gets home. Would you like to stay down here with me until then? I'll make us some tea. How about that lovely lemon tea you like?"

Charlotte snuffled back a tear and nodded as she gently stroked Marty's fur.

Poor Little Doggy

At five-thirty, Charlotte finally heard her dad walk through the front door. At 5:31, Charlotte threw herself at him. He stumbled backward as she grabbed his arm and dragged him into Miss Pierce's apartment.

"Dad, Marty's really sick. I mean *really* sick! We have to take him to the vet, like, right now!"

Charlotte's dad took one look at a limp Marty lying

curled up on the sofa and said, "You're right. He doesn't look like himself at all." Scooping Marty into his arms, he ushered Charlotte toward the door.

"Have these two been down here with you all afternoon, Miss Pierce?" he asked.

"Yes, Charlotte came down directly when she discovered Marty in such a state. Do let me know what the vet tells you, Mr. Ramsey."

"Of course," he promised her. "And, thank you, Miss Pierce, for staying with the *kids*." As a single dad, Mr. Ramsey was grateful for the kindly landlady's support.

"Thank you so much!" Charlotte called out, never taking her eyes away from Marty's sad face.

A Mystery Illness

When Charlotte, Mr. Ramsey, and Marty walked through the door at the Precious Paws Animal Hospital, the receptionist's face creased with concern. "What's up with Marty? This little guy's not his usually bubbly self."

"That's why we're here." Charlotte sighed as she rubbed Marty's ear. "We think he's very sick."

The receptionist nodded at Charlotte and her dad. "Go ahead and take a seat. The doctor will be with you as soon as possible."

The animal clinic spilled over with animals of all shapes and sizes. A gray-haired woman by the door held a cockatoo in a cage on her lap. A fat bulldog squatted at the feet of a man reading a magazine. When the bulldog saw Marty, he lumbered to his feet, obviously anticipating a yap hello. Nothing. Marty was just too weak to greet his favorite park pal, Louie.

Charlotte began to get fidgety. It seemed like Dr. Clayton was never coming. Even the talking cockatoo wasn't funny anymore.

"If that bird asks 'what's your problem?' one more time, I'm going to answer him," Mr. Ramsey whispered to Charlotte. "Should I tell him about my student who's failing, or my terrible singing voice?"

"Mr. Ramsey?" interrupted a friendly voice. It was Dr. Clayton. "Let's check this little guy out."

The vet directed them to an examination room, and Marty stood on the exam table obediently, watching Charlotte with a sorrowful expression while Dr. Clayton checked his heartbeat, eyes, and temperature. He didn't even throw a fit when the vet had to poke him with a needle. It was as if all off Marty's feistiness had leaked out of him!

The doctor left the examining room with a tiny vial of Marty's blood.

"Do you think Marty has . . . you know . . . a serious medical condition?" Charlotte asked in a worried voice.

"I just don't know, honey," her father answered. "Yesterday he seemed perfectly fine, and that's a good sign. Whatever it is, I'm sure it's nothing Dr. Clayton can't handle." He gave her a reassuring hug.

Charlotte nodded, but looking at Marty's hunched-up little body, she wasn't really sure she believed him.

When Dr. Clayton returned, she was smiling. "I don't think there is anything seriously wrong with Marty."

Charlotte heaved a sigh of relief. "But," Dr. Clayton continued, "he does seem a bit subdued."

Hello. Subdued! thought Charlotte. *Marty is practically a zombie!*

Dr. Clayton gave Marty a reassuring scratch behind the ears. "Let's keep an eye on the little guy this week and make sure he drinks plenty of water and gets some exercise and rest. If he doesn't perk up in a few days, bring him back in. We'll do some more tests."

"Thanks, Dr. Clayton," said Mr. Ramsey.

Charlotte scooped Marty off the table and buried her face in his fur. "Thanks," she mumbled.

During the drive home, Marty slept in Charlotte's lap, snoring softly.

"I don't understand, Dad," said Charlotte. "What's wrong with him?"

"I don't know, kiddo. We'll just watch him and see if he improves, like Dr. Clayton said. The good thing is that he's not in any danger at this point. Why don't you see if he wants to play outside when we get home? The doc said exercise would be good for him."

When they got home, Marty definitely wasn't in the mood to play. Even pulling the leash out didn't generate any doggy excitement. Charlotte left him snoozing in the living room and went downstairs to tell Miss Pierce the news. She was sure she would want to know.

She rapped lightly on the door and waited. Moments later, the door opened and Miss Pierce stood in the entrance. Charlotte blinked. Miss Pierce had on makeup—wine-colored lipstick, muted eye shadow, pink blush—even a little foundation. Miss Pierce hardly ever wore makeup. She also had on slim black pants, a white blouse, and a silver star-shaped necklace.

"Wow!" Charlotte blurted out. "You look really snazzy."

The new-and-improved Miss Pierce's eyes twinkled at the compliment. "Thank you, my dear. And how is our friend Marty?"

"Uh . . . he's fine. At least, that's what the vet says . . . but I'm still not sure. He's so . . . lethargic."

"Perfect description, dear. Marty did seem to have lost his spark." She nodded as she held the door open.

"Little dog not have spark?" a gruff voice said from inside the apartment.

Charlotte peered around the landlady. "Yuri!" she exclaimed. When she had first met the Russian man who owned Yuri's Fruit Stand, he'd seemed like a grouch. But he turned out to be Charlotte's first friend in Brookline, offering her a piece of fruit every day as she passed his stand on the way to school. Even his rough tone couldn't hide Yuri's concern for Marty's well-being.

Charlotte remembered how worried Yuri got when Miss Pierce went on a secret mission for NASA and no one knew where she was. The BSG thought something was up then, and now Charlotte actually had proof! The way Yuri looked at Miss Pierce could melt an iceberg.

Miss Pierce's face turned several shades of pink as she followed Charlotte's gaze. "Charlotte. Would you . . . would you like to come in?"

Yuri rose from the sofa and stood there with his hands

shoved in his pockets. "What is news? How is little dog?"

"Uh . . . the vet says he's okay, but he's really not acting like himself."

Yuri's mouth spread into a huge smile. "No worry, Charlotte. That little dude rock it out."

Charlotte stifled a giggle. Yuri always sounded so funny mixing up modern expressions with his thick accent.

Miss Pierce's hands fluttered off her pants, plucking invisible lint.

I should give them some space, Charlotte suddenly realized. *And tell the BSG that we were right all along about Miss Pierce and Yuri!*

"Well . . . I should go check on Marty again." Charlotte turned and fled upstairs. Talk about some news! This was something she definitely needed to share with her best friends ASAP. Too bad she also had to break the bad news about Marty. Avery would be really upset. She was completely crazy about dogs, and Marty in particular.

"What do you want for dinner, Char . . . ?" Mr. Ramsey's voice trailed off as she zoomed past him and headed toward the stairs.

"Oh . . . anything, Dad," Charlotte called down from her room as she logged on to the computer.

skywriter: Do u want the good news or the bad?

Kgirl: bad news??? better get it over with

lafrida: wait, where is Maeve?

4kicks: no clue. probably tired . . . tough game today, but we won, thanks to Maeve's goal!!!

skywriter: really? we should all high-five her tomorrow!

lafrida: Char, what's the bad news?

skywriter: Marty's been acting really funny

lafrida: how?

4kicks: is he telling jokes? ha-ha

skywriter: this is serious. My dad and I thought he was sick, so we took him 2 the vet

lafrida: oh, no! What did the vet say?

4 people here

skywriter
lafrida
Kgirl
4kicks

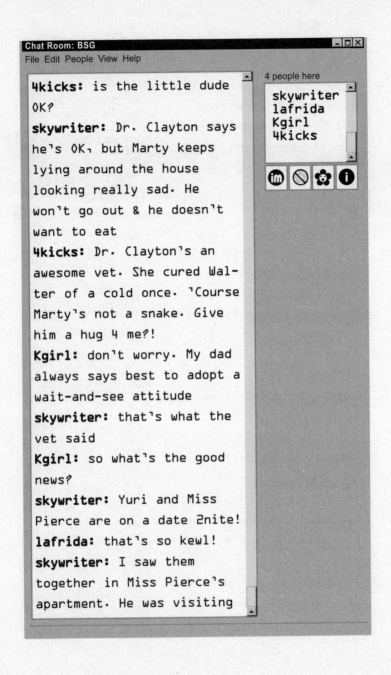

Chat Room: BSG

File Edit People View Help

4kicks: is the little dude OK?

skywriter: Dr. Clayton says he's OK, but Marty keeps lying around the house looking really sad. He won't go out & he doesn't want to eat

4kicks: Dr. Clayton's an awesome vet. She cured Walter of a cold once. 'Course Marty's not a snake. Give him a hug 4 me?!

Kgirl: don't worry. My dad always says best to adopt a wait-and-see attitude

skywriter: that's what the vet said

Kgirl: so what's the good news?

skywriter: Yuri and Miss Pierce are on a date 2nite!

lafrida: that's so kewl!

skywriter: I saw them together in Miss Pierce's apartment. He was visiting

4 people here

skywriter
lafrida
Kgirl
4kicks

CHAPTER

6

Courage in the Serengeti

fter dinner, her dad asked Charlotte to watch a special on the Serengeti with him. When they'd lived in Africa, her father had written a book called *Serengeti Summer . . . or, How I Survived an Elephant Stampede*. If she closed her eyes, Charlotte could still hear the sounds of the thundering animals.

"Dad, someday I'm going back to Africa," Charlotte suddenly blurted as she watched a mother elephant charge a jeep that had gotten too close to her baby.

Mr. Ramsey smiled and nodded. "I believe that you will, Charlotte. You were always drawn to the wildlife there, and you have the heart of an adventurer."

Her dad glanced down at Marty, who sat by their feet, his nose resting on his paws. Mr. Ramsey's smile melted into a look of concern. "But the wildlife around here still seems a little, well, less than wild," he said as he tried to get Marty to liven up by waving Happy Lucky Thingy in front of his face. Marty just turned his head away.

Charlotte frowned. "Dad, something is definitely wrong with Marty. He's crazy about Happy Lucky Thingy! Now he doesn't even care that you're waving it in front of his nose."

Happy Lucky Thingy was a toy that used to belong to Avery. The little pink character had traveled with her from Korea to the U.S., when Avery was adopted by her parents. The really weird thing about him was that he had a happy face on one side and a mad face on the other. Marty was obsessed with him.

Mr. Ramsey reached down and scratched the little dude behind the ears. "Don't worry, Charlotte. We'll take him back to Dr. Clayton if he doesn't bounce back soon."

Charlotte bent down to stroke Marty's fur. Staring mindlessly at the television screen, Charlotte tried to concentrate on the show again, but it was hopeless. And it wasn't just because of Marty. A teeny, tiny little worry started growing in Charlotte's mind. *Where was Nick after school, anyway? Was he talking to Chelsea the whole time?*

Charlotte chewed her nail as the worry got bigger. Chelsea *was* acting a lot more friendly and confident these days. Everyone had noticed it.

Aside from the BSG, Nick and Chelsea were probably her best friends in Brookline. So what if . . . what if . . . Charlotte didn't even want to think it, but she couldn't help it: *WHAT IF NICK LIKES CHELSEA?*

The idea was so uncomfortable, it made her sit up suddenly on the couch. What if Nick hadn't asked her to the dance yet because he didn't want to? And because . . . because he was going to ask Chelsea to the dance instead?

The thought made her feel like someone had just punched her in the stomach and she was about to turn green. Nick was the only boy she really wanted to go to the dance with. She couldn't imagine going with anyone else. . . . she'd rather go alone!

"What's up, Charlotte?" her dad asked in a concerned voice, breaking into her thoughts. "You look like you just saw a ghost."

Charlotte scratched Marty's ears. "Nothing. Just thinking," she said.

Mr. Ramsey reached for the bowl of microwave popcorn sitting on the coffee table. "About what? This show is about your favorite place in the whole world, and you're not even paying attention. What's going on, kiddo?"

Charlotte shook her head. Talking to her dad about boy stuff felt weird. It was at a time like this that Charlotte really missed her mom the most. Times when she needed advice that only a mom could give. But . . . looking at her dad's concerned expression, she decided that just maybe he might understand.

"Oh, Dad. It's just that . . . well . . . there's this, uhhh . . . boy."

Mr. Ramsey put the popcorn bowl down and turned toward her, his eyes serious. Charlotte took a deep breath. "I kind of like him and there's a big Valentine's Dance on Friday and I'm just thinking that, well . . . maybe he doesn't want to go with me." Her words came out in a rush.

Her dad smiled reassuringly. "Well, how do you know? Maybe he just hasn't worked up to asking you yet."

Charlotte leaned against him, resting her head on

his shoulder. Marty jumped down from her lap and scrambled out of the room. "What do you mean?"

Mr. Ramsey gave her a quick hug. She looked up at him.

"Well, it takes a lot of courage to ask a pretty girl like you to a dance . . . probably more courage than walking up to that lion on the screen there," he joked.

Charlotte smiled up at him. "Oh Dad, I'm just a regular girl. You should see some of the girls at school. They're *really* beautiful."

Mr. Ramsey turned to face his daughter. "Charlotte, you are a bright, beautiful girl! And I mean on the inside, too." Charlotte opened her mouth, but her dad put up a hand to stop her. "I know, I know, parents say this stuff all the time, but just listen one more time, okay? Humor an old guy."

She closed her mouth again and gave her dad a chance to finish. "Someone can be the most beautiful person on the planet," he went on, "but if they're unkind or selfish, it doesn't matter how beautiful they are on the outside. Eventually no one will want to be around her."

Immediately, images of Anna and Joline popped into her head. The Queens of Mean were two of the prettiest girls at Abigail Adams, but their personalities kind of reduced the dazzle of their looks. Charlotte imagined for a minute the Queens of Mean turned inside out . . . without their designer clothes and perfect makeup, but polite, friendly, and cheerful. Wow, what a crazy, mixed-up world that would be!

Mr. Ramsey reminisced. "I remember the first time

I planned on asking your mother out. I was a nervous wreck. I kept thinking about how I was going to ask her and whether she would say no. Trust me, kiddo. When a guy wants to ask a girl to a dance, it's not the easiest thing in the world. Especially when the girl is as beautiful as my incredibly lovely daughter."

Charlotte laughed and took a handful of popcorn. "I think you're a little blinded by love, Dad."

Mr. Ramsey crunched up his forehead. "Could be! But don't worry. I have a funny feeling that Nick Montoya just needs little more time to work up his nerve."

Charlotte gagged on the popcorn. Her dad gave her a few whacks on the back. When she finally got the popcorn down, she gazed at him with alarmed eyes. "Dad, how did you know—I mean, what makes you think I'm talking about Nick?"

Mr. Ramsey grinned and threw up his hands innocently. "I'm kidding! I'm kidding! I only said Nick, you know, as an example. Could be anyone. What do I know? I'm just your *clueless* dad."

Charlotte's face burned as she stared at the TV. Was her crush that obvious?

Finally her dad reached over and squeezed her shoulders. "I'm sorry. I shouldn't have teased you about it. It's just that I'm so sure everything will turn out okay. So let's get back the Serengeti, huh? Looks like that water buffalo is about to run down a zebra with a mean look in his eye."

When she went up to the Tower later that evening, Charlotte's worries returned in full force. Sure, her dad thought she was beautiful and everything, but that was the thing: He was her *dad*. What if Nick didn't think she was pretty? What if he thought of her as just a friend . . . a friend he had things in common with? What if he thought *Chelsea* was cool? Nick always asked to see Chelsea's latest photos, and now they were working on that Sentinel project together. . . .

Maybe if I write to Sophie, I can stop obsessing over this, she thought, shaking her head as if that would make all the unpleasant thoughts fly out her ears. Sophie lived in Paris, one of the many places Charlotte and her dad had lived, and was one of her best friends. Charlotte still really missed her French friend, especially right now.

```
To: Sophie
From: Charlotte
Subject: Nick & Marty


Dear Sophie,
I just have to tell all my thoughts to
someone or I'm never going to get to
sleep tonight. Ma chere, do you like
my cool new stationery? Those little
dogs doing backflips look just like
Marty! I'm sending a photo so you can
compare. But the real Marty hasn't
done a backflip all day. I just don't
know what's wrong with him. He is not
himself. The vet said he's not sick,
but I'm really worried. The little dude
```

just lies around like a sad rag doll.
And that's not the only thing going
wrong. I think Nick has been avoiding
me lately. There's a Valentine's Day
Dance this Friday, and I don't know
if he's going to ask me. He's been
hanging around my friend Chelsea a
lot. I don't want to be jealous, but
I can't help it. I mean, I thought
Nick kind of liked me. But maybe I'm
wrong. I wish I was back in Paris with
you right now! A box of our favorite
chocolates would make me forget all
about this crazy dance, I just know
it. Until then . . .

Au revoir!
Charlotte

Ice Cream and Secrets

Writing to Sophie about chocolate inspired Charlotte
to wander down to the kitchen in search of some double
chocolate chip ice cream. She never quite understood the
secret of ice cream. The creamy treat seemed to have the
power to make everyone feel better, and chocolate chips
put the dessert over the edge of perfection. *Whoever thought
of adding chocolate chips to ice cream should get the Nobel Peace
Prize,* she thought happily as she pulled open the freezer.

"What a day!" she said out loud. There was no ice
cream. Not even a Popsicle!

Charlotte let out a lion-sized sigh of disappointment and walked over to the note pad by the phone to add "ICE CREAM!" (in capital letters) to her dad's shopping list, but a red blinking light caught her attention. *A message! Could it be Nick?* That would definitely make up for no double chocolate chip ice cream!

Charlotte lifted up the phone and pressed play.

"Hi, Richard! Sorry I missed you." Normally Charlotte would hang up the phone at Richard—her dad got calls from other professors all the time—but this woman's voice sounded familiar. "Friday at eight is perfect. Le Bistro Français is my favorite restaurant! How did you know? I'll see you there!" The woman ended her message with a lighthearted laugh.

Charlotte's hands flew up to her mouth to stifle a surprised yelp. Only one person she knew laughed that way: Bif Madden, Avery's mom! But why was *her* dad meeting Avery's mom at Le Bistro Français? The restaurant was a trendy, cozy café with dim lighting and romantic little booths.

Oh, my gosh! My dad is going on a date with Avery's mom! Charlotte stiffened. She didn't know if she *wanted* her dad to have a date with Avery's mom. It was beyond weird. *Mrs. Madden going out with my dad?* And something told her that Avery wouldn't be too thrilled with the idea either.

Suddenly, thoughts of her dad and Avery's mom sharing a single strand of pasta like Lady and the Tramp floated through her brain. To keep that way-too-weird image from her mind, Charlotte headed back up to the Tower to start working on an outline for her *Sentinel* article. But all she could do was stare at the computer screen. "Serious case of writer's block," she said out loud to the empty Tower room. *How am I going to write an article about the Valentine's Day Dance when my dad can find a date that night, but Nick Montoya doesn't even like me anymore?*

Marty was cowering under Charlotte's desk, looking just as miserable as she felt. Lifting him into her lap, Charlotte scratched behind his ears.

"It's okay, Marty. We'll get through this. Somehow."

Charlotte's Journal
My Top Ten Things to Do Alone on
Valentine's Day:

1. *Eat double-chocolate-chip ice cream. (Make sure there's some on hand ahead of time.)*
2. *Take Marty to the park and play a game of fetch. (This only works if the little dude isn't moping around looking just as depressed as me!)*
3. *Write in my journal. (Only one paragraph of self-pity allowed.)*
4. *Watch a National Geographic Special on TV. (Avoid talking to Dad about his date.)*
5. *Go to the Book Nook and spend my allowance on a brand-new novel (fantasy or science fiction?).*
6. *Read all day.*
7. *IM with the BSG. They'll cheer me up.*
8. *Start a new story. (Set in Paris? Characters? A woman in a purple raincoat?)*
9. *E-mail Sophie.*

10. *Go to the Tower and watch the stars. (Ask Miss Pierce to show me the nebula she's researching.)*

Charlotte closed her journal. She was about to shut down the computer and go to bed, when a blinking light in her e-mail program alerted her: *one new message.*

To: Charlotte
From: Sophie
Subject: re: Nick and Marty

Bonjour, Charlotte,
Marty is *très* adorable! Thank you for
to send this new photo of him. I am
hoping you and the BSG can discover
why he is so sad. And you, my friend!
Do not be sad or worry. If Nick does
not like you, then he is crazy! But
you are *très magnifique*! I am sure he
will ask you to the dance. If he does
not, you can find a more handsome boy.
I will help you. What are you wearing?
Purple is your best color, but
something long and dark to contrast
your hair? Do you have snow? If snow,
light purple, I think!

Au revoir, mon amie,
Sophie

CHAPTER

7

MFT the Great!

Maeve opened the door to AAJH feeling so much better than she had the night before. *I mean,* she thought confidently, *what's a little face plant in the mud when a girl is wearing a super outfit?* Maeve felt so fabuloso that she had to restrain herself from dancing down the hallway.

The night before she and her mother had picked out her new boot-cut jeans, a white-and-pink-striped V-neck sweater, and soft pink loafers to match (boots were sooo yesterday, anyway) for Maeve to wear to school.

Her mother, after spending a half hour wiping sticky mud off Maeve's face with her special lavender-rose face lotion, explained that when you were having a terrible, awful day, looking good could make you feel so much better.

Maeve had gone to sleep glowing with the happy memory of her winning goal (minus the face plant, of course). Her sleepy vision included a cheer and a sweet kiss on the cheek from Dillon for an extra dollop of dreaminess.

Remembering how her mother had cheered her on—"You

are MKT! You kicked in the winning goal. So, dress for the success you are and no one will remember your little mud mishap"—Maeve felt ready to tackle whatever came her way. In fact, she was all set to continue her campaign to get Dillon to ask her to the Valentine's Day Dance.

Suddenly, she heard one of her least-favorite voices at AAJH.

"Hey, it's MFT!" Anna (QOM#1) pointed from her locker across the hall. Joline (QOM #2), stood giggling beside her, hiding her mouth with her hand.

Maeve flushed, but no way was Anna going to ruin her moment!

"Excuse me?" she retorted as she shifted one hip. "It's MKT for those in the know, but I'll let it pass this once, Anna. You're probably just upset about your *loss* yesterday."

"I don't think so, MFT. Do you, Joline?" Anna snickered and arched her eyebrow at her witchy partner.

Maeve began to walk away. Katani always said if you were going to defend yourself, do it quickly and move away before Anna and Joline worked up a head of steam. But then Maeve heard Joline's reply.

"Yeah, MFT! You know, Maeve—Mud Face Taylor. It kind of suits you," Joline spat out. And then they both cackled, their laughter filling the hallway.

Maeve gasped and spun around, her face burning with humiliation. It was all she could do to keep from screaming, "I'll get you, my pretties," in her best imitation of the Wicked Witch of the West. She had been practicing that line on her little brother Sam for years, and he always ran away whenever she whispered it behind him. She had to whisper it because her mother threatened her with a week's worth of grounding for scaring Sam. But this was different—Anna and Joline deserved a good scare.

"No, a name like that doesn't suit Maeve at all," a stern Mrs. Fields reprimanded. All three girls spun around to face the principal of AAJH.

"And if I hear it from anyone ever again, I'll know just whom to call to my office. AAJH does not allow name calling . . . ever."

Maeve looked up at Mrs. Fields, her face flushed with gratitude.

Mrs. Fields seems to have this knack for ferreting out hall trouble before anything bad really happens, Maeve thought admiringly. And the principal was smart enough not to give special attention to the student who was being picked on. It was like she knew that any sympathy from her would cause problems for the victim later on.

"Now, get moving, girls. You will be late for class. And this ends right here and now. Am I understood?" She looked sternly at all of them. Maeve nodded, and so did Anna and Joline. Of course they pouted too, Maeve noted smugly. But she was relieved. Nobody messed with Mrs. Fields—the Queens of Mean included.

Maeve paused while the QOM flew off down the hall on their brooms. She gave a quick smile to Mrs. Fields, who simply said, "Nice goal."

As she headed toward class, Maeve hoped that Anna and Joline hadn't spread their little joke at her expense. All of sudden she had a horrible thought. *What if Dillon and Avery are calling me MFT too?*

Maeve paused at the door to first-period science class and took a deep breath, suddenly afraid that when she walked into the classroom, everyone would laugh at her.

"Maeve, I heard . . . " Isabel said, but before she could finish, Avery jogged up, followed by Charlotte and Katani.

"What were you doing with Anna and Joline and Mrs. Fields in the hallway? Yurt said Mrs. Fields looked really mad."

"I don't want to talk about it," Maeve grumbled.

"Were the QOM on the attack?" Avery asked, concern in her voice.

"I said I don't want to talk about it," Maeve answered sharply. She'd had enough for one day.

"Let's just go in and sit down?" Charlotte, sensitive to her friend's discomfort, suggested when the bell rang. The rest of the class had already filed past, into the room. Maeve thought everyone would be looking at her, but no one was. Maybe Mrs. Fields really had saved the day.

Mixing up Some Love Potion

"You're in luck, people," Mr. Moore said. "I'm going to be Mr. Nice Guy and let you choose your own lab partners today." *Oh, lovely,* Maeve thought. *Who will want to work with Mud Face Taylor!* Suddenly her mother's words popped in her head and she decided to just try to pay attention to the science teacher. She was MKT. She was!

Mr. Moore picked up a huge stuffed cow from his desk and gave it a squeeze. It let out a long, loud "Moooooooooo."

His bright orange tie, decorated with purple cows, looked to Maeve like a traffic cone with an awful disease. Mr. Moore was kind of obsessed with goofy-looking cow paraphernalia, but he was a good teacher.

Riley walked up to her desk so quietly, Maeve jumped when he spoke. "Want to be partners?" Maeve scanned the room for Dillon. He was talking to Henry Yurt. What was he saying? Her stomach began to churn. Her hopes for a date with Dillon were fading fast.

"I guess." Maeve sounded so unfriendly, Riley hesitated for a moment. But when she scooched her stool over, Riley put down his backpack and stared at his shoes. "Um, I heard about your goal—"

"What?" Maeve snapped. "Wait, never mind. Don't tell me."

"No, I mean, your goal rocked!" Riley grimaced when he saw Maeve's horrified expression. "I didn't know you could play soccer."

"I can't." Maeve stared hard at Riley's face. Was he actually trying to make her feel better? Weird. They were kind of friends, but they usually just chatted about music. "I stink at soccer," she said.

"Maeve, you rock at everything you do." He grinned, and Maeve felt some of her frustration washing away. She pulled out her lab notebook and started reading the directions for Love Potion #9 out loud to Riley.

A Confident Girl

Katani strolled over to Reggie's desk. "Want to work together?"

He nodded. "Sure thing."

Chelsea watched Katani, wondering how that girl managed to be so calm and confident. Her ease with Reggie gave Chelsea an idea. This was a perfect opportunity to work with someone different. Someone like Trevor. He sat on the other side of the classroom, stuffing some papers in his notebook with a look of concentration that set Chelsea's heart pounding in her ribcage. *I'll ask if he wants to work together, and maybe we'll get talking about photography again! Maybe I should tell him about the action shots I got of him playing soccer?*

Chelsea opened her mouth to call out Trevor's name. But she never got the chance.

"Hey, T-Dawg," Avery said, bouncing over to him with a grin. "Wanna work with me?"

Trevor caught Chelsea looking at him from across the room and gave her a nod. But he turned right back to Avery. "Sure." He scooted his stool over so that Avery could slip onto the one beside him.

Chelsea's hope faded like a flower drooping and turning brown. Did Avery have to be buddies with every guy in the school? Chelsea turned to ask Charlotte to be her partner, but Char was talking to Isabel. Then she noticed Nick sitting alone. Maybe he'd be her partner.

Worse than a Klutz Attack

"Char, do you think Maeve is okay?" Isabel asked.

"Yeah, I think so. . . ." Charlotte's gaze drifted to a certain dark-haired boy. "Izzy, do you mind if I ask Nick to be my lab partner?"

Isabel looked over at Nick and Chelsea. "Better go quick!" she replied.

Charlotte made her way across the room, stopping to ask Avery a quick question about her dog depression research first. She didn't want to look too obvious . . . but she was ready to take Sophie's advice. Of course Nick still liked her. He and Chels were just friends, and she was friends with both of them.

"Hey, Nick." Charlotte smiled. "Want to be my partner?"

Nick's eyes opened wide for a second and he played with his pen, flipping it over and over in his fingers. "Ummm . . . sorry, Char. I'd love to, but Chelsea and I are kind of working together already, but . . ."

Charlotte stumbled away before she heard the rest of Nick's sentence. Charlotte wanted to go to the nurse's office and lie down. It was so obvious, and there was absolutely no denying it now: Nick definitely liked Chelsea. Charlotte glanced around the room, sweat breaking out on her palms. Whom could she work with? Isabel gave her an apologetic smile. *I thought you were working with Nick!* she mouthed from her stool next to Kevin.

Mortified, Charlotte realized not having anyone to work with was definitely worse than a klutz attack! It was a ticket to loserville!

"My, my!" Mr. Moore walked over to Charlotte. "It seems we have an odd number today. Would you like to be my lab assistant?" It was now official: Charlotte Ramsey was a loser!

Mr. Moore didn't wait for a yes or no. He handed

Charlotte the stuffed cow and perched on the edge of his desk. "In honor of the holiday this weekend—I think you all know the one I mean—today we are going to perform an experiment, making a mixture I like to call "Love Potion Number Nine."

The class erupted into laughter. Charlotte smiled weakly.

The Yurtmeister waved his hand in the air. "Hey! What happened to the other eight?"

Everyone giggled.

Mr. Moore rolled his eyes. "Very clever, Mr. Yurt. It comes from an old song—'Love Potion Number 9.' Ask your grandparents."

Mr. Moore took out a jar of pickled red cabbage, opened it with a flourish, poured a little bit into a beaker, and handed the jar to Charlotte. She wrinkled up her nose at the strong smell.

"Do you know what this substance is?" Mr. Moore asked.

"Smells like dirty gym socks!" the always wisecracking Dillon shouted. Henry Yurt gave him a high five.

"Oh, it's even better than that! This cabbage juice is an acid-base indicator. Would you like to hand me the baking soda and vinegar, Charlotte?"

Trevor lifted a hand in the air. "We made volcanoes out of baking soda and vinegar at my old school."

Mr. Moore nodded. "I bet you'll like this experiment better. Prepare to be amazed! Charlotte, pour in a pinch of that baking soda."

Charlotte gritted her teeth with concentration. This

was the perfect opportunity for disaster, but her hands held steady, and to her surprise, just the tiniest sprinkling of baking soda caused an explosion of blue-green foam!

"Cool!" several voices called out from around the room.

Mr. Moore whisked the beaker over to the sink by his desk before any foam got on the floor. "Now the vinegar!" His tie was stuck sideways in one of his buttonholes, but he didn't seem to notice. Charlotte walked over to the sink and tipped the bottle of vinegar over the green foam.

Pink froth bubbled up, completely covering the green!

Cheers and whistles erupted from around the classroom. Mr. Moore took a bow, put the beaker down and, recognizing Charlotte's discomfort, led her over to Maeve and Riley.

"You'll be a group of three. Now everyone get to work! Your job is to explain *why* Love Potion Number Nine changes color. If you get up to page three before the end of the period, I have some other household items you can drop in your beakers for extra credit. Tums, ammonia, lemon juice . . . have a blast, and, *may the force be with you!*"

Mr. Moore was both a cow lover *and* a card-carrying member of the official Star Wars Fan Club. He never let a class period go by without trying to include some dialogue from the movies. That was just part of his weirdness, and most of the students loved it.

Usually Mr. Moore's quotes made Maeve laugh. Not today. She studied the handout, her brow wrinkled in concentration. Math and science always made her brain fog. Why did there have to be so many numbers and symbols? What if Riley thought she was stupid? At least Charlotte was in the group to save her from complete embarrassment.

"Maeve, the experiment's easy," Charlotte promised. Despite her own misery, Charlotte knew that numbers always put Maeve into a panic, and she couldn't stand seeing one of her best friends get upset.

"Yeah, but look at these questions!" Maeve bit her lip. "What the heck is this word? Looks like Nacho-Three."

"There's a chart on page one," Riley flipped back. "$NaHCO_3$ is baking soda, I guess. Why don't they just say that?"

"That's what I was just thinking!" Maeve grinned, but her smile faded when she heard Dillon laugh. He was goofing around with Avery. They kept flicking green foam across the table—until Mr. Moore came along and told them to cut it out or they'd have extra homework that night.

"Uh . . . Maeve?" Riley said, putting the beaker down on the lab table. It quietly *clinked*. He followed her eyes and saw what had drawn her attention. Charlotte watched Riley stare at his hands under the table. She felt bad, but how could she explain to him that this was just how Maeve was? She'd be over Dillon eventually, and then some other boy would get her attention. Maybe it would even be Riley. You never knew with Maeve.

Charlotte added a spoonful of vinegar and watched pink froth bubble over the side of the beaker. *Excellent*, she thought. *Maybe my love potion will work on Nick. Then he'll ask me, not Chelsea, to the dance, and everything will be perfect.*

If only love potions really existed, she thought wistfully as she marked notes on her lab sheet.

A loud laugh broke her concentration. She whipped her head around to see Chelsea fidgeting on her stool beside Nick. Charlotte wished she had earplugs.

Green Foam and Romance

On the other side of the room, Reggie and Katani worked with their heads close together. They had finished the main experiment, and had the extra-credit ingredients arranged in a neat line. The Tums didn't cause nearly as much green foam as the baking soda.

"Our stomachs are acidic," Reggie explained. "Baking soda changes the chemistry completely to a base, which isn't good. That's why we take Tums, 'cause they only cut back on the worst acid."

Katani shook her head. "Reggie, you're the super kind of nerd! I think you'll be famous one day . . . like Bill Gates, even."

Reggie shook his head, but Katani could tell he was pleased by the comment. "Nah. I just like to learn about how the world works . . . that's all." He picked up one of the soft pink tablets and stared at it intently. "You're pretty intelligent yourself."

Katani looked up from her calculator, completely missing his awkward blush. "Well, my grandma is the principal. She'd be so disappointed in me if she saw I wasn't trying my best. Anyway, if you want to be successful in life, you've got to study hard. I mean, Reggie, how else am I going to start my own business if I don't learn everything I can while I'm in school? And I have to start my own business," she said, an urgent tone in her voice. "I just have to."

"You will. You've got it all going for you, Katani. You're organized, smart, pretty . . . " Reggie looked down at the Tums again.

Katani leaned over the beaker and whispered, "That's about the nicest thing anyone has ever said to me." Reggie squirmed under her gaze and accidentally dropped the Tums into the beaker.

Green froth splashed out, spattering on Katani's perfect notes and speckling her smile with flakes of foam.

"Oh, my gosh, I'm so sorry! I'll get you a paper towel." Reggie, his face red, jumped up, but Katani touched his shoulder and took a yellow handkerchief out of her school bag.

"Reggie DeWitt, do you want to go to the Valentine's Day Dance with me?"

"Sure!" He shrugged, trying to be a little cool. Katani smiled, and caught Charlotte's gaze. Katani just asked a boy to the dance! Just like that! And it didn't even matter that she had green foam on her nose!

CHAPTER

8

Secret Notebooks
and Girl Talk

When the bell rang, Charlotte tripped over Riley's backpack in her hurry to talk to Katani. One well-worn notebook dropped out and spun across the floor. Charlotte bent to pick it up, then looked around for Riley. He was ducking out the door, his open backpack slung over one shoulder. Maybe he hadn't noticed? She opened the cover and saw the handwritten lyrics of a new song, underneath a doodle of the logo of his band, Mustard Monkey.

Furniture Boy
by Riley Lee
The girl I love thinks I'm a piece of furniture.
She can't see me even though I look at her.
Help me, help me, find a way to win her heart.
Keep her close and never ever ever part.

My life's crazy 'cause she'll never ever see.
Furniture boy — that's me.
The Furniture Boy — that's me. . . .

Charlotte quickly closed the cover. This was private. She shouldn't be reading it at all!

Katani walked over, her bag slung casually over one shoulder.

"What was that look for, girl? And what's that you're holding?" Katani made a face at the scuffed, stained, and torn state of Riley's notebook.

"Oh, nothing," Charlotte held the notebook behind her back. "Did you really ask Reggie to the dance?"

"Of course! Girl power. We need to take control." Katani frowned at Charlotte's expression. "When are you asking Nick?"

Charlotte shrugged and looked at the floor.

"We need to have a talk." Katani put an arm around Charlotte and led her out of the room. "Just you and me. After school in the Tower?"

Charlotte nodded okay and looked around for Riley. "See you in math class?" She forced a smile, and Katani reluctantly let her go.

Riley was kneeling next to his locker, frantically searching through piles of notebooks and papers. Charlotte held out his collection of lyrics. "Umm, is this yours?"

Riley snatched the notebook. He said nothing, but first his ears and then his cheeks flushed red.

"I didn't read it," Charlotte whispered. As she walked

away, she wondered if a boy would ever write song lyrics about her.

After about a million years, the last bell of the day rang and Charlotte joined the crowd of students flooding into the hallways. When she reached her locker, she rummaged inside it, looking for her social studies book. She checked her hair in the mirror, her spirits sinking. Maybe it was time for a makeover. She'd been wearing her hair the same way forever. Katani could give her some tips this afternoon—for something more glamorous and grownup. Avery's mom had once told her she should try a curler, at least for the ends.

Avery's mom! Charlotte leaned her head against the locker. *I still have to break the news about my dad's date to Avery!*

"What's up, Charlotte?" a familiar voice called behind her. A voice that for some reason made her insides turn into lime Jell-O.

Her heart jumped as she turned around to look at Nick. He stood there with a nervous smile on his face.

"Yes?" she asked, and chewed her bottom lip.

"You wanna meet tomorrow morning at Montoya's before school?" He smiled and waited, his backpack slug over one shoulder.

Charlotte felt her own expression brightening. She couldn't keep her excitement inside! *He wants to meet me tomorrow morning? Yes! Yes!* Maybe the whole Nick-and-Chelsea thing was just a figment of her imagination! "Sure," she told him. "I think I can make it."

This is it! she thought. *Tomorrow morning, he's going to ask me to the Valentine's Day Dance, and I'm going to say yes!*

She turned to shut her locker, but accidentally caught her finger in the locker door. "Ouch!" she shouted, rubbing her finger as she felt her face turning red.

"Are you okay?" he asked.

Charlotte gritted her teeth. "Uh . . . yeah. I'm fine."

Nick looked concerned. "Tomorrow morning at seven thirty. Okay? Want to walk home together?"

"I can't!" Charlotte regretted the words as soon as they came out. But it was true—she couldn't leave before talking to Avery. "But I'll see you in the morning!" She blew on her sore finger as Nick nodded and waved good-bye.

Charlotte found Avery after a fifteen-minute-long search through the hallways. She was in the gym, shooting baskets with Dillon and the Trentini twins.

"Ave! Can you stop for a second?" Charlotte called out.

Avery landed a perfect layup, then trotted over. "Hey, Char. What's up?"

"I need to talk to you." Charlotte twisted her hair around her fingers.

"Okay, shoot!" Avery tossed a pretend basketball to her friend.

"Not now!" Charlotte lowered her voice. "Can you come to the Tower later this afternoon? Just you."

"I'm practicing with these guys till four, but I can come right after. Is that cool?" Avery frowned. "Is everything okay?"

"Yes . . . fine. See you later?"

The Ultimate Makeover

Charlotte walked home looking forward to a few minutes of quiet time curled up with a good book and Marty. *That's just what I need after a day like today.*

But there was Katani, already sitting on the front steps, wrapped in a stylish wool coat, a hand-appliquéd messenger bag resting by her feet.

"Where have you been, girlfriend?" Katani tapped her watch. "I was just about to leave."

"Oh!" Charlotte exclaimed. "I'm so sorry. . . ." She unlocked the door, realizing maybe Katani's kind advice and style tips would be more helpful than escaping into a book. "I got caught up after school." She couldn't tell Katani about meeting with Avery, because their parents dating seemed like the kind of thing that deserved some privacy—even from best friends. She was sure Avery would feel the same way.

"No problem." Katani took off her coat and opened the messenger bag so Charlotte could see the neat rows of little pink containers, brushes, and spray bottles inside. There was even a curling iron! "Let's go up to the Tower," Katani suggested. "I've got everything we need right here!"

Katani unloaded her bag on the windowsill behind the lime green swivel, her favorite styling chair. Charlotte thought there seemed to be plenty of makeup items lined up there already, but what did she know about makeovers?

Katani folded her arms just so. "Okay, Char, let's get this show started!"

Charlotte sat down and touched her hair. "What's your game plan?"

Katani grinned. "Charlotte Elizabeth Ramsey is in need of a new, confidence-boosting, life-changing make-over so she can get up the courage to ask her dream date to the dance!"

Charlotte giggled, "Katani, I think it's time you had your own talk show."

"There, that's better already, and we haven't even started yet!" Katani leaned down and gave Charlotte a hug. "I saw what happened in science lab today. And, honestly, Char, I don't think you have anything to worry about. Nick Montoya is just not the kind of boy to ditch a girl without saying something first. He just isn't!"

Charlotte smiled. "He does want to meet me at the bakery tomorrow morning."

"Am I right or what?" Katani joked. "Now, sit back and relax while I work my magic."

Charlotte felt her super-tight nerves release as Katani's hands worked through her hair.

"Tomorrow morning is the perfect opportunity!" Katani let go of Charlotte's hair and took out several tubes of cream blush. "Are you dusty rose or peach?"

"Do you really think he'll ask me to the dance?" Charlotte asked.

Katani stopped with a blob of peach blush on her fingertips. "Oh, no . . . YOU will ask HIM."

"I will?" Charlotte squeaked.

Katani nodded and started dabbing at Charlotte's cheeks. "Remember, blush is an accent! Not too thick, and rub it in evenly." Katani spoke as if she were already in a TV studio giving directions to a rapt audience of fans.

Charlotte closed her eyes and pictured walking into Montoya's, sipping hot chocolate with Nick, and asking him . . . what? "What would I say?" Charlotte asked.

"Here." Katani pulled over the chair from Charlotte's desk. "I'm Nick, and this is a hot chocolate." Katani held up a bottle of hairspray. "Good morning, Charlotte," she said, making her voice a little deeper.

Charlotte burst out laughing.

Katani, eyes twinkling, said in a stern but kind voice, "This is serious business! Learn from me. I'm Charlotte now. You've had half a mug of hot chocolate, and there's a meaningful pause in the conversation. You ask: 'Nick Montoya, do you have any plans for the dance on Friday'?"

"Ummm, no?" Charlotte said, stifling the giggles that threatened to burst out.

"Would you like to go with me?" Katani leaned in close, still holding the hairspray. "Now you try."

They repeated the scenario four or five times, then Katani fussed her way through about seventeen different shades of nail polish, eye shadow, and lipstick.

"Now remember, you've got to walk with attitude when you get in there. Make eye contact and look confident," Katani said as she demonstrated the correct way to apply the sparkly eye shadow she was wearing. That was good because Charlotte was pretty much hopeless at putting on makeup. But with Katani's masterful tutoring, Charlotte learned how to spread on the eye shadow with a light touch so she didn't look like a raccoon. Charlotte was having a great time, but she kept glancing at the clock by her desk. What if Avery showed up and Katani was still here?

Katani sighed with satisfaction as she finished curling the ends of Charlotte's hair. "This is what I love to do—help people reach their full fashion potential."

Charlotte knew all about her friend's dreams for Kgirl Enterprises. "I can see it all now," she said. "Kgirl fashion and style stores in every major city in America! No—in every major city around the world!"

Katani played along. "Ladies who need some serious help in the style department will stampede to my stores and I will hook them up with the coolest clothes and makeup the world has ever seen!"

Charlotte stood up. "And then Kgirl Talk, the number-one TV talk show all over the world!"

"You mean number-two, after Oprah!" Katani scolded. Oprah was her idol and she would never want to dethrone the queen of all talk shows!

Katani held out a hand for Charlotte and directed her friend over to the full-length mirror.

"You look fierce," she said, staring at Charlotte with pride. Her friend's hair was down and curled just the slightest bit at the ends. Sparkly lilac eye shadow complemented her light pink nail polish. "You're going to knock that boy dead."

"Thanks, Katani," Charlotte told her, and gave her a quick hug. "I should take Marty out now."

"What about your outfit?" Katani asked.

"Didn't we decide I'd wear my favorite purple sweater?" The minute hand inched forward. It was almost four-fifteen! Avery would be there any minute.

"Yes, but you've got to try it on!" Katani pointed toward the steps down to Charlotte's room.

"Okay . . ." Charlotte dashed down to her room, threw on the sweater, and sprinted back up to the Tower.

"Perfect!" Katani gave the outfit two thumbs-up. "Not too dressy. Comfortable and sophisticated."

Charlotte gave a quick glance at the clock. "I usually take Marty out right away when I get home . . ."

"Do you want me to come?" Katani asked.

"Oh, no!" Charlotte said. "I mean, you'd get your nice shoes all muddy, and it's really not a big deal. Thanks sooo much for your fashion wisdom! I'd be lost without you." She threw her arms around Katani and gave her a big hug.

"I'm always there for my BSG!" Katani gave Charlotte a funny look, wondering why she seemed so eager to get her out the door. *It's probably just nerves*, Katani thought. "I have a lot of sewing to get done on my dress for Friday, anyway," she said as Charlotte walked her down to the front door.

"I've done all I can," Katani announced as she waved good-bye. "Now it's up to *you* to take control!" She didn't notice a small figure sprinting down the street from the other direction.

CHAPTER

9
Sister Act

W here's the Kgirl running off to?" Avery asked as she
dropped her backpack by the front door.

"She had to go home and I needed to talk to you.
This is very important. Let's go upstairs." Charlotte started
up the stairs.

"What's going on, Char? It's not more bad news about
Marty, I hope," Avery asked as she hurriedly scrambled
after Charlotte.

"No—it's not that. Although the little guy is still not
himself." Charlotte sighed over her shoulder as she made
her way up to her bedroom.

"Whoa, that's some makeup job, Char," Avery said, getting a closer look at Charlotte's face. "I hope you didn't call
me over to talk to me about *that*! I'm not wearing makeup
to the dance, no matter what anyone says. I hate the way
it feels on my skin," she complained.

Charlotte shook her head no and plopped down onto
her bed. Marty was curled up in a pathetic doggy blob at

the foot of the bed. He managed to give a small wag of his short little tail when he saw Avery.

"Awww!" Avery knelt down and reached into her pocket. "Poor little dude. I stopped and bought you some treats." She offered one to Marty, who snarfed it down as he whined pitifully.

Avery dumped two pocketfuls of dog treats on the bed. "The little dude is a lot worse that I thought. You sure he's okay?"

Charlotte leaned over to scratch his belly. "I don't know. It's like he knows everything is going wrong."

Avery stared expectantly. "What's going wrong? What are you trying to tell me?"

"Your mom left my dad a phone message last night," Charlotte said.

Avery shrugged. "So?" She offered Marty another treat, which he promptly gobbled up despite his droopy state.

"Geesh, Charlotte. I don't think Marty has lost his appetite. He's going after these treats like an alligator." As if he understood what Avery was saying, the little dude rolled over on his side and stared at both girls with sad doggy eyes. The effect was so comical that both girls began a fit of giggling. With that, Marty jumped up and ran under Charlotte's bed.

"I think Marty needs a doggy shrink," a stunned Avery remarked. "He's never acted like that before."

"All three of us might need a shrink when I finish telling you about your mom and my dad." Charlotte looked at Avery pointedly.

"This sounds serious," Avery said, a little frightened.

"If you think your dad and my mom going on a date for dinner to Le Bistro Français at eight o'clock Friday night is serious, then it is! *Super* serious," Charlotte added for emphasis.

Avery's eyes widened. "Wait a minute. Are you trying to tell me your dad's meeting my mom at that fancy restaurant?"

"In a word, yes." Charlotte took one of Avery's dog treats, reached down, and fed it to a waiting Marty.

Avery's eyes grew even wider. "The one where it's kind of dark and they have candles and guys walking around playing violins and stuff?"

"That's the one," answered Charlotte as she flopped back on her pillow. "It was bad enough when we caught my dad and Lissie McMillan sharing a candlelit dinner on our trip to Montana . . . and it turned out they were just friends."

"Yeah, that was weird," Avery agreed. "But this is even weirder. My mom and Mr. Ramsey," she mumbled as she plopped down on the floor. She tried to coax a wounded Marty with more treats to come out from his hiding place.

"What if my dad and your mom get *married*?" Charlotte put her hands over her face, trying to push away all the distressing thoughts that surfaced.

"Wow!" Avery said, fiddling with a hair elastic that she found on the floor. "That would be so weird."

Charlotte looked at her, exasperated. "Is 'weird' all you can say?"

Avery turned to look at her. Her mouth opened. Shut. Opened again. "They . . . they're going . . . on a . . . a date," Avery stuttered. "My mom's dating your dad and she didn't even tell me."

Charlotte sat up a little, resting on her elbows. Pushing away the thought that she might have to call Mrs. Madden "Mom."

"Yeah, my dad didn't tell me, either. That really bothers me."

"Yeah, I know what you mean. I mean . . . not your dad . . . not telling me . . . my mom . . ." a very confused Avery rambled. "Gosh, this is so weird."

"If you say 'weird' one more time, I am going to put . . . makeup on you," threatened Charlotte.

"No way!" Avery yelled.

Marty yelped quietly. "See, even Marty doesn't like that idea!" Avery said, and fed him another treat. Marty sat up a little and delicately snatched two more treats from Avery's hand.

Charlotte folded her arms. "Well, I think we've established the fact that your mom and my dad going out is totally strange. The real question is: What are we going to do? I mean, do we tell them that we know?"

Avery popped up, her eyes wide. "No way, dude! I'm not going to talk to my mom about this. I mean . . . she's my mom! I can't tell her who to go out with. Remember when I was visiting my dad in Colorado and he was dating Andie?"

She looked up at Charlotte with a devilish grin, "At least you're not Crazie Kazie." Kazie was Andie's daughter, and she and Avery were definitely not on the same page. Avery couldn't imagine having to deal with Kazie as a sister! Avery jumped up, realizing something important. "Wait! If they get married, we'll be related!"

Charlotte sat up straight and gasped. "We'd be sisters!"

Avery jumped up and threw her arms around Charlotte. "A sister! That would be so cool. Scott and Tim would love it too."

"Yeah!" Charlotte said, a grin spreading across her face, "I've always wanted a sister too. It's kind of lonely being an only child. Never anyone to talk to, and no one to listen to you talk about all your problems. Hey! Maybe this won't be so bad after all. . . ."

Avery pulled away from her. Her animated face suddenly grew serious—something Avery rarely was. "Wait a minute. We can't tell the rest of the BSG yet. I mean, with Maeve's parents getting a divorce and us not knowing everything."

Charlotte nodded. "I agree. Let's make a pact. Hold your right hand up, palm facing me."

"Why?'

"Just do it, Avery," Charlotte said with a serious tone to her voice.

"Okay. Okay. Chill!" Avery raised her right hand, palm facing Charlotte. Then Charlotte raised her right hand and faced her.

"Repeat after me," said Charlotte. "I promise."

Avery made a face but repeated. "I promise."

"That I will not . . ."

Avery rolled her eyes. Oaths were cheesy, but this was for a good cause. "That I will not . . ."

"Reveal to anyone that our parents are dating," said Charlotte.

Avery echoed Charlotte's words, and the two girls sat staring at Marty. He'd eaten the last of Avery's treats and was lying on his back, whining softly.

"What would happen to Marty if my mom moved in?" Avery said, concerned. "She's allergic."

Charlotte didn't know what to say to that, but Marty did. He suddenly gave a huge doggy burp.

"Eeew!" Charlotte held her nose. "I think we fed him too many treats!" She stood up and opened the door. "Speaking of treats, I've got a chocolate bar in my desk drawer up in the Tower. Want to go up?"

The two of them climbed up the Tower stairs. And while Avery munched on her half of the caramel milk chocolate bar, Charlotte pulled up her e-mail at her writing desk.

"Wait a sec, Ave. I have to e-mail Sophie. Then let's take Marty to the park? Maybe all those treats gave him some energy."

Avery nodded, happy with her chocolate and a burping Marty.

While Charlotte wrote, she rubbed the sleeve of her mom's vintage denim jacket, the one Katani always said was so retro chic. From her desk she could see out the window toward the Boston Public Gardens and, beyond that, the Atlantic Ocean.

She began typing as Avery lay on the floor next to Marty.

To: Sophie
From: Charlotte
Subject: re: Dance

Hey, Sophie. I have big news. *Mon amie* Katani talked me into it—I'm asking Nick to the dance. I'm meeting him 2morrow morning at his family's bakery. Katani helped me curl my hair in the most adorable way. She says not too much makeup, though, and she gave me this sparkly eye shadow that you would love. I hope I don't mess up!!! I'm so nervous, Sophie. What if he says no? Katani says it's not possible, but I don't know.
Au revoir, Charlotte

P.S. I think my dad is secretly dating my friend Avery's mom. Strange, huh?
P.P.S. Have you seen Orangina? If you ever catch a glimpse of that rascal cat, say *bonjour* from me! Marty's still moping around. Avery and I are going to take him to the park, gtg! I miss u sooo much!!!

A Doggy Shrink

February wasn't the greatest time of year in Amory

Park, but the warm weather spell had all sorts of people out jogging, pushing strollers, or chatting on cell phones as they walked their dogs.

"I brought Happy Lucky Thingy from the Tower," said Avery, fishing the toy out of her pocket and tossing it toward a picnic bench.

Charlotte gasped. "Avery! You can't just throw Happy Lucky Thingy around! He's a thingy, not a ball!"

Avery laughed and crouched down beside Marty. "Go get it, Marty. Go get it, boy!"

But Marty only stood next to them, his head bent low, his ears drooping, and his tail sagging. He whined a bit, a mournful sound as pitiful as a baby crying.

"Hey, isn't that Ms. Pink and La Fanny?" Avery picked up Happy Lucky Thingy and pointed down the path past the bench.

Marty perked up suddenly, and gave a little yip.

"Yeah, and that's her new boyfriend, Zak, with the rottweiler." Charlotte waved, but the couple didn't seem to see. "Isabel and I saw them just the other day."

"Come on, little dude!" Avery tugged Marty's leash. "Let's go say hi to your girlfriend!"

Marty sat down suddenly, and his mournful whining deepened into a growl. Charlotte watched Ms. Pink's brightly colored hair disappear behind a pine tree.

"What is wrong with you, Marty man?" Avery tugged the leash, and the dog flopped down on his stomach, paws digging in the dirt as Avery dragged him forward. She was strong, but Marty was obviously determined not to go anywhere.

"Bizarre," Charlotte said. "He won't go. They're gone now, anyway."

"I think Marty might be depressed," Avery said sadly as they trudged out of the park, the little pup trotting beside them on his leash.

"Is that even possible?" Charlotte asked.

"Who knows?" Avery knelt down to give Marty a hug before taking off down her street. "I'm going straight home to do some research!"

Avery's Blog

After some serious scientific research (ten minutes online, ha-ha), I have determined that the strange phenomenon of dog depression really does exist! Here are some signs to look out for. Your dog may be depressed if he or she:

1. *Doesn't want to play*
2. *Avoids eye contact*
3. *Refuses to move*
4. *Eats less*
5. *Runs away from you*
6. *Doesn't like being held*
7. *Acts more aggressive than usual*

It looks like our pal Marty only had the first three symptoms. Here are some possible cures for a depressed doggy:

1. *Lots of extra love and attention*
2. *Find other dogs to play with. Your pet needs friends too!*

3. *Visit a veterinarian*

Why do dogs get depressed? For basically the same reasons people do:

1. *Someone they care about died or went away.*
2. *A huge change like moving from one place to another*
3. *A new baby, pet, or person they don't know moves in.*

But none of those applies to Marty! So what's wrong?

CHAPTER

10

Breakfast at the Bakery

Charlotte couldn't help smiling as she surveyed herself in the mirror. Her favorite purple sweater brought out the color of Katani's sparkly lilac eye shadow, and her new jeans hung perfectly on her slender frame. She pronounced Katani's style makeover a major success.

As she made one final twirl she thought, *I'm ready to ask Nick to the dance today*—even though her heart hammered in her chest, her knees wobbled, and she didn't know if she'd be able to eat a single bite of anything at Brookline's famous bakery.

Just then, she heard a knock on her bedroom door.

"Come in, Dad," Charlotte said, smoothing down her hair—still warm from the curling iron—with nervous fingers.

Dad poked his head in and whistled. "Wow, sweetie! You're dressed up. What's the occasion?"

Charlotte pushed back a sliver of hurt. Her dad was keeping the important news about his date from her, but he wanted to hear about her life. Charlotte didn't feel like she could share right now. "Uh . . . Dad, there's no special occasion. I just wanted to look nice this morning."

Mr. Ramsey held up his hands and smiled. "Well, you look beautiful . . . as always. Come on into the kitchen. I'll fix you some breakfast."

Charlotte danced over and gave him a peck on the cheek. "Sorry, Dad. I'm going to Montoya's this morning. Thanks, anyway."

"Well, give my best to the BSG." Her Dad smiled, gave her a little wave, and walked back to the kitchen.

Charlotte rushed downstairs and out the door. She felt a tad guilty that she had let her dad believe that she was dressing up for no reason, but she was so excited about seeing Nick that she had to concentrate on keeping herself from skipping down the sidewalk.

Be cool; be confident, she told herself. Just like Katani said. Except Charlotte wasn't really the calm, cool, collected type. She was the nervous, klutzy type, and anything could happen on an important morning like this. *Just breathe*, she whispered to herself as she began to race down Beacon Street to her destiny!

Ten minutes later a breathless Charlotte arrived at Montoya's, exhausted from running. *So much for breathing*. She sighed as she stood at the bakery's entrance trying to collect her jumbled up thoughts . . . and build up her courage.

Hi, Nick. What are your plans for this Friday? she practiced in her head, going through the dialogue Katani had helped her prepare.

But the mouthwatering smells of freshly baked cinnamon rolls and cappuccino drifting in the air distracted Charlotte, and prompted a growl from her hungry stomach. *A nice croissant with some hot chocolate would be delicious right now, but first I need to find Nick.*

Scanning the busy bakery, Charlotte saw bleary-eyed college kids sipping lattes, businesspeople in suits, moms with babies in strollers, standing in line for cappuccinos. But where was Nick?

Charlotte decided to take a seat at the BSG's favorite table and wait for him. It would give her some time to prepare herself to do what she had never done before—ask a boy, and not just any ordinary boy, but a very special boy, to a special dance.

Pulling a notebook from her school bag, and one of her favorite purple pens, she began to jot down her thoughts. Charlotte loved to write. For her, writing was sometimes easier than talking. This was one of those times.

Hi, Nick . . . She chuckled. *Good beginning.* She looked up, hoping no one had heard her laugh. She didn't want anyone to think she was talking to herself. *Your mom makes the best croissants—would you like a bite? Well, how about that Valentine's Day Dance? Everybody's talking about it. Would you like to go with me? Please say yes so I don't have to feel like a complete goof.* She added a smiley face for good measure.

Just then Charlotte felt eyes looking over her shoulder. She quickly closed the notebook and turned around. It was Fabiana, Nick's sister. Charlotte suppressed a gasp. Had Fabiana seen her note?

"Hey, Charlotte. How's it going? Would you like

something to eat?" Fabiana asked coolly, like she hadn't seen anything at all.

Charlotte smiled up at her and managed to spit out, "That's okay. . . . I'm just waiting for Nick."

Nick's sister was one of the most popular girls at the high school, and a star in all the school musicals. When she sang "Tonight" in *West Side Story*, the whole audience stood up and applauded in the middle of the musical. Of course Maeve practically worshipped the ground Fabiana walked on.

While she collected some empty coffee mugs from a nearby table, Fabiana asked, "Did Nick know you were coming? 'Cause he said he was going to meet Chelsea this morning, and he already left."

Did he know I was coming . . . meeting with Chelsea . . . Charlotte froze. *Act normal, don't lose it.* She bobbed her head up and down. Her mouth formed an *Oh*, but she wasn't sure if she actually said anything.

Fabiana looked at her with alarm. "Are you okay, Charlotte?"

Charlotte forced herself to speak, but her voice came out all rusty and cracked. "Um . . . I'm . . . fine. I . . . I needed help with some homework. . . ." Charlotte couldn't go on. A lump the size of Nebraska had formed in her throat.

"I'm sure he's waiting for you at school," Fabiana said as she rested a hand on Charlotte's shoulder.

Charlotte quickly stood up and, before Fabiana could say anything else, she fled the bakery, her book bag banging against her side.

Misery to the Max

When Charlotte arrived at school she saw them: Nick and Chelsea. They were laughing and smiling at each other as they stood in the hallway. Nick was interviewing the Trentini twins while Chelsea was adjusting the lens on the camera. Suddenly, Nick and Chelsea began howling as the Trentini goofballs posed like super athletes for the camera.

Charlotte felt like an elephant had trampled her heart. *How could Nick do this to me?* she thought wildly. *He's supposed to be my friend! And Chelsea, too!*

She quickly walked past them, her head down.

Nick looked up and saw Charlotte briskly moving past him.

"Sorry. Gotta go," he said to Chelsea, and raced after Charlotte. But it was too late. She had already disappeared into the crowded hallway. And even though she heard him call out to her, she wouldn't look back. Not today.

Cornered

I wonder why Nick took off like that, Chelsea thought as she aimed her camera at a group of girls holding pictures of celebrities they absolutely loved. *Weird.*

She shrugged and snapped the picture. The girls laughed and waved at Chelsea as they trooped down the hallway. *I have to find more examples of "Love Is in the Air,"* Chelsea thought. *Something that represents how fantastic it is to love something or . . . someone.*

She felt a tap on her shoulder. She turned around.

"Trevor!" she said, feeling her whole face light up.

Chelsea, chill on the over eager stuff, she scolded herself. But it was hard not to smile at Trevor. *He's so cute and nice and sweet and . . .*

"Hi, Chelsea. What's up?"

He stood with his hands in the pockets of his jeans. His black T-shirt looked so good with his blond hair! Did he have any idea how adorable he was?

"Oh, nothing," she said. "Just taking pictures for my *Sentinel* project."

Trevor nodded and stared at her with sparkling eyes. "Oh, yeah. Cool."

He looks at me as if he is completely interested in every single word that comes out of my mouth. Does he do that to everyone he talks to?

And he's still talking to me. Pay attention!

"We should hang out together sometime. What kinds of things do you like to do?" Trevor asked.

Chelsea's knees began to wobble She shrugged, trying to look cool. "Oh . . . anything. Movies, the mall, museums—stuff like that."

"Do you like skating?" he asked.

"Sure," said Chelsea.

She was really trying to be more physically active, hoping to become healthier. Ever since she'd started eating a more balanced diet, she'd found she had more energy to do stuff like bike riding and skating. And, to her surprise, she'd discovered she actually loved being active. It made her feel happy and positive about herself—which was just what Jody, her favorite camp counselor from Lake Rescue, had told her would happen.

"Hey, Chelsea," said a voice behind her.

Chelsea's shoulders hunched up to her ears. It was Joline Kaminsky.

"Hey, Chelsea," said another sickly sweet voice.

Great, thought Chelsea. *The double whammy. QOM times two.*

"Uh . . . hi, Joline, Anna."

The Queens of Mean moved closer to Chelsea and Trevor. All Chelsea could think of was two lionesses moving in on their prey. Both of them flashed huge tooth-whitened smiles at Trevor as they flipped their perfect hair over their shoulders.

Could their skirts possibly get any shorter? Chelsea thought, eyeing the girls' matching red skirts and white baby tees. They reminded her of the set of twins on the new gum commercial everyone was imitating lately.

"Hi, Trevor," the Queens of Mean chorused, then turned their stalking eyes back toward Chelsea.

"Chelsea, you look great," Joline gushed, her voice incredibly fake. "I can't believe how much weight you've lost!"

There it is—the sneak attack. Chelsea felt her face grow hot.

"Yeah," Anna said with fake admiration. "You've totally slimmed down."

Joline stifled a smirk behind her hand. "I guess it's great not having to go into the plus-size stores anymore."

Chelsea simply turned on her heel and raced away, pushing her way through the crowd of kids on their way to homeroom. *Yes, let's all laugh at the fat girl! It's so much fun!* There was no way she was going to stick around for that. She brushed a tear from her eyes. But crying wasn't what she really wanted to do. She wanted to scream at Anna and Joline to *find your own friends!*

Frowning as Chelsea took off, Trevor began to walk away, but not before throwing a dismissive look to the Queens of Mean. "What's your problem, dudes? Chelsea's a nice kid."

Anna and Joline watched him go, their faces flushed with embarrassment. "He is so erased off my list of top-ten hot guys," Joline said.

Anna bit her lip and twirled a lock of hair around her finger. "Totally."

Recipe for Heartbreak

Ten O'Clock Study Hall: Montoya's Bakery Recipe for a Disastrous Non-Date

> *Charlotte's Journal*
> *1 cup favorite outfit*
> *½ cup of Ultimate Makeover courtesy of Kgirl*
> *1 tsp. of dodging Dad's questions about why so dressed up*
> *1 tbsp. of frantic dash to meet a really cute crush*
> *2 tsp. of waiting around for, like, forever*
> *A dash of really cute crush's big sis seeing a private note about crush*
> *3 cups of missing Nick Montoya!*
> *5 cups of feeling like a complete nerd as everyone watches you run red-faced out of bakery*

Mix ingredients well and bake in an oven of embar-
rassment for forty-five minutes
Serves one

Comfort and Fruit Salad

The BSG sat around the cafeteria table, trying to console their friend. But it wasn't working.

"And then I found him already at school, laughing and talking with Chelsea. He was helping her take pictures and they were having the best time," a wistful Charlotte described as she picked at her fruit salad. She had totally lost her appetite.

"I just don't understand it." She looked up at her friends. "I thought . . . I thought he liked me. What happened? Did I read Nick all wrong? I read in a magazine that you can tell if a boy is crushing on you just by reading the signals he sends you."

Avery looked totally confused. "What do you mean . . . signals? Like in baseball? Charlotte allowed herself a tiny chuckle. It ended in a hiccup.

Katani glared at Avery. "Clue yourself in, girl! You know the kind of signals she means. Boys teasing you, walking beside you in the hall."

"Sorry," Avery mumbled, and took a bite of her ham sandwich.

Charlotte sent Avery a watery smile. "No, that's okay. I needed to laugh right now."

Isabel patted Charlotte's hand. "I'm sure you read his signals just fine. There has to be a logical explanation for all this. Nick has liked you as long as I have been here."

Katani leaned forward on her elbows. "This is a lesson for all of us. A girl has to be able to stand on her own two feet. You know—be strong and confident. It's SSGP Rule number one!"

"Uh, Katani, now *I* am really confused. What does SSGP mean? Inquiring minds really do want to know," Maeve asked.

Katani looked around at her BSG and performed a little dance in her seat. "Super Star Girl Power!" she sang in her off-key voice.

"You know, ladies," she continued, "we gotta be like in the old Destiny's Child song: 'Independent Women.' That should be every girl's anthem."

"I love that one!" said Avery.

At that, she stood up and began to sing the song as she flailed about. This was Avery's attempt at dancing.

"Avery, sit!" Isabel grabbed Avery's shirt and pulled her back down. "You're totally embarrassing us!"

"What?" Avery asked innocently. "What happened to SSGP?"

Katani grimaced. "I don't think that applies to dancing like a chicken in the middle of the cafeteria."

Isabel leaned her elbows on the table and propped her chin in her hands. "Well, my *abuelita* always says you really do have to make your own happiness. Having a boyfriend is fine and dandy, but you need to be able to find happiness on your own. It's what makes you a beautiful woman."

"Well, I'm done with boys," Maeve blurted out. "They just make you miserable. Playing with your heart and stomping all over it till it . . . bursts like a balloon!"

"That's kind of harsh, Maeve," Avery commented.

Maeve's chin quivered as she placed her hands flat on the table and stood up. "And another thing. It isn't cool for friends to steal other friends' crushes. That is the ultimate in betrayal. It's just like that Bette Davis movie *All About Eve* where the famous actress becomes friends with the girl who wants to be an actress too, and the other actress tries to steal away her boyfriend and take away her roles and . . ."

The BSG stared at her in confusion.

"Maeve. What in the world *are* you talking about?" Katani asked.

Maeve threw up her arms in frustration. "Bette Davis was a famous movie star a long time ago, and she . . . you should see the movie." Maeve pointed at Avery, a suspicious hint of tears in her eyes.

Suddenly the table went silent.

Avery felt a hand on her shoulder.

"Dude!" Dillon said. "Pete Wexler was dissing the Brady Man, and I need someone with solid Patriots knowledge on my side. Come on."

Avery gratefully let him drag her over to the boys' table. She'd rather talk about football than deal with Maeve's sudden attack of weirdness.

Maeve stared after them in silent outrage. Finally she jumped up from her seat. "That's it! I'm out of here." She flounced out of the cafeteria.

"Oh. My. Gosh," Isabel said in a hushed voice. "It's a love triangle."

Charlotte momentarily forgot about her own problems and nodded. "I think you're right. This is terrible. Maeve likes Dillon, Dillon likes Avery, and Avery likes . . . who?"

"Avery's in love with fun," Katani said, wiping the corners of her mouth with a napkin.

"Maybe Avery is secretly crushing on Dillon?" asked Charlotte.

"Well, she *is* always hanging around the boy," Isabel said. "And they're always goofing around a lot, punching each other and stuff. Isn't that one of the signals?" She took a bite of her sandwich and slowly chewed as she mulled the whole thing over.

"Poor Maeve," said Charlotte. "I totally know how she feels. When you think your crush has been stolen away from you by a girl you thought was your friend . . . it really hurts."

"Charlotte?"

She looked up from her sandwich, her body stiffening. *Nick.* "Yes?" she said, trying to keep her voice from trembling.

Nick looked down at his shoes. "Uh . . . could I talk to you for a minute?"

"I'm kind of busy now," Charlotte said abruptly.

Nick looked at Katani, who looked at Isabel, who looked at Charlotte, who looked down at her hands. Nick turned and walked away.

"Charlotte!" her friends gasped.

"What?" She shrugged.

❀ ❀ ❀

To: Sophie
From: Charlotte
Subject: Crying myself to sleep

Sophie I can't believe it . . . I
waited at the bakery for half an hour
this morning and Nick never came. He
forgot about me. He was at school with
Chelsea the whole time! I almost ran
back home to hide under the covers
all day. He tried to talk to me at
lunch and I ruined everything. . . .
I think he hates me now.
Can I please escape to Paris with
you??? We can hop on a boat and make
our way around the world together.

Charlotte

Part Two
Dance to the Music

CHAPTER
11

Matchup Mayhem

Izzy, are you sure you don't want to come play basketball? We really need another player for four on four," pleaded Avery. "Besides . . . we could totally use the famous Isabel Martinez jump shot!" She laughed.

"I can't, Ave," answered Isabel, sorry to disappoint her friend. "I really wish I could play, but I'm on the decorating committee, remember? We're going to turn the basketball court into a Valentine wonderland!"

The last bell of school had just rung, and Avery and Isabel were standing at their lockers. Kids streamed all around them, opening lockers, shouting to friends, and pointing to Isabel's pink posters advertising the dance.

"Friday night—dance fever, dude!" an eighth-grader shouted to his friend across the hall. "You coming?"

The friend nodded. "Sure thing!"

Isabel smiled. This *was* going to be such an awesome dance. Everyone was getting really excited! She couldn't wait to go shopping with her sister.

She and Avery walked down the hall together, and Isabel stopped at the door to the art room. When she opened the door, the scent of watercolors mixed with white glue and paper wafted through the air. "This smell always gets my creativity flowing," she told her friend.

Avery peeked around the door, too. All the long, wooden tables were cleared off except one, which was full of bags from the local craft shop. Betsy was dumping them out, frantically looking for something.

"I'm sure I bought a ruler!" the head of the decorating committee exclaimed, to no one in particular. "How can we make sure the hearts are symmetrical without one?"

"The art room has rulers," a short, dark-haired boy said, holding one up for Betsy to inspect.

Betsy rubbed a finger along the ancient wooden edge. "It's full of dents."

Isabel held back a laugh. She was totally messy when it came to art . . . papers and brushes and paint flew everywhere, and she never needed a ruler! In fact, *reminder for later,* she was going to have to tell Betsy that the hearts would look more fun if they were all different shapes and sizes and a little off kilter. But she would do that in a minute, *after* Betsy calmed down.

"Are you seriously going to attack the hoops with all that pink stuff?" Avery pointed to the pile of pink and red streamers, balloons, glitter, and metallic papers Betsy had dumped out of the shopping bags.

"Not today," Isabel assured her sporty friend." Today we're just making decorations. We'll put them up tomorrow."

Avery took a few steps away from the door. "Well, it's wayyy too much pink for me! If you finish early, Dillon and I could really use you at b-ball." And with a wave, she was off to the gym.

"Ave, wait!" Isabel followed her out into the hall, letting the art room door close. Ever since lunch yesterday she'd been meaning to talk to Avery. Isabel wished Charlotte had said something about Dillon—she was so much better with words—but Charlotte was too upset about Nick to pay attention to anything else.

"Look," Isabel said. "I have to ask you something, and it's a little . . . awkward . . . but . . . I guess . . . well, here goes. . . ." She took a deep breath. "How do you feel about Dillon?"

"Uhhh . . . he's my friend," Avery answered, looking at Isabel like she had two heads. "Why?"

Isabel looked around to make sure no one was in earshot. "Do you like, *like* him?"

Avery stared at Isabel, a confused look on her face. "Yeah, everybody likes Dillon!"

"Ahh." Isabel sighed. This was going to be more difficult than she had anticipated. Avery Madden clearly was not processing the subtleties of romance. She was just going to have to spell it out for her. Isabel looked around the hall again to make sure no one was listening.

"Izzy, I have to go," Avery said impatiently. "The guys are waiting for me." And she began walking away.

"Just a sec, Ave. This is important." Isabel lowered her voice and followed Avery.

"Here it is in a nutshell, Ave. Maeve likes Dillon as

in, really *likes* him, as in, has a huge crush on him." Isabel explained. "But he only ever pays attention to you, so she's, well, I think she's pretty jealous."

Avery fished a quarter out of her pocket and ran it along the grate on a nearby locker. "So that's why she's been acting all bizarre-o around me."

Isabel shrugged. "Yeah, I guess." She was a little surprised at Avery's laidback response to the situation. But, that was Avery.

"So what am I supposed to do?" Avery spun the quarter around in her fingers. "Dillon's my friend. I can't just stop hanging out with him!"

"I don't know." Isabel sighed, glad that she'd finally said something. "Maybe talk to Maeve?"

Avery nodded. "Sure. I can do that. We wouldn't want our buddy Maeve moping at the dance! I'll talk to her later. Gotta go." With that, she bounced off down the hall.

Isabel headed back into the art room hoping she had done the right thing and wondering whether Avery understood how complicated a "love triangle" could get.

A Forget-Me-Not

Isabel was hard at work painting a gigantic cardboard heart when a familiar figure strolled into the art room.

"Kevin!" she waved.

He lifted a drawing out of his portfolio and laid it on the table next to her. "Hey, what's up?"

"Hearts, hearts, and more hearts!" Both of them laughed. Isabel's table was covered with pink and purple hearts of all shapes and sizes.

"You definitely have a heart-fest going on," Kevin commented with a wry grin.

Isabel looked over his shoulder. He was working on a black-and-white portrait of an older woman sitting on a beach chair near the ocean. There was a photograph taped above the drawing, and the resemblance was remarkable.

"What do you think of these waves?" Kevin asked. "I'm having trouble making them, you know . . . frothy. . . . It's for my grandmother," he added, a little embarrassed. "So don't make fun of my froth," he joked. But Isabel knew that he was really serious. Kevin's art meant a lot to him and he wanted things to look the way he thought they should. The way he saw them in his mind.

"Did you try a kneaded eraser?" Isabel found one in her backpack. It looked like a wad of chewed-up gray gum, but it was her favorite art supply. When she wasn't drawing, she could twist and shape it like a tiny piece of clay. She showed him the technique on a corner of notebook paper.

"This is great, Isabel," he told her, his face brightening.

While Kevin worked on his waves, Isabel mixed up a magenta color for the next cardboard heart. "Aren't these decorations fabulous? I'm so excited about the dance! Are you going?" she asked, expecting the "yeah" answer she'd been hearing in the halls all day.

She'd kind of had a vision running through her head all day. It seemed really simple. Kevin would show up in the art room like he almost always did after school, they'd talk about the dance, and somehow, they'd end up going together.

But that's not what happened.

Kevin put down the eraser and looked up at her with a confused expression. "Isabel," he said. "You *can't* go to the dance."

"I can't?" she responded, not really understanding.

"No!" Kevin looked at her strangely. "Don't you remember . . . ?" he asked.

"Remember what?" Isabel asked nervously. Her hands began to shake as she wondered what she had forgotten that was so important that she couldn't go to the dance.

"You know . . . art night at Jeri's Place," he prompted. "You said you would go."

Best Buddies

"Dude, I can't believe we couldn't play basketball," Avery complained, walking home with Dillon and the Trentini twins. They'd gotten to the gym only to discover all the hoops raised up into the ceiling in preparation for the dance the next night. Even worse, the janitor was in there sweeping and wouldn't even let them practice passing and dribbling.

"Yeah, seriously, couldn't they wait until tomorrow to clean the place?" grumbled Billy.

A winter breeze whisked around them, causing the tree leaves above to sway and tremble with each gust, but the air remained unusually warm.

"If only it would snow!" Avery complained. "I'd teach you guys some of the freestyle board tricks I learned in Colorado. . . ."

She picked up a pebble and skimmed it across a muddy

puddle. "Oh, well," she joked. "I guess an essay about my favorite poem is just as much fun. . . ."

Dillon laughed. "Dude, you have a favorite poem?"

"No way." Avery grinned. "I have to call Charlotte to help me pick one."

"What's up with Ms. R and that assignment?" Billy Trentini groaned. "She never gives homework over the weekend."

Dillon knelt down to tie his shoe. "Teachers act like kids have nothing better to do than homework. I mean, when are we supposed to have fun?"

Josh Trentini jumped up and touched a low-hanging tree branch overhead. "Yeah. A guy should have the right to relax all weekend without worrying about doing more schoolwork."

"Josh, you're not even going to start your essay until Monday morning, so why are you complaining, dude?" his twin brother, Billy, quipped, and gave him a friendly shove.

Josh stumbled into Avery, knocking her off balance for a moment. "Hey!" she shouted. "Watch it, guys!"

The Trentini twins grinned. "Sorry, shorty," Josh said as he ruffled her hair.

Avery glared as the twins took off down the street toward their house. Sometimes Josh Tentini really got on her nerves. It seemed like he never let a day go by without reminding her she was vertically challenged. *What a dweeb,* Avery thought as she adjusted her backpack.

"So are you going to the basketball game?" Dillon asked, kicking a small rock down the sidewalk as they went along.

Avery brightened. "You mean the one at Brookline High?"

"Yeah."

"Definitely. My brother Scott says they're gonna go all the way to the state championships this year."

Dillon grinned at her. "Okay. If you had to choose only one sport to play and you had to give all the others up, which one would you choose?"

"Oh," Avery said. "That's a no-brainer. Soccer, of course! What about you?" She shook out her ponytail and looked up at the sky. If it didn't snow, maybe they'd be able to organize another pickup soccer game. Only she'd be sure not to let anyone make fun of Maeve this time. That is, if she even wanted to play!

Dillon thought for a moment. "I don't know. In a way, I think I'd have to stick with basketball. I mean, I can totally see myself becoming the next Michael Jordan."

Avery chortled. "Dream on, dude."

Dillon ignored her like he always did. "But then again, I'm really into soccer, too. I mean, I could take on David Beckham."

Avery looked at him like he had two heads. "What world are you living in, boy? There's only one Beckham," she challenged him.

"But maybe you could be his teammate or something. After all, you are definitely the best player in our league." Avery smiled over at Dillon. She believed in telling the truth about someone's sports abilities.

The two friends crossed the street, dodging a kid on a bike who was too busy listening to his iPod to realize he was about to turn them into pancakes.

"You really think so, Ave? I could play with Beckham?" The usually confident Dillon actually sounded a little surprised that Avery thought he was that good. "But"—he looked over at her, a devilish smile on his face—"check this out: Dillon Johnson, star pitcher at the World Series!" he bragged, and threw a pebble across the park.

Avery cuffed him on the arm. "Now you're getting delusional."

Dillon turned to her and gave her a goofy grin. "Or I could always become a tenth-degree black belt at tae kwon do."

Avery rolled her eyes. "I think you should focus on graduating from junior high first."

Dillon shrugged. "Hey, a guy can dream, right?"

They walked in silence for a while. Avery loved this time of day, when everybody started coming home from school and work. She was finally free to jump and shout and do whatever she wanted, and this warm thaw made her feel like running the rest of the way home.

"Come on, Dillon!" she shouted. "Race you!"

As she ran, taking huge gasps of air, she thought about what Isabel had said: "Do you like, *like* Dillon?" He was extremely easy to hang out with, and never seemed to care how she looked or what she said. The two of them could just chill out, like buddies. *Does that mean I like him?*

She felt a hand on her shoulder. "Slow down, dude!"

They stopped, leaning against the wall of a shop. Dillon said something, muffled by his heavy breathing. It sounded like, "Want to show ants?"

"Huh?" Avery asked. "What did you say?"

Dillon ran a hand through his blond hair. He looked at her, his eyes crinkling at the corners. She stood straight.

"Avery, you're such a spaz sometimes. I said, 'Do you wanna go to the dance?'"

"The dance?"

Dillon playfully punched her in the shoulder. "Yeah, the Valentine's Day Dance. You're going, right?"

"Of course I'm going," she said calmly, but inside she was shaking. *Oh. Wow*, Avery thought. *Dillon is asking me to the dance. Oh, boy. Trouble on Beacon Street.* Maeve would totally flip out if she said yes, but how could she say no? Dillon was, like, her best friend after the BSG!

Shaking her head back and forth, she looked up at him, her entire body twitching. "Hold up. I can't go with you. You *have* to go with Maeve!"

Dillon stared at her with his mouth open. "What are you talking about?" he gasped. "Not *Maeve*. She . . . well, she's just too, well . . . she wouldn't go with me!" he stammered.

"You are so goofy." Avery shook her head. "Maeve is totally crushing on you right now. And I mean, totally."

"Totally?" He looked concerned.

She stood with all her weight on one leg, her hands on her hips. "Totally, dude."

"But—"

"But, nothing," said Avery, glaring at him. "Maeve really likes you, so there's no way I'm going to the dance with you. Period. She'd be absolutely miserable, and I could never do that to one of my best friends. So you need to ask her to the dance." She narrowed her eyes. "Because if you don't . . . I might have to join another pickup soccer team."

Dillon backed away from the determined glint in her eye. "Uh . . . okay . . . okay, Avery. Don't go all psycho on me. Chill." He grinned and put his palms up.

Avery's face transformed as a victorious smile spread across it. "So, you'll ask her. Right?"

Dillon said, "Yeah. Sure. Maeve's okay. Besides, Billy would pulverize me if you quit. You're the best forward we have right now."

Avery smiled, relief washing through her. Everything was going to be okay. "That's right. Trust me. You'd be meat loaf."

They started walking again—not saying anything. Avery chewed on her lower lip, suddenly feeling very weird about what had just happened. She had turned down Dillon Johnson—Mr. Popular—and made him promise to take Maeve. *Is there something wrong with this picture?* Avery wondered as Dillon stared at his sneakers. *I don't have a crush on him, Maeve likes him, so he should ask Maeve. Right?*

"Well, uh . . . gotta go. See ya!" Avery turned and ran down her street as fast as she could. She just knew that if she didn't escape now, she would say something stupid. Besides, what if Dillon like . . . like, LIKED her?

"See ya!" Dillon called as she raced away, her sneakers pounding on the sidewalk.

Absolutely Everyone Is Going

Isabel's paintbrush dripped magenta all over the cardboard heart, and she didn't even notice. "I know about art night at Jeri's Place, but why can't I go to the dance?" Isabel asked, wishing Kevin would stop frowning like that. What was going on?

"Jeri's Place," he repeated. "Valentine's Crafts."

"Yeah! Okay, Saturday at seven, right?" Isabel insisted. Kevin had asked her about a month ago if she could help him out teaching art to little kids at the homeless shelter. But what did that have to do with the dance?

"It's not on Saturday. It's tomorrow, Friday, at seven." Kevin sounded annoyed. He kept pulling her eraser apart and squishing it back together while his drawing lay on the table, untouched.

"What? You never said Friday!" Isabel's face grew hot. She could have sworn it was Saturday! She never would have promised to do something the night of the Valentine's dance.

"It was *always* Friday," Kevin answered, his voice rising. "You said you could come, and I promised we'd be there."

Betsy looked over from a table across the room where she was trying to measure something with one of the art room's less-than-perfect rulers. Isabel ignored her. "I'm almost done with these hearts!" Betsy said, and turned away when she saw Isabel's expression.

"But everyone's going to the dance!" Isabel protested. "Everyone!"

"I'm not going," Kevin answered in a firm voice. "I made a promise, and those kids are expecting us!"

Isabel felt her stomach lurch. What about her posters? And her decorations? And the shopping trip with Elena

Maria and the BSG this afternoon? All she'd been thinking about for a week was this dance, and in just five minutes— poof—she wasn't going?

"I . . . I . . . have to get going," she said, backing toward the door. "My sister's waiting for me."

"Isabel, you promised," Kevin called after her.

CHAPTER

12

Sometimes a Girl
Needs a New Dress

When Avery reached the front porch of her house, her breath was coming in quick gasps. And it wasn't just because she had been moving fast enough to outrun a cheetah. Dillon was cool—he gave her noogies, talked about the Patriots, and raced her to the cafeteria after science class. But suddenly things had changed. Dillon had asked her to the dance. He wanted to go with *her*—Avery Koh Madden—who never thought about going to the dance with anyone. But then again, he seemed okay about taking Maeve to the dance too!

What a crazy, mixed-up situation, Avery thought. She fished the house key out of her backpack, opened the door, and charged into the front hallway, dropping her backpack on the floor with a thud. She knew her mom would make her pick it up as soon as she saw it, but for now, Avery just couldn't be bothered.

Then she heard her mom's music. *Oh no, not the Cyndi Lauper CD again.* Avery groaned to herself. All her mom's favorite singers from the 80s and 90s sounded like they needed looser clothing and a serious reality check.

Avery ran upstairs toward her mother's bedroom and knocked on the door. *Maybe Mom can give me some advice on the Dillon situation,* she thought.

"Come in," her mom's voice rang out above the synthesizers and drum machines.

"Is that a new dress?" Avery asked, her eyes widening. Her mom looked drop-dead gorgeous—like one of those ladies on TV advertising hair products.

Mrs. Madden flashed Avery a huge smile. "Yes, it's new." She turned back toward the full-length mirror and primped in the glass. "Do you like it?"

"It's all right," Avery admitted grudgingly. "But why did you buy it?"

"Sometimes a girl just needs a new dress!" Mrs. Madden announced, like her daughter understood this feeling exactly. "I saw it in the store and couldn't pass it up. It's a perfect dinner dress, don't you think?"

Dinner! Avery remembered. The secret date with Mr. Ramsey! That's why her mom bought that dress. That's why she was posing like a model in front of the mirror in teetering high heels.

"Sure, Mom. It looks good," Avery said, backing out of the room. She mentally scratched her mom off the list of people she could talk to about the whole Dillon-Maeve thing. It looked like her mom had her own romantic business to worry about . . . which Avery didn't really want to think about yet. Thinking about her mother and Mr. Ramsey gave her a headache!

"Don't forget, sweetie!" her mom called down the hall. "Isabel's sister is coming by in half an hour so you can all go to the mall to shop for your big dance! We should take a picture together when you get back. Two beautiful Madden women!"

"Uh . . . okay." Avery had completely forgotten about the mall. Elena Maria had offered to take them all on Monday. *A dress is the last thing in the world I need right now.* She retreated into her room and closed the door, then cranked up her own music—loud enough to drown out her mom's tunes from the age of the dinosaurs, and then took Walter, her snake, out of his terrarium. Walter always made her laugh.

All Alone

Charlotte dragged her feet the whole walk home from school. Nick had tried to talk to her again, more than once, but she didn't want to hear his apologies or excuses. They would only make it all worse.

A gust of wind swept up her new Kgirl hairdo and slapped the neatly curled ends against her nose and chin. The warm weather spell seemed to be ending, and a slight chill in the air made her think of snow. *Maybe it will be a blizzard, and they'll cancel school tomorrow,* Charlotte thought, picking up the pace a little. *No school, no dance!*

She climbed up to the Tower to check her e-mail before taking Marty out. Sure enough, there was a message from Sophie.

To: Charlotte
From: Sophie
Subject: Bisous

Charlotte, my darling friend!
Please, do not cry. Perhaps there is
some mistake? This whole year you
have told me Nick, Nick, Nick, and
I feel I know this boy would not
hurting you without good reason. I
am joking when I say to find more
handsome boy. You must talk to this
girl Chelsea. Find the truth. She is
trying to steal him or no? My mama
always says to, how do you say it
in America? "Keep your cool." You
are a cool girl, very strong and
confident!
I found these dresses online. Every
one will make all boys to fall in
love with you!
I regret to say I have not seen
that bad cat. Perhaps he traveled
somewhere else. He is so tricky. I
hope he will write a book about his
travels! Or you can write for him?

Beaucoup de bisous,
Sophie

Charlotte hit reply and stared at the empty text box. But there was nothing she really wanted to say. *I'll think of something on Marty's walk,* she told herself, and went down to her bedroom to find the little dude.

"Come on, Marty," Charlotte sang in her happiest voice. "It's time for your walk!"

Marty was still curled up under her bed. To get him to eat, she had to slide his bowls into the dust-strewn darkness. It looked like a nice place to be: in a cave, alone, where no one could find him, except those he loved most.

Marty stuck his nose out from beneath the bed skirt and whined a little.

"I know, I promise we'll come right back." Charlotte grabbed his leash and held out a treat from her pocket. Marty followed her out the door into the gusty street.

"I thought Nick liked me," she told Marty as they walked toward the park. "Sophie says he still does, but she's in Paris."

They passed a gate where remnants of snow still hung to the metal bars. Marty trotted along, head down, not at all interested in sniffing the gate. Charlotte sighed. "What's wrong with us, Marty?"

You Can't Always Get What You Want

"Yum! I just love Montoya's hot chocolate! It's just the absolute best in the world." Maeve took a sip of her favorite drink from her favorite bakery and grinned at Riley, who sat across the tiny table with a sandwich and a glass of orange juice.

Maeve watched him drum his fingers on the smooth

surface. *Was he tapping out the rhythm to a new song?*

"Hot chocolate, hot chocolate, what would I do, without you?" Riley sang to his finger drum beat.

Maeve laughed and inhaled the heavenly scents of brewing coffee, fresh-baked pastries, and, of course, hot chocolate. She could almost forget that the dance was tomorrow night and not a single boy had asked her. Or that the rest of the BSG were going to the mall this afternoon to shop for dresses, but she had dance class . . . the one activity in her hectic life that she didn't want to miss, even for shopping!

It was amazing what a ginormous chocolate chip cookie and a hot chocolate could do for a girl with a lot on her mind. Maeve pictured the dress she'd seen at Think Pink, the one with a flared skirt in a daring color only the boldest redhead would ever wear. . . .

"Maeve?" Riley finished the last bite of one of the bakery's special ham and pickle sandwiches.

"Hmmm?" She leaned forward, hoping he would make up another funny song, or something. Or maybe they could talk about that cool new indie band he had mentioned at school. I mean, that was why he suggested she come hang out with him, right? But as soon as she looked at him, Riley started looking everywhere in the bakery except at her.

"What's wrong with you?" Maeve demanded, noticing that Riley's face had suddenly paled. "You're not sick or something, are you?"

Riley looked up, startled. "What? Huh? No! I'm not sick . . . I'm just . . . just . . . thinking."

"Good. We don't want anyone getting sick before the

big dance," Maeve said as she took another long sip of her perfectly delicious hot chocolate. She had to admit, Riley always seemed a little bit nervous whenever she talked to him. Maybe that was just the way he was.

"What were you thinking about?" she asked. Studying Riley over the brim of her mug, she couldn't help but notice how he was looking really cute that afternoon. His dark green T-shirt accentuated the color of his eyes.

Riley leaned forward, his elbows on the table. "Maeve, uh . . . I'd like . . ."

Before he could finish, she sprang from her seat, her face alight with barely contained excitement. "OMG! It's Dillon!" She tucked some hair behind one ear and ran the tip of her tongue over her lips. It wouldn't do for her to approach him with chocolate smeared across her mouth. Definitely not cool. "I'm going to ask him to sit with us."

After all, Maeve thought, *what is it my dad always says: "It ain't over till it's over." Maybe I still have a chance . . . for a date to the dance!* She giggled at her rhyme.

"Maeve, wait!" Riley said as she bounded away, but in her excitement, she didn't hear him call out. Rushing through the bakery doors, she practically tackled Dillon, who stumbled backward as she dragged him inside Montoya's.

"Dillon!" she gushed, her blue eyes twinkling. "What a surprise! Why don't you join Riley and me for some . . . light refreshments?" Maeve loved the sound of "light refreshments." It sounded like something Audrey Hepburn, her favorite old-time movie star, would say.

"Huh?" asked Dillon as he allowed himself to be ushered into a chair next to Maeve's.

Riley mumbled, "What's up, man?" and knocked fists with Dillon in greeting.

Maeve didn't even notice how flustered both boys looked. She sat down gracefully, rested her chin in her hands, and gazed at Dillon with a dazzled expression on her face. "It's so good to see you again, Dillon."

"Uh, we just saw each other a few hours ago at school," Dillon said as he scooted his chair a little farther away from hers.

Maeve laughed, her best sparkling, actress-y laughter, making quite a few customers turn in their seats to see what was going on. She tried to quiet the thudding of her heart. *Okay, Maeve. Play it cool*, she told herself. *Pretend you're Audrey in* Sabrina—*sophisticated, clever, mysterious.*

"So . . . Dillon . . . what brings you here?" she asked as she tossed her red curls over her shoulder.

"Well, I was just passing by . . ." Dillon paused, glancing around. Riley was glowering. Both Maeve and Dillon noticed. What was up with that? They both shrugged at the same time.

"Uhhh . . ." Dillon continued, "you pulled me in here . . . so . . . you want to go to the Valentine's Day Dance with me?"

Maeve squealed with delight and bounced in her seat. "Oh, my gosh, Dillon. I'd absolutely adore going with you to the dance. How kind of you to ask me!"

"Great!" Dillon stood up. "I'll be going, then—"

Riley suddenly slammed his glass down on the table. Both Maeve and Dillon jumped.

"You okay?" Maeve asked. "You really aren't acting like yourself, Riley."

"Yeah, dude." Dillon agreed. "You look kind of weird."

"I'm fine," Riley mumbled tensely, once again looking everywhere except at Maeve.

"Anyway," Maeve said, and without missing a beat, went on. "Dillon! I need to go shopping for a dress and we'll have to color-coordinate our outfits so that we don't clash and you know I'm a redhead so we have to be very careful as to what color we choose to go with . . ."

Dillon looked around like a squirrel trapped in a cage while Maeve rattled on. *Fa la la la,* she was singing to herself in her head. *Everything is turning out just like I imagined!*

"Well, I gotta go, Maeve," Dillon announced, and jumped up.

"Me too! I think my mom's out there waiting to take me to dance class. Feel better, Riley," she called out as she tagged after Dillon.

"I'm not sick," he mumbled, then slumped down in his chair and opened up a battered notebook. He took out a pen and began to write.

New Lyrics for Mustard Monkey
Valentine Song
by Riley Lee

I want to go to the dance with you.
I can't help it . . . no other girl will do.
I will be the guy you want me to be,
Just come to the dance with me.
Yeah, come to the dance with me.
We'll share hot chocolate, me and you.

No one else will be forever true.
I won't go with any, any other girl.
You are my whole world!
I want to go to the dance with you.
I can't help it . . . no other girl will do.
You'll be the one that I'll always adore.
Dance with me forever more.
Yes, dance with me forever more!

In the car on the way to dance class from the bakery, Maeve opened up her laptop. "Mom," she announced. "Dillon Johnson has asked me to the Valentine's Day Dance! There is so much to do, I just have to get it all down before I forget!"

Maeve's Notes to Self
1. *Buy fantabulous Valentine's Day Dance dress at Think Pink.*
2. *Find perfect shoes for my fabbity-fab-pink Valentine's Day Dance dress. Should I go with silver? Or my personal fave . . . pink! Too matchy-matchy???*
3. *Find perfect accessories. Make sure to buy a necklace and earrings.*
4. *Take Dillon shopping with me so we can match our outfits.*
5. *Study for Pre-Algebra quiz. Help!*
6. *Ask Riley about his new songs.*
7. *Rename the guinea pigs. Napoleon and Josephine? So royal!*

CHAPTER

13

Words of Wisdom

$\mathcal{A}$very lay on her bed, studying the ceiling, Walter wrapped around her arm. There was a tiny spidery crack in the plaster, a reminder of the time she and her brothers were playing basketball in her room and Scott threw the ball too high. It cracked some of the ceiling, and her mom had grounded them all for a month.

As if psychic, Scott popped his head inside her room. His messy hair flopped into his eyes.

"Hey, Bean Head. Nice tunes. Who is it? Let me guess . . . a baby-face teen pop sensation?"

Avery let Walter slither back into his cage, then turned down her iPod speakers and threw a pillow at her brother. "How many times have I told you to knock before you come in here, Goober!"

Scott caught the airborne pillow and tossed it back at her. "I did knock. You just didn't hear me."

Avery shrugged, holding the pillow on her knees. "So what's up?"

"Nothing," Scott said, leaning on the door frame. "What's up with you?"

"You don't want to know. Too much drama." As soon as Avery said the words, the scene with Dillon came flooding back. Had she done the right thing?

Scott sauntered into her room and perched on the edge of her bed. "You're only in seventh grade—how bad can it be?" Scott saw the look on his sister's face and turned suddenly serious. "You know, if someone's giving you a hard time, I can take him out for you."

Avery laughed and shook her head. "No, no." She looked down at the floor and noticed she had a hole in the toe of her left sock. Her big toe poked out of the opening.

Scott grabbed the pillow and bopped his sister lightly on the head. Instead of fighting back, Avery just pushed the pillow away and sighed again. "Come on, Scott. Not now."

"What is with you?" He sat down next to her, and Avery looked up, expecting to see a teasing glint his eyes. But he really looked concerned. She'd always been able to talk to him before, so after taking a deep breath, she told him everything. About Dillon and Maeve and the Valentine's Day Dance.

"Wow! That bites," her brother commented after she had finished the whole story.

"I didn't even care about going with anybody!" Avery exclaimed. "Why did Dillon have to ask me?"

"He likes you, Ave, *obviously*." Scott ruffled his sister's hair and grinned. "Everyone likes you!"

Avery felt blood rushing to her face. "Was it a total loser move to say no?"

"He'll get over it. This is just one dance and you're going to have an awesome time. My sister is *not* a loser."

"Thanks," Avery said with a watery smile.

"A goofball, maybe," he continued with a smirk, "but not a loser."

Scott picked up a neon green super ball off Avery's desk and started tossing and catching it. "So who's this Dillon? Do I know the dude?"

"He's pretty cool, I guess. You've probably seen him at my games. He has some killer moves on the soccer field . . . he thinks he's Beckham," she snorted.

One corner of Scott's mouth quirked up. "And that's his best quality, huh?"

Avery nodded. "Uh-huh."

"You are so weird," he said with a laugh.

"It's not like I *like* him!" Avery protested. "I don't think I like *anybody* that way." As soon as she spoke, a memory of snow and a hawk spiraling up in the air reminded her of her last moments with her friend Jason in Colorado. *Maybe I like Jason, but I don't know. . . .*

Avery took a deep breath and continued. "I just want to hang out and have fun. Why does everyone have to go to this dance with somebody? What's up with that?"

Scott tossed her the super ball. "All right, I'm going to give you some serious wisdom from one who has been there, done that."

"You have wisdom?" Avery dribbled the tiny ball on her bedside table.

"Of course! Listen up. I didn't have my first crush till I was fifteen. It's totally normal, woo-hoo, no big deal. You don't need to like anyone, and you don't need a date just 'cause all your friends have them."

"Yeah, I guess you're right," she muttered. "But what about Maeve?"

Scott shrugged. "Good kid, but I don't understand a single thing that girl does. She lives in movieland. Hopefully she appreciates you giving up Dillon for her."

Avery nodded. "That was nice of me, huh?" A smile crept across her face. Scott punched her shoulder affectionately and grabbed the super ball, tossing it higher and higher toward the ceiling.

"That's not all that's going on." Avery's smile faded. She'd promised Charlotte not to tell anyone, but . . . Scott deserved to know.

"Yo, you weren't kidding about drama," Scott made a face.

"Only this time it's about Mom."

Scott froze, and the ball came down right on top of his head, bouncing off into the mess of clothing and comic books all over Avery's floor. "What about her?"

"She's going out with Charlotte's Dad," Avery said, feeling weird that she was even saying something like that out loud.

"You mean Charlotte Ramsey—Charlotte who also might not have a date to this dance?"

Avery sighed. "That's the one, all right."

Rubbing the top of his head thoughtfully, Scott stared down at the Patriots blanket. Long ago Avery had announced that even though her mom made her have such a girly four-poster bed, she could at least let her have a really cool football blanket on top of her lacy bedspread. "Okay. Now I wasn't prepared for that one. Uh . . . how do you know this?"

Avery stood up and the words tumbled from her mouth. "Charlotte listened to a phone message Mom left for her dad. They're meeting Friday at Le Bistro Français!"

Avery watched Scott's eyes widen. "You're kidding me!"

"Why would I joke about something like this?" Avery said, throwing up her hands.

"But that's the fancy restaurant where it costs about five dollars for a glass of water."

Avery shot him a look, her eyebrows raised quizzically. "And how do *you* know that?"

"I took a girl there once. We had to leave after I saw the prices on the menu. Way embarrassing, let me tell you. The girl broke up with me after that. Said I was cheap."

Avery rooted through the piles on the floor, looking for the neon green ball. "Mom also bought a brand-new dress today and was trying it on when I got home. It's all slinky and black, like something out of one those celebrity fashion magazines Maeve is always reading."

"Huh," Scott grunted.

Avery found the ball and threw it at her brother's head. "So what do we do, Mr. Fountain of Wisdom?"

Scott caught the ball easily and shrugged. "I'm gonna pretend like I don't know. I mean, Dad goes on dates with Andie all the time. Why can't Mom go out with whoever she wants? We can't run her life."

Avery fell backward on the bed with a groan. She

stared up at the crack in the ceiling again. "But shouldn't she at least *tell* us?"

Mrs. Madden's musical voice called up the stairs: "A-ver-y! The girls are here!"

"Got to go . . ." Avery gave her big brother a quick hug. "My friends are dragging me to the mall. If I don't make it back alive, take care of Walter and Frogster for me?"

Scott glanced over at the cages holding his sister's pet snake and frog. "Sure thing, Bean Head. Have fun!"

Secrets at the Mall

Charlotte ran her hand along a satiny lavender gown. The fabric had little white hearts embroidered along the waist and neckline. It was beautiful, and she loved anything having to do with the color purple, but what was the point? She fought back the lump in her throat, the one that just wouldn't go away.

"Charlotte, come look at this!" Katani urged. She was standing with Avery, Isabel, and Elena Maria by a rack of lime green and yellow dresses. "I can't believe they ruined such a perfectly good design with such outrageous colors! Imagine this in muted violet, or indigo. It would be perfect." Katani sighed at the world's obviously lacking fashion sense.

"Ooh," Elena Maria said, pointing out the same lavender gown Charlotte had been standing next to. "Look how it brings out your complexion, Charlotte. You just have to try it on! What's your size?"

"I'm not sure, with dresses like these. . . ." Charlotte flipped over the price tag. "And it's awfully expensive."

"What's the matter, Char?" Avery asked. When her friend didn't respond, she lifted the gown off the rack and held it up, batting her eyelashes. "Don't I look gooorgeous?" she imitated Maeve, which made Isabel and Katani crack up, but Charlotte's lips barely twitched at the corners.

"I . . . I don't think I'm going to go," Charlotte whispered.

"What?!" Katani took the dress from Avery and draped it over a pile that was growing on one arm. "No way is one of my BSG going to back out of this dance! We're all going, and we won't let any boys stop us from having fun! It's girl power all the way!"

No one noticed Isabel's downturned face. Elena Maria and Katani were having too much fun commenting on all the styles to notice. *How am I going to explain about Kevin?* She sighed.

"Hey, Char," Avery piped in. "Dillon asked me, and I said no! I don't need to go with a boy, so neither do you!"

Isabel looked uncomfortable. "Dillon asked you to the dance?"

"Uh-huh." Avery stood up as tall as she could, which wasn't very tall. "I told him to ask Maeve, just like you said!"

"Oh, no!" Suddenly Isabel had something to worry about in addition to Kevin and the homeless shelter. "That's not what I said, Avery!"

"It's not?" Avery slumped a little.

"Did Dillon ask her to the dance yet?" Katani questioned.

Avery shrugged.

Charlotte ran a hand through her hair. She was stilling wearing it down, curled at the ends like Katani had taught her. "Avery, if Maeve found out Dillon only asked her because you told him to . . . let's just say, it would not be good."

"But I thought it would make her happy!" Avery protested. Sometimes she just did not understand her friends at all. Boys, at least, told you what they meant and stuck with it. And if they got mad at each other, they roughhoused for a while and that was that. It happened with her brothers all the time.

"She wants Dillon to *want* to ask her," Isabel explained patiently.

"Am I understanding correctly?" an amused Elena Maria broke in. "Maeve's crush asked her to the dance, but only because this crazy *chica* here told him to?"

"Well, maybe he hasn't asked yet." Katani whipped her cell phone out of her purse. Do you have Dillon's number?" she asked Avery, who concentrated hard at trying to remember the digits. She hardly ever called him, just texted him sometimes.

Just then, a hip-hop beat announced a new message on Katani's phone.

> **flikchic:** guess what??!??!?!!!!!?
> Dillon asked me 2 the dance! Tell
> every1 for me!!! Silver or gold
> jewelry w pink? I forget. Gtg,
> dance class.

Katani's thumbs flew as she typed a reply.

> **Kgirl:** congrats! silver, and not
> 2 much, your hair is the key fea-
> ture. show it off. wish you could
> be here <3 BSG

Katani passed the phone around so everyone could see.

"What do we do?" Isabel asked.

Everyone just stood there. A sales associate came by and asked, "May I help you?"

Charlotte shook her head no, then whispered to the group, "I think we have to pretend we don't know he asked Avery."

"You mean . . . lie?" Avery gasped.

"Well, it's not so much a lie as a white lie to save a friend's pride," Elena Maria explained. "Sometimes you need to bend the truth a little, to protect your friends from being really hurt."

Katani tilted her head thoughtfully. "Is this worth breaking the Tower rules?" She quoted from memory: "We will be loyal to our friends and won't lie to them even if they make a mistake or do something totally embarrassing.'"

"I think my sister's right this time," Isabel pointed out. "It's not really a lie. We just aren't telling her something that might upset her. Maybe Dillon really *does* like her, but just didn't have the nerve to ask her."

"Fat chance," Avery exclaimed, and Katani gave her a stern look.

"Sorry," she said. "I really messed up, huh?"

"Don't worry about it." Charlotte gave her a hug. "You really meant well, and that's what counts."

"Thanks, Char," a grateful Avery said with a smile. She *had* done a nice thing for Maeve.

Katani picked a plain black dress off a nearby rack. "Let's all go try something on. We've been here for almost an hour and we still haven't narrowed down the choices!"

In the dressing room, Charlotte discovered a sweet lilac dress abandoned on a hanger. Sophie had sent pictures of dresses in all shades of purple attached to her e-mail. She knew Charlotte's feelings about the color, and she'd chosen well. *If only Sophie could see this dress!* Hanging alone and forgotten, the dress seemed like it had been left just for Charlotte. It had thin straps, a high waist, and the satiny fabric fell in rippled folds like cool water against the back of her hand. *Could it be my size?* Charlotte wondered.

She slipped it on and spun around in front of the mirror. It fit perfectly, and it actually shimmered as she twirled around!

She stepped out of the dressing room, and Katani applauded. "We have a winner! It's perfect, Charlotte. I wouldn't change anything."

Katani didn't have to try anything on. She'd sewn her own dress, a sunshine yellow dress with a halter neckline. She'd started it around Christmas with some fabric her parents let her pick out as a gift, and then hurried to finish it in time when she found out about the dance. Now, it was hanging in her closet, ready to go.

Charlotte smiled. "I love it too, Katani. I think I may just *have* to go to this dance." Katani was right! A girl had to make her own good time.

Next, Avery came out, picking at the black sash on a simple white dress.

"It's too girly," Avery complained. "Everyone will laugh."

"You look beautiful!" Isabel exclaimed. The black sash drew attention to her tiny waist while the cap sleeves showed off her toned arms.

"*Muy bonita*," Elena Maria agreed as she clasped her hands together.

Avery stared at her reflection in the mirror, grumbling about ridiculous frilly dresses that didn't have any pockets, but she had to admit to herself that she actually felt pretty. The dress wasn't too fancy or too plain. She spun around in a circle. The dress felt really comfortable, too. "Hey, guys—look! I could probably play soccer in this," she shouted, and kicked her sweater into the air.

Elena Maria urged Avery back into the dressing room warning her, "You are going to ruin that dress if you are not careful."

"Sorry." Avery laughed, then looked over at Isabel. She hadn't tried on a single thing! "Come on, Izzy. I tried on, like, six dresses. Your turn!"

"Yeah," her sister added. "What is the matter with you, *chica*?"

But Isabel just shook her head. "I can't . . ." she started.

"This isn't about your allowance, is it?" Elena Maria demanded. "I said you could pay me back later. *No problema*."

"No . . ." Isabel hesitated. "See, it's Kevin . . ."

"Not boys again!" Katani threw her hands in the air. "We need to make a new Tower rule, I think . . . 'boys do not control the show!'"

"Katani . . . ," Charlotte began.

"I'm just kidding," Katani said, and put a hand on Isabel's shoulder. "Tell me, what's wrong?"

"Well . . . I guess I made a promise to Kevin . . . about a

month ago . . . that I'd go to Jeri's Place with him and teach kids a Valentine craft."

"That's awesome!" Avery bounced up and down in her dress. "You've got to go!"

"But one of us messed the date up . . . and it's the same night as the dance," Isabel said, and burst into tears.

"Oh, no . . ." Charlotte put her arms around Isabel. Avery looked horrified, and Katani paced in front of the mirror.

"Well, you could split your time! Or, call the shelter and reschedule. There have got to be other volunteers who want to go to the dance. . . ."

Elena Maria stood quietly, biting her lip.

"No!" Isabel sobbed. "I thought of *everything* already, and it won't work. This is a special event and the kids are really looking forward to it, and if I don't go, Kevin won't be able to get anyone else. . . ."

"Can't Kevin handle a bunch of five-year-olds by himself?" Avery asked.

"Avery!" Katani put her hands on her hips. "That's not the point."

"Yeah," said Charlotte. "Isabel made a promise . . ."

"I wish I hadn't," she whispered.

"Hey, don't talk that way!" Elena Maria picked up her purse and took her sister's hand. "Come, *mi hermana*. First, let's get some dinner. Then go home. Mama will know what to do." Purse swinging from her arm, Isabel's older sister led them out of the dressing room.

CHAPTER

14

Be My Valentine

By the time Charlotte got home, it was already eight o'clock. She climbed the stairs and poked her head into her dad's office. She found him typing away on his laptop while Marty lay curled up at his feet, gently snoring.

"Hey, Dad," she greeted him affectionately. "It looks like the little guy is feeling a bit better."

"Yeah, he crawled out from under your bed when he smelled my chicken nugget dinner cooking." Her dad laughed. "Did you find a dress?" He looked at Charlotte with such a concerned look on his face that C harlotte wanted to fling herself into his arms and tell him her whole sad tale.

Instead, she opened up her shopping bag and pulled out the shimmering light purple dress.

"Wow! Smashing!" He smiled and reached out to touch the smooth fabric. "You will definitely steal the show tomorrow night." He gave her a big thumbs-up.

"Oh, Dad, you always think I'm the best," Charlotte

teased, but glowed a little inside. "I'm going up to the Tower, but wanted to let you know that I'm home." Charlotte reached down to pat Marty on the head before heading up to her writing desk.

"Wait," her dad called as she turned to go. "You had several phone calls this evening. Nick Montoya's trying to reach you. Maybe you should give him a call?" Her dad raised one eyebrow, but Charlotte just shook her head and backed out of the room. That awkward lonely feeling came rushing back, just when she thought she had conquered it. *I wonder why* he's *calling now,* she thought as she dashed up to the Tower, with Marty following close behind.

At her desk, she opened the chocolate drawer first, then remembered that she and Avery had finished off the caramel bar. All she had were a few Hershey's Kisses with almonds left over from a sleepover. As she booted up her computer, Charlotte opened one up and popped the slightly crunchy chocolate into her mouth.

One new message. *Maybe Sophie wrote again!* Charlotte sighed with relief as she opened up the e-mail. She could use some of her French friend's wit and wisdom right now!

Her heart leaped—the e-mail wasn't from Sophie.

From: Nick
To: Charlotte
Subject: Apology

Charlotte,
Hope you get this!!! I owe you big-
time for the other morning. See,

when I asked you to meet me at the
bakery, I forgot that I'd already
promised Chelsea to meet and work on
our *Sentinel* project and I ran out in
a hurry when she called from school,
wondering where I was. It's a bogus
excuse, I know . . . I should have
called or IMed or something, but I was
so late for Chelsea and I figured I
would see you in school, anyway. And
then I didn't.
I'm really bad at apologies, but
I'm, like, really sorry . . . and I
understand if you don't want to talk
to me.

Your friend,
Nick

P.S. Your hair looked nice today.

By the end of the e-mail, Charlotte had a huge smile
on her face. *What a dork I've been for ignoring him!* she realized. *He had no idea I got all dressed up just to ask him to the
dance.* Usually it wouldn't be a huge deal if one of them
didn't show at the bakery. And then she hadn't really
given him a chance to explain, because she had been
sure he liked Chelsea. This dance thing was just making
everyone crazy!

Then another thought crept out in between all the

others. *He noticed my hair!* Charlotte grinned down at Marty. "Nick Montoya liked my hair! What do you think of that, Mr. Marté?" she picked up the little dog, and Marty reached out his tongue and licked the tip of her nose. Charlotte giggled. "I'll take that as a 'very beautiful, darling,'" she said, wiping the slurp off her nose.

Then the phone rang. Charlotte listened to the faint tone downstairs, then the click of her dad's shoes walking up toward the Tower.

A lump began to expand in her throat. Charlotte felt like she was on the edge of something amazing and strange and fantastic all at the same time. *If it's Nick, what am I going to say?*

Mr. Ramsey handed his daughter the phone. "There's a young gentleman who wants to speak with you," he said in a formal voice, then turned to leave.

"Okay, thanks, Dad," Charlotte gulped, struggling to keep huge waves of excitement from crashing through her voice.

"Charlotte?" Nick's voice on the phone was muted, soft even. Charlotte thought she could just sit there and listen to him say her name again and she would be happy. "Charlotte, you there?" he said again.

She smiled. "Yes, it's me."

He was quiet for a little while, and she listened to him breathing.

"Ummm . . . ," he said finally. "Did you get my e-mail?"

"Yes." Charlotte lay back on her windowsill with the cordless phone in one hand, watching cars go by on the street below. "And it's okay, I was being a dork too. I thought . . . well, it doesn't matter!" she laughed, and Nick laughed with her.

"Charlotte?"

"Yes, Nick?"

"I really missed not talking to you this week. You're, well . . . you're really . . . special . . . interesting. You know."

"Special? And interesting?" She liked the way those words sounded.

"Yeah, you, well . . . you understand me. Maybe this is weird, but I think sometimes you know me better than anyone else. You really get that whole adventure thing I have. . . ." He fumbled for words.

"I do?" Charlotte curled up with her knees against her chest.

"Yeah . . . it's hard to explain. . . ." Nick's voice trailed off.

"I think I know what you mean," Charlotte answered him, feeling all the words she'd held up inside so long come pouring out. "I like to talk to you . . . I mean, because I know you listen and you're, like, really interesting and different from most boys."

They both laughed again. This time, a relaxed laugh, not a nervous one.

"You know, isn't it weird what this Valentine's Day Dance is doing to everyone?" Charlotte joked, all of her worries washing away. "I mean, Betsy's going with Yurt, and Isabel can't go, and Maeve's going crazy and . . . well, I guess I was acting pretty crazy too."

"It's okay," Nick soothed. "While we're on the subject, can we go together to the dance?" he asked. "I've been trying to ask you all week, and somehow, with all this craziness, it never happened."

"Really?" Charlotte's voice came out all high. She was smiling so hard, she couldn't help it.

"Really," he assured her.

"Oh. Well, okay. I mean sure, of *course* I will go to the dance with you!" Charlotte sat up and leaned forward, cradling the phone against her shoulder. It seemed so ridiculous and silly now that she had been so afraid to talk to Nick.

Nick laughed. "Cool! What time should I come by to walk to the dance with you, then?"

"Oh, anytime . . ." Charlotte switched the phone to the other ear. "Maybe six forty-five? The BSG are all coming to the Tower beforehand to get ready, and then a group is coming to walk to the dance."

"Right. Awesome."

"Okay, see you then?" Charlotte said.

"Yeah. See you tomorrow, okay?"

"Okay." Charlotte held the phone against her ear for a few minutes after she heard the *click*, then jumped straight up in the air.

"Yesssss!" she shouted to the empty room. Marty jumped away and barked a few times. Charlotte picked him up and spun him around. "I'm going to the dance with Nick!" she sang while the little dude yipped along. "I have a Valentine!" Then she kissed Marty right on the nose, not even minding his salty dog smell.

Promises to Keep

Isabel and Elena Maria opened the door to the

welcoming smell of frying tortillas. Mama and Aunt Lourdes sat together in the kitchen, laughing and listening to the radio. Isabel hadn't seen her mother so animated in days. She had multiple sclerosis, which made it hard for her to move around sometimes. Today was one of those days. She sat in her wheelchair while the girls' aunt flipped the home-made tortillas, but her laughter was genuine and happy.

"We're home!" Isabel and Elena Maria chorused, and they both ran over to give their mother a big hug.

Mrs. Martinez kissed each daughter on the cheek. "You're just in time! The tortillas are almost finished."

"Oh, Mama, we already ate. . . ." Elena Maria touched her mother's dark hair with one hand.

"Now you eat again!" Aunt Lourdes smiled and thrust a tortilla-covered plate at her oldest niece.

"Oh, Aunt Lourdes"—Elena Maria looked over at Isabel with a mischievous twinkle in her eyes—"I am so stuffed with pizza, but I am sure Isabel would like one. Wouldn't you, Izzy?" Elena Maria knew that Aunt Lourdes would flip out that they preferred pizza to her tortillas.

But Isabel was not in the mood for Elena Maria's little jokes this evening and said through gritted teeth, "I'm not really hungry either."

"Well," her aunt responded in a huffy voice, "I made enough for four."

Then she scolded both girls, "How many times do I tell you? You change your plans, you call. We pay for your cell phone, no? It is not for talking to boys, it is for calling your aunt and mother who are slaving away in the kitchen making everyone's favorite tortillas!" She put her hands on her hips and glared at her nieces, "So what do you have to say for yourselves . . . eating pizza?"

"We're sorry, Aunt Lourdes," they apologized in unison.

Aunt Lourdes was completely over the top, especially when it came to pizza versus tortillas. In her mind there was no comparison. Isabel had to bite her lip to keep from giggling. She glanced at her sister, who was doing the same thing.

"Lourdes . . ." Mama held up a hand for her older sister to calm down, then looked into Isabel's eyes. "Isabel, honey, let me see your dress."

Isabel shook her head slowly as tears leaked from the corners of her eyes. Mrs. Ramirez looked to Elena Maria with an expression that said, *What did you do to your sister?*

"You tell Mama, Izzy. Tell her your promise." Elena Maria dropped her purse on the table next to the untouched plate of tortillas, and began to move toward the door.

"What promise?" a suddenly alert Aunt Lourdes asked.

"Aunt Lourdes," Elena Maria interrupted, "do you think you could help me in the bedroom with the new dress I bought? I think it might need to be hemmed."

Lourdes hesitated for a second, looking back and forth at each sister. Then she said, "Oh, of course, Elena Maria. Let me just take my apron off."

That's the thing about Aunt Lourdes, Isabel thought as she sat down next to her mother. Her aunt might be strict and a little cranky sometimes, but she was a nurse and she loved taking care of people, especially her family. The sisters knew that anytime they asked, Aunt Lourdes would drop everything to help them, even if was just about a dress.

Isabel flashed her sister a grateful smile as Elena Maria grabbed Aunt Lourdes's arm and disappeared into the bedroom she shared with Isabel.

"So, *mi hija*, what is this promise you have made?" Her mother looked at her younger daughter with a sympathetic smile.

While Isabel explained about Kevin and the dance, Mama filled a tortilla with steaming chicken and vegetables waiting in separate bowls.

"Mama, I have to go to this dance!" Isabel cried, wiping her nose with the back of one arm. "My friends are all going, and I made the posters, and the decorations, and . . ."

"And you don't have a dress," Mama pointed out.

Isabel shook her head. "But I could borrow one of Elena Maria's old dresses, she said so."

"That is not the point. You will not be borrowing a dress," Mama said gently. "You already made your decision, no? You gave your word. And this boy . . . Kevin . . . is he not counting on you to help him?"

Isabel rested her head on her mother's shoulder. "But . . ."

Mama nodded once, a smile on her lips. "You are my responsible daughter. You know what is the right thing to do."

"I know, Mama, but this is *so* hard. All my friends will be there and I really wanted to go. The dates got mixed up . . . it's not my fault!" She leaned her head on her mother's shoulder.

"I know," her mother said, patting her daughter's arm. "But one dance will not make up for the bad feeling that you will have for breaking a promise to a friend."

Isabel understood what she had to do.

```
From: Isabel
To: Kevin
Subject: Art Class

Kevin,
I'll will meet you at the homeless
shelter on Friday. Thank you for
inviting me to help and I'm sorry I
got so upset in the art
room . . . but I really thought it
was on Saturday. ☹ Oh, well. The
kids will be so happy, and that's
what matters.

See you tomorrow,
Izzy
```

flikchic: sooo · · · how was the mall????
4kicks: i survived, lol
Kgirl: ave and char got dresses · · · they r so beauteous!
skywriter: and I have news
flikchic: oooh good news i hope?
skywriter: nick and i made up
lafrida: really?! i am so happy 4 U
flikchic: did he ask u to the dance?!?!
skywriter: yes ☺
Kgirl: !!!!!!
4kicks: so it's just me w/ out a boy?
flikchic: well what about izzy?
lafrida: i can't go to the dance
flikchic: what?!?!
4kicks: so you're going to the shelter w kevin?

flikchic
4kicks
Kgirl
skywriter
lafrida

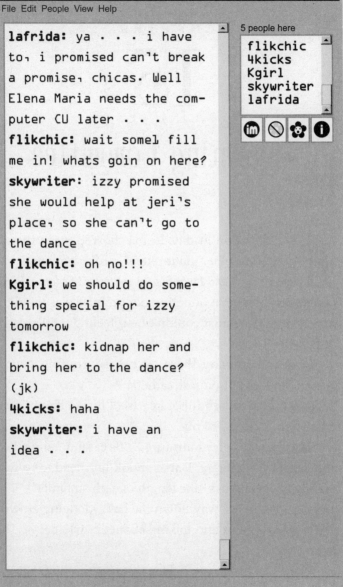

Chat Room: BSG

File Edit People View Help

lafrida: ya · · · i have
to¬ i promised can't break
a promise¬ chicas. Well
Elena Maria needs the computer CU later · · ·
flikchic: wait some1 fill
me in! whats goin on here?
skywriter: izzy promised
she would help at jeri's
place¬ so she can't go to
the dance
flikchic: oh no!!!
Kgirl: we should do something special for izzy
tomorrow
flikchic: kidnap her and
bring her to the dance?
(jk)
4kicks: haha
skywriter: i have an
idea · · ·

5 people here

flikchic
4kicks
Kgirl
skywriter
lafrida

CHAPTER

15

Decorating Committee

After school on Friday, Isabel showed up in the art room to face her giant pile of cardboard hearts. *All this work . . . and I won't even get to see the dance.* Even though she knew that honoring her promise was the right thing to do, Isabel just couldn't help feeling a little sorry for herself.

Betsy was already there, of course, fretting over a tangled mass of hot pink streamers.

Isabel lifted an armful of hearts. "I'll take these down to the gym," she called out.

"Mm-hmm," Betsy murmured. "Be careful," she called after Isabel. *Poor Betsy.* Isabel shook her head. She was actually obsessing over the length of each streamer.

Isabel made her way down the halls, dodging crowds of kids hanging out and talking about . . . what else? The dance.

"Ooh! Can I have one?" Henry Yurt danced up behind Isabel, trying to grab the purple heart on top.

"No!" Isabel swung her creations away from the class clown. "They're for the dance."

"Duh . . . Betsy asked me to help you guys set up. So can I have one?"

Isabel sighed. "Just don't bend it or anything. I worked hard on these."

"Yes!" Henry held up the heart and cheered. "Dudes, look, I earned a purple heart!"

"Henry, you better be careful or I will sic Betsy on you." Isabel almost laughed out loud when she saw his shaken face.

"Oh, don't do that, Isabel." He got down on one knee and pressed the purple heart to his chest.

"Betsy is my Valentine," he pleaded.

"Yurt," Isabel laughed, "join the drama club. They need goofballs like you."

Isabel hurried ahead while Henry followed her like a puppy dog down the hall. The first thing she heard as she approached the gym was a throbbing hip-hop beat and giggling voices that sounded very, very familiar.

"BSG!" she shouted as she burst through the door. There was Maeve, playing with the settings on a CD player, and Katani, studying the gym walls with a calculating look. Avery was tossing a tennis ball against the wall while Charlotte watched the door. When Isabel walked through, Charlotte ran over and reached for the pile of painted cardboard hearts.

"What's this all about, Char?" Isabel asked, so startled, she managed to drop most of her hearts on the floor instead of handing them over.

"I'll get those!" Katani picked one up and held it up to the wall, turning slowly.

Charlotte took Isabel's hand. "We're here to help you decorate, Izzy! It's not fair that you have to do all this work, then miss the dance! So Maeve brought the tunes, and we're going to have our own little decorating dance party."

Just then, Henry Yurt burst through the door, trailed by a few other kids carrying shopping bags full of supplies. "Hey! Nice music!" He grinned, grabbed a roll of masking tape out of his pocket and taped his purple heart next to the door. He couldn't reach any higher.

"People will knock it off if you put it there, Henry," Katani pointed out, and easily moved it up higher.

The Yurtmeister jumped and grabbed for it, but he couldn't reach. "Hey, that's my purple heart!"

"Come on, dude," one of his friends called, setting his bag down on the gym floor. "There's a ton more stuff back in the art room."

The boys left, and Maeve ran over to see what was in the bags.

"Ooh, look! Streamers! Glitter, cupid cutouts . . ." She dumped everything on the floor while Katani found masking tape, scissors, and string.

"Let's get to work, girls!" she announced. In a matter of minutes the gym was a beehive of activity. At one point Isabel reached over and hugged Charlotte. "I just can't believe you all decided to do this. I have the best friends in the world."

When Betsy finally made it down to the gym twenty

minutes later with the last bag of decorations and a note-book detailing exactly where every last streamer and heart was to be placed, she stopped in her tracks. "What," she exclaimed, "is going on?!"

Henry rushed to her side. "Betsy, your committee has fulfilled your dream. This place is going to rock. Check it out!"

Maeve was dancing to her favorite song with a mask-ing-tape bracelet on her wrist, handing rolls of tape up to Charlotte, who was standing on a chair and hanging hearts and cupids all over the walls, according to Katani's directions. Avery was in the middle of the floor with a roll of pink streamers. Squinting to get her aim just right, she wrapped a length of streamer around her tennis ball, and tossed it up into the basketball hoops. A pink rocket shot up, then down on the other side.

"Bull's-eye!" she shouted, and ran to pick up the ten-nis ball. Streamers were hanging through all the hoops, irregular and twisted.

"Betsy!" Isabel ran up to her, eyes shining. "Isn't it wonderful? We're almost done!"

Betsy shook her head soundlessly and opened her note-book. "But, but . . . I had it all planned out! The streamers are for the doorways! And the hearts are supposed to be lined up in a *pattern* above the bleachers! I even got the key to the janitor's closet to get a ladder!"

"Chill, girl!" Katani laughed. "It's going to look great."

Charlotte stepped down from her chair and dashed over to the pile of backpacks next to the CD player. "I know just what you need, Betsy!" she returned with a bag of Swedish fish in one hand, and M&M's in the other. "Refreshments!"

Maeve grabbed a handful of Swedish fish, laughing. "You're right, that's *exactly* what I need!"

Betsy eyed the candy suspiciously. "Well, I guess . . . I guess the hearts look okay . . . but we *have* to do something about those streamers!"

"This is only step one!" Avery protested as Betsy headed toward the janitor's closet for a ladder. "Maybe if I used a basketball?"

Everyone laughed, even Betsy.

Isabel looked around at her friends, "You guys are the awesomest ever!" she shouted, then spun around in a circle as a new song came on the radio. This was the greatest decorating dance party ever!

The Tower Princesses

That night, Charlotte stood in the middle of the Tower room with Katani and Avery. Katani looked absolutely fabulous in the halter-top sunshine yellow dress with beaded detail at the neckline that she had sewn herself, and Avery wore her simple but elegant white dress with the black sash. Charlotte was spinning around in front of the mirror, admiring her lilac perfection, shimmering with little rainbows of light as she moved.

"Girls, the BSG are looking fierce tonight!" Katani announced.

"We're like princesses preparing for a ball!" Charlotte laughed. Nick was coming in half an hour, along with a bunch of other friends, but it was mostly the thought of seeing him again that put her in a giddy mood. She'd talked to him at school, of course, all through lunch and study hall! But that seemed like such a long time ago.

"You can be a princess," Avery said. "But I'm a dance ninja . . . watch this!" she made a high-pitched squealing noise and sliced the air in front of Marty with one foot. The little dog jumped back and barked softly. Then Avery broke into one of her signature dance moves. She flailed her arms and legs, bobbed her head, hopped on one foot, and completely failed to look like the guys in the rap videos.

"Avery," Katani said, bent over with laughter, "you *need* to stop."

Charlotte warned, "Watch out, innocent bystanders of Abigail Adams Junior High, Avery Madden is on the loose!"

Even Avery lost it at that comment, and the girls collapsed together in a huddle of colorful fabric and jewelry, shaking with laughter. The fancy dresses were forgotten for a moment as they relished their moment of zany togetherness.

"Didn't Maeve give you lessons a few months ago?" Katani asked in between gasps of air.

Avery grinned and spun away from the group. "Yeah, that ended when I broke her mom's favorite antique vase."

Marty whined at Avery, and she patted his head. "Poor Mr. Marté! I didn't mean to scare you, little guy. How is the little dude doing?"

"He's a little better," Charlotte sighed and then turned and asked Katani, "So where's Maeve?"

"If Maeve ever arrived on time," Katani said, "we'd know the world was about to end."

"Okay, everyone, remember . . . we can't say a thing about why Dillon asked her!" Charlotte reminded them. "We have to pretend we don't know."

"Uh-huh," Avery promised. "But I still think it's not a big deal. I mean, we're all walking over in a big group, right? What does it matter who goes with who?" Avery picked at the sash on her dress, managing to undo the bow.

Katani sighed. "Let me fix that," she straightened Avery's dress.

"It matters because . . . well, because it just does!" Charlotte commented, realizing that, for once, she couldn't think of the right words to explain.

Avery looked at her like she had two heads. "Whatever you say. . . ." Avery reached up and tightened her ponytail.

Katani frowned. "Hmm . . . we have to do something about that hair! I can't let any of my girls walk out of here looking less than fab. I have my reputation to protect, you know."

Avery plopped herself in the lime swivel styling chair. "I like my ponytail," she pouted. "But if it will make you happy . . ."

"Hey!" Charlotte called out. "Look, everybody."

Avery jumped out of the chair and stood on tiptoe to see over her friend's shoulder.

"Avery!" Katani waved her hairbrush and a bottle of glitter, then gave up and looked out the window too. "Isn't that Yuri?" she asked.

"Yeah," said Charlotte. "I've never seen him so dressed up before. I wonder . . ."

The Russian fruit seller was walking up to Charlotte's front door wearing a dark blue suit, a spiffy red tie, and carrying a single red rose.

"Ooh—he's got a flower!" Katani said, the palms of her hands pressed against the window.

The melodious bong of the doorbell echoed up to the Tower.

"Should we answer?" Charlotte asked.

"What if it's for you, Char?" Avery joked as she bounced up and down on her toes, trying to get a better look.

"It's not for me, Avery." Charlotte knew whom the rose was for.

"Talk about romantic," said Katani.

"Look!" Charlotte pointed out the window. "It's for Miss Pierce."

The BSG peered down at the sidewalk just in time to see Charotte's landlady, the very shy astronomer who never left her basement lab, step out the front door. Charlotte almost didn't recognize her in the breezy light blue dress, her hair done up in a glamorous French twist. She took Yuri's arm and smiled up at him.

"Very interesting," said Katani, tapping her index finger against the windowsill. "Love is definitely in the air."

"Hey, girls!" Maeve's fiery hair suddenly appeared at the top of the ladder-like stairs, followed by glittering earrings and the top of a pink spaghetti-strap dress with an embroidered yoke. Maeve jumped off the final step, twirled around on one of her pink-heeled sandals, held up her arms, and bowed, tossing her red curls dramatically.

"Oh, Maeve," Charlotte said. "You've definitely got some serious fabulosity going on!"

"Thanks! This is all so exciting! It's almost as wonderful as going to a premiere of my very own blockbuster movie!" Maeve bowed again. "But, wow, have I got some huge news! I mean, huge! Huge! Huge! I just saw Miss Pierce and Yuri together like they were going out on a date! And get this! He gave her a red rose. That proves he's totally into her."

"We know!" Charlotte said. "I saw them together the other night, too."

"Do you think they'll get married??" Maeve exclaimed. "Oh, that would be so enchanting!"

It was unbelievable. Miss Pierce never left her computer monitors, stars, and secret NASA assignments, but now she was going out on a date with Yuri the human bear.

Avery sat back down in the swivel. "I still think they're too old."

"Avery!" Katani exclaimed. "Old people can fall in love."

Maeve spun around so that the skirt of her dress flared out around her. "But I have some more news! Extra-super-front-page-special-announcement-huge! Dillon is coming to walk me to the dance! And he's going to wear the baseball tie clip I found for him! I'm so happy, I could just die! Isn't it great?"

"Wow, Maeve, that's . . . awesome!" Charlotte looked around for support, but Katani was brushing Avery's hair like it took all her concentration.

"What's a tie clip?" Avery asked.

"It's a little clip that a man uses to hold his necktie to his shirt," Katani explained. "My dad has some. Does Dillon even *own* a necktie?"

"Of course!" Maeve proclaimed, imagining Dillon in a full suit and tie, wearing a silver tie clip that matched her earrings. They were walking together up a pathway lined with rosebushes to her very own mansion in the Hollywood hills. Maeve danced around the lime green swivel chair, lost in her fantasy. *Dillon leans down and plucks a rose, just for me! Then he whispers in my ear . . .*

"Are you okay? Maeve?" Charlotte did not belong in the Hollywood hills. The roses faded.

"I've never been better, darling!"

"It's really too bad Izzy couldn't be here," Charlotte sighed, relishing the feeling of being in her favorite place in the world with the friends she loved best.

"I brought a camera!" Maeve reached into a tiny purse that looked like it couldn't even hold a tube of lipstick, and fished out a slim silver case. "It's my mom's. She said to take *tons* of photos! Let's take one right now, for Izzy."

Katani nodded. "I'm almost done with Ave's hair."

Charlotte and Maeve watched with admiration as the Kgirl put the finishing touches on her latest makeover subject. Finally, Katani gave Avery a thumbs-up, and she bounced out of the chair.

"Ta-da!" she shouted, and looked in the mirror. Katani had turned her hair into a shimmering cascade, like a waterfall at midnight.

"I guess we really are princesses," Avery admitted.

"Say cheese!" Maeve exclaimed, and held out the camera with one arm.

The flash caught Avery with her eyes closed and cut off half of Katani's head. "Try again! Try again!" she shrieked, looking at the preview window.

It took at least twelve more tries before they got the perfect picture.

"I'm going to frame that and put it on my writing desk!" Charlotte exclaimed. "It's the perfect memory for a perfect night."

Not one of them thought for a second that everything might not stay perfect. . . . The night had only just begun.

CHAPTER

16

Have a Heart

I sabel waited for Kevin at the entrance to Jeri's Place, the homeless shelter in Brookline. The small gray building at 76 Parker Street seemed deserted from the outside, but inside the swinging glass doors, Isabel knew, it was buzzing with life. She had been there before.

In her first weeks at AAJH, she'd offered to help Maeve make blankets for a community service project at Jeri's Place. But the two of them were so hopelessly disorganized that "Project Thread" almost didn't happen. Lucky for them and the shelter, Katani had stepped in and helped them deliver a pile of colorful fleece blankets as promised.

"Hey," Kevin greeted her.

Isabel spun around and watched as he came walking toward her from behind the building.

"Were you waiting long?" he asked.

Isabel suddenly felt a little awkward. She hoped Kevin didn't think she was mean or something for wanting to go to the dance instead of keeping her promise.

She shook her head and rolled a pebble under her sneaker.

Kevin smiled.

Mmm . . . good sign. Isabel smiled back.

"Umm . . . I'm really sorry you had to miss the dance," he said, looking down at his feet.

"It's okay." Isabel gave him a reassuring smile.

"We're good then?" he asked.

"We're good," she said with a nod, then gave a little tug on his jacket. "Let's go in."

Kevin opened the door and gestured for Isabel to go in first. "Wow," he exclaimed, seeing all the people milling about. "I had no idea this was such a big deal."

"These events mean a lot to the people who live here," Isabel explained. "It makes them feel that people remember them. That's what the owner told Maeve and me when we were here for Project Thread."

"Well, I'm happy to be here." Kevin squeezed her hand.

A little shocked, Isabel turned away and quickly took off her coat and hung it on a hook near the door. She was suddenly glad that she was wearing her favorite jeans and the green sweater that Elena Maria said "makes your skin glow."

Right then she thought, *my friends are all dressing up in shimmery gowns and fancy jewelry* . . . but somehow that didn't matter anymore. There wasn't time to feel sorry for herself. Kids of all ages and sizes had swarmed into the carpeted lounge, their laughter and high-pitched voices surrounding the two seventh graders.

One of the kids, Isabel noticed, carried a fleece blanket from Project Thread. She couldn't wait to tell Maeve. It would make her feel so proud. For all of Maeve's dramatics, she really did have a heart of gold.

In a common room off to the right, Isabel could see more kids and even a few adults. They were playing board games, reading books, and flipping through magazines. By the far wall, a group clustered around a large TV.

When Isabel had first visited, she'd worried that everyone might be sad and quiet. It had come as a surprise how bright and cheerful everything was. Now, she couldn't imagine Jeri's Place any other way. She waved to the girl with the blanket and pointed out a sign on the wall to Kevin.

"I made that on the computer," she said. It described Project Thread and gave a phone number for anyone who wanted to participate.

Kevin nodded. "You and your friends have done a lot to help. I only started getting involved when my cousins in Florida lost their home in a hurricane. They had to stay in a shelter for a few weeks, and it wasn't as nice as this one."

Isabel frowned. "I didn't know that!"

"Yeah, it was really hard on them." Kevin turned slowly toward a young woman who was making her way through the sea of kids. It was Lorelei, the daughter of the director of Jeri's Place.

"Oh, great! You guys made it!" She grinned at Kevin and Isabel, her eyes bright. "The kids are so excited." That did it for Isabel. Any remaining thoughts of the Valentine's

Day Dance flew out the window. She was ready to make hearts . . . lots of them.

"Look what I made for you!" A little boy held up a construction paper heart to Isabel, while the girl with the blanket clung to one of her legs.

"Thank you." Isabel smiled at the kids.

"Do I get anything?" Kevin joked.

"Okay, you can have this!" Another little boy, probably only four years old, handed him a piece of paper decorated with a scribble of blobs and lines.

"Is this you?" Kevin asked.

"Me and Mommy!" said the boy.

Lorelei called to the kids. "Listen up, everyone! The art teachers, Kevin and Isabel, are here. Let's all go to the workshop room."

The kids laughed and jostled Kevin and Isabel as they made their way to a large, airy room with huge windows. A flurry of excitement built inside Isabel's stomach as she surveyed the workshop room. Construction paper, tissue paper, markers, crayons, glue, scissors, and various other art supplies sat on long tables flanked by gray folding chairs.

"So what do you need us to do?" Kevin asked Lorelei.

"There are a few different projects," she said. "I'll be at this table helping the kids draw cards for their parents, another volunteer is helping them make their own chocolate lollipops, and you two can take over the heart magnet table," Lorelei pointed to a table covered with newspaper, cups of paint, and lots of plain white ceramic shapes.

"We made the shapes in molds yesterday with the

older kids," Lorelei explained. "All you have to do is help them paint, and tomorrow we'll use the glue gun to stick magnets on the back."

Ten minutes later, Isabel found herself handing out paintbrushes with one hand while helping a little girl with wavy red hair almost like Maeve's mix white paint with the dark blue to make light blue.

"I'm making an Easter egg!" she announced.

"It's *Valentine's Day*, dummy," scowled a boy across the table. He was a few years older, and had decided to paint his magnet like a robot.

"My name's not Dummy. It's Sylvia. And this is a Valentine Easter Egg." She continued painting happily.

Isabel placed a hand on the girl's shoulder. "It's very beautiful! Your mom is going to love her magnet."

"I know," said the girl. "But I'm not really good at art," she whispered.

Isabel sat down in an empty chair next to the girl and shook her head. "Yes, you are! Look, hold your brush like this."

She guided the girl's tiny fingers to make a squiggly line across the middle of her egg, and was rewarded by the girl's blinding smile. "Thanks, Izablue!"

"Izablue? Why Izablue?" Isabel laughed.

"Because, silly." The little girl looked up from her egg, and in a very serious little voice explained: "Blue is my favorite color, and you are my favorite teacher. You belong together."

Isabel reached over and hugged Sylvia, telling her, "you're the best."

Mama was right, she realized. *Helping out at Jeri's Place is worth missing the Valentine's Day Dance.* Here she was really making a difference, brightening the lives of little kids doing something she liked best—art.

Isabel waved at Kevin. He was sitting across the table, helping the boy with the robot magnet clean up a huge blob of black paint he'd spilled on the table. Kevin glanced up and gave her a quick smile.

"Who is that boy smiling at you?" Sylvia asked.

"He's my friend Kevin," Isabel said as she ruffled the little girl's hair.

"He looks nice," she pronounced, and went back to painting her Valentine's Easter Egg.

"He *is* nice . . . very nice." Isabel looked over at Kevin, his head bent close to the little boy who was at that moment crying because some of the black paint had dripped onto his shirt.

Isabel took a deep breath. One of the most popular boys at Abigail Adams Junior High would rather volunteer to teach art at the local homeless shelter than go to a school dance. *I hope my friends are having as much fun as Izablue!*

Isabel chuckled to herself and dipped her paintbrush into a lovely shade of sky blue paint.

Ready, Set, Go

At six o'clock, the doorbell rang again. Charlotte ran downstairs to greet the dance posse.

"Hi, everybody," she said as she opened the door and ushered in Dillon, Reggie, Riley, Chelsea, the Yurtmeister,

Betsy Fitzgerald, Henry Yurt, Billy Trentini, Chase Finley, and Nick Montoya. Everyone looked so dressed up....except Dillon, Billy, and Chase, who wore matching Red Sox jerseys.

More than anything Charlotte was excited to see Nick, who wore a white button-up shirt. She glanced sideways at him as he stood close beside her. Nick's invitation to the dance still echoed in her ears. *He could have asked Chelsea, but he didn't,* she thought. *He asked me . . . Charlotte Ramsey. I don't know how I could have doubted him before.*

Meanwhile, the excited chatter of her friends caused the yellow Victorian to ring with energy. *It's probably been a long time since this house was crammed with so many kids at once,* thought Charlotte. She hoped that Miss Pierce wouldn't mind all the noise. But then she remembered that she had just left with Yuri. The noise wouldn't matter tonight!

Chelsea was carrying something in a large frame wrapped in bright tissue paper. "Hey, what's that, Chels?" asked Avery, who had run down the stairs behind Charlotte. Chelsea just smiled mysteriously and laid the package up against the wall, warning all the kids not to touch it.

"She won't tell you, dude. It's huge . . . like, a huge surprise," Dillon joked as he reached over and tried to give Avery and Chelsea each a noogie on the head. They both ducked.

"Dillon's been trying to peek inside all the way over here," Chelsea explained.

As the group began heading upstairs, Dillon pulled Charlotte aside. "Where's the little dude? He always comes to the door." He smiled appreciatively at Charlotte's dress. "You look nice, by the way."

Charlotte smiled and said, "Gee, thanks." She was surprised that Dillon Johnson would actually notice her dress. But her smile faltered when she told him about Marty. "He's hiding somewhere. He's being acting really down lately. We don't really know what's wrong with the little guy."

At the top of the stairs Katani stood next to Chelsea, who had decided to wear a rose-colored dress that brought out the beautiful light brown color of her eyes.

"Hey, where's Marty?" Chelsea asked worriedly. She was big dog lover too. "Is he okay?"

"I think he's depressed," Avery answered as she joined the crowd in the living room. "He just sits around all day looking really mopey."

"Who ever heard of a depressed doggy?" Chase Finley, Charlotte's least favorite boy at AAJH, asked with a snort.

"Dude, I've done research on the Internet," Avery challenged, her hands on her hips. "Dogs can get depressed just like people."

"I can see it now," Chase said. "Marty lying down on the psychiatrist's couch as he talks about his childhood."

"You mean puppy-hood, dude," Yurt added with a grin.

At that moment, Mr. Ramsey walked in. "Well, it looks like AAJH is going to rock tonight. You all look great." Charlotte looked at Katani and rolled her eyes. Nobody said *rock* anymore.

Her dad high-fived a few of the boys, winked at Charlotte, then went back to his office, but not before adding, "Have a great time, and stay safe, everyone."

The boys laughed, but the girls all began to talk worriedly about Marty and his strange behavior. They all agreed that Charlotte should keep an eye on him to make sure he didn't get worse.

"Maybe you should get another puppy," Dillon offered. "I read somewhere that dogs get lonely too."

Maeve whispered to Katani, "Dillon is so sensitive . . . just like a real Prince Charming."

"He probably saw that on my blog. . . ." Avery joked to the girls.

"You *read*, dude?" Billy Trentini teased, a big smile spreading across his face.

"Hey, don't be talkin' trash, comic book boy," Dillon retorted as he waggled his head and shoulders at Billy like he was starring in his own music video.

"Well, Maeve, maybe not *exactly* Prince Charming," responded Katani with an arched eyebrow.

Maeve sighed in frustration. She was just going to have to take over. Her romantic vision of a perfect Valentine's Day Dance was not going to be ruined by the antics of two goofy boys, especially since one of those boys was her dream date. She stomped over with her hands on her hips and glared at Billy and Dillon. "I hope you boys are going to behave yourselves. We have a very important event to attend."

The room grew silent as Dillon backed away from her, his eyes wide.

Nick, who was standing next to Dillon, said, "Dude, you are toast. Say something nice." Dillon looked around the room for Avery. But Avery was deep in conversation with Riley.

"Sorry, Maeve . . . ?" Dillon, on the spot, fumbled around and finally blurted. "Your pink dress looks cool with your red hair."

Maeve eyed him suspiciously. *Does he think redheads shouldn't wear pink?* Her vision of a perfect evening with Mr. Popular was starting to look a little blurry.

Lucky for both of them that just then Billy Trentini threw himself on the living room floor as he tried to mimic a classic wave move. Everyone hooted, including Billy, who unfortunately managed to smash his nose in the process.

"That's bogus, man!" Chase yelled.

Groaning and with blood dripping from his nose, Billy sat up. It was like a scene from *Emergency Room Doctors*. The girls scattered when they saw the blood. Katani held on to the skirt of her hand-sewn dress, grimacing at the mess, and Maeve let out a scream.

"Everything okay out there?" Mr. Ramsey's voice echoed from his office down the hall.

"We're fine, Dad!" Charlotte called back.

"We are?" Maeve didn't look so sure.

The truth was, Betsy Fitzgerald loved *Emergency Room Doctors*. She sprang into action just like her favorite physician Dr. Cathi Tidwell did every Thursday night.

"Everyone—stand back," Dr. Betsy directed with a firm wave of her hand. Then she sat down behind Billy's head and told him, "Lean your head back. That will stop the flow of blood. Charlotte, please run and get a cold cloth with some ice, if you can, please. Katani, hand me those tissues."

Betsy grabbed a handful of tissues and held them tight against a grateful Billy's nose.

"Isn't my Valentine date wonderful," a proud Henry Yurt exclaimed. "Let's give that girl a round of applause."

Giggling, everyone began clapping, "Woohoo for Dr. Betsy!"

"Sit still, Billy," Betsy commanded. "You don't want your nose to start bleeding again, do you?"

"She could probably skip medical school and go straight to the emergency room from eighth grade," Avery snickered to Katani, who burst out laughing.

"It's not funny," Billy sputtered, his voice muffled from all the tissues Betsy still had firmly planted against his nose.

At that moment Charlotte came rushing back into the room with a cold ice pack. Betsy told Billy to hold it on his nose for a few minutes. Then she stood up and pronounced to the group, "My work is done. I want to go to the dance. Henry, let's go have some fun."

"Whatever milady wishes." Henry bowed, then he and Betsy headed out the door and downstairs, promising to see everyone there.

"Dudes, that girl is waaay too much! I don't think 'fun' is in her vocabulary," Chase said snidely as he watched Dillon and Nick help Billy to his feet.

Betsy heard him and spun around. Her eyes flamed,

which actually made her look very pretty in her soft blue dress that flared from the waist.

Folding her arms and lifting her chin, she stared defiantly at Chase. "For your information, Chase Finley, I do so know how to have fun . . . a lot of fun! Don't I, Henry?" She looked over at Henry Yurt for confirmation.

"Absolutely!" he responded. "They should give you an honorary degree in fun."

Betsy looked at Chase with a smug expression, grabbed the Yurtmeister's hand, and marched downstairs.

For once in his life, Chase Finley was speechless.

Katani glanced at her watch, the one she found at the second-hand shop and had tied to her wrist with a blue satin rhinestone studded ribbon, and announced. "We all better go. It's getting late."

Everyone herded downstairs. Charlotte stopped, however, when she heard her dad coming down the steps behind them. Mr. Ramsey was all dressed up in a dark gray suit and tie, and his hair was neatly combed and gelled in a new style.

Chelsea squeezed Charlotte's elbow. "Wow, Char, your dad looks kind of handsome. Where's he going?"

"I . . . don't . . . he . . ."

Chelsea looked at her strangely and walked out the door.

Charlotte couldn't believe her dad was going out and he wasn't even going to tell her where he was going. Of course, she already knew where he was going, but that wasn't the point.

Mr. Ramsey walked over to Charlotte and gave

her a quick hug. "You look wonderful, sweetie."

She couldn't help herself. She had to ask. "Thanks, Dad . . . uh . . . where are you going?"

Mr. Ramsey straightened his tie. "You're not the only one going out on the town. I'm heading out this evening too." He gave her a reassuring pat on the shoulder. "But don't worry. I'll be back before you get home from the dance."

Mr. Ramsey walked out on the porch and said good night to all of Charlotte's friends.

"Have a good time," they all called out to her dad as he headed down the street.

He's going out on his secret date with Avery's mom, Charlotte thought. *What is Avery going to think?* she wondered. She peeked out the door, but Avery was chatting it up with Maeve and Dillon.

Nick came back in to get Charlotte and took her hand. The gentle pressure of his fingers made butterflies flutter in her stomach. As if by magic, she felt at peace again. What was it about Nick Montoya that made her feel so happy? Her heart started to pound when Nick looked into her eyes. How had she never noticed his long eyelashes and the freckle on his left cheek?

"Are you ready?" he asked.

Because Charlotte couldn't speak, she nodded.

The two of them walked down the stairs and, hand in hand, followed their friends down the street. They both doubled in laughter when they heard Maeve ask Dillon, "Isn't it a glorious night for a dance?" and Dillon answer, "Yeah, sure, Maeve. It's, like, just glorious. . . ."

Halfway to the dance, Avery stopped to slide on a puddle that had frozen into a delicate web of ice. As she kicked glasslike shards of ice across the sidewalk, she noticed Chelsea trailing behind, lugging her wrapped-up surprise and camera bag.

"Hey." Avery trotted back to walk with Chelsea. "What's up? Need help with that stuff?"

Chelsea smiled a little. "It's not a big deal. I'm fine."

"You sure?" Avery studied Chelsea's downturned eyes and decided she was definitely *not* fine. "Look, this dance is gonna be awesome! Aren't you psyched?" She spun around, jiggling her arms in an attempt to make her friend laugh. "What's under all that tissue paper, anyway?"

"I can't show you yet! It's really a surprise." Chelsea lowered her voice. "So . . . do you think Trevor will be at the dance?" she asked, trying to be nonchalant.

"The T-Dawg?" Avery found another icy puddle and this time smashed it with one fancy black shoe. "I heard Anna asked him."

"He isn't going with her, is he?!" The tone of Chelsea's voice startled Avery.

"No clue." Avery stopped in her tracks. "Wait, you like the T-Dawg?"

Chelsea paused, setting her package down for a second. "Well . . . yeah, I do. He's so cool . . . he likes photography and every time we talk, he's really nice to me. . . ."

"He *is* a cool dude," Avery agreed.

"But he didn't ask me to the dance." Chelsea sighed. "We're, like, the only girls in our group who didn't get

When in doubt ...
DANCE!

Isabel M.

asked to the dance, Avery! Doesn't that bother you even a little *tiny* bit?"

"Not at all," Avery said. "Besides, Dillon asked me to the dance and I said no." Suddenly she covered her mouth with one hand, looking around frantically to see if Maeve was in earshot. Thankfully, she was way up ahead of everyone, talking Dillon's ear off. *Oops,* Avery thought. *So much for not saying anything. . . .*

"Really?" Chelsea couldn't believe it. "Dillon's one of the most popular guys at school!"

"Yeah, but don't tell anyone." Avery held out her hands. "I don't get it, but apparently Maeve will murder me if she finds out I told him to ask her instead."

"You didn't!" Chelsea giggled.

"I did." Avery grinned. "Anyway, it doesn't matter! We're here with all our friends, having a great time, and we're going to dance all night, right? Boys or no boys!"

Chelsea smiled in spite of herself. Avery was right. The whole point of going to a dance was having fun. It didn't matter if you went with a boy or not. Still, at least someone had *asked* Avery. . . .

"Chels?" Avery interrupted her thoughts.

"Yeah, Ave?"

"Don't say anything about the Dillon thing, okay?"

"No problem." Chelsea took out her camera and snapped a picture of Avery skipping backward down the sidewalk. "That's one for the paper!" she declared.

CHAPTER

17

Sorta-Kinda Like
Romeo and Juliet

T he BSG and all of their friends arrived at the dance
to find the Abigail Adams Junior High gymnasium
transformed into a pink-and-red explosion of lights
and sound. Couples were spinning, music was blaring,
and a kaleidoscope of twirling fancy dresses created a diz-
zying effect.

"It's absolutely magical!" Maeve cried, her eyes shining. "Like something right out of a dream!" She grabbed
on to Dillon's arm, who for once looked equally dazzled.

"Maeve," Katani exclaimed, "we hung every single
one of these decorations a few hours ago."

"I know. But with the lights and everything, it looks
different . . . better!"

When Katani looked out at the dance floor, she, too,
had to admit that the gym looked transformed—into a fes-
tive ballroom filled with fairytale dancers. The only thing

that reminded her of the old gym was the pair of basket-ball hoops hanging from the backboards. But even they were decorated with pink and purple streamers.

"Wow! You guys did an amazing job," Nick commented as he tried to take in the sudden blast of color and activity. He stood right next to Charlotte, where she could just barely feel his arm against her jacket. Charlotte felt her heart began to beat to the rhythm of the music. *Oh, yes*, she tapped her foot. *This is going to be one incredible night.*

"Leave your coats on the rack, here!" a jubilant Betsy, who appeared out of nowhere, directed them. And then, with a wave of her hand and a smitten Henry Yurt following behind her, she disappeared into a group of decorating committee friends milling around by the entrance.

Most of the boys in their group peeled off too, rushing to the far wall where the refreshments were. The lure of Party Favors cupcakes and pepperoni pizza proved irresistible. Dillon was about to follow when Maeve tossed him her coat. She almost knocked him off balance when she threw her arms up in the air with a dramatic flourish and trilled, "Let's dance!"

Dillon, Charlotte thought, looked like a deer in the headlights, while an oblivious Maeve clasped her hands below her chin and spun around. "This is the part of the movie where a really cool song comes on and then suddenly all the kids in the room break out the same dance, hitting all the moves, and then a space opens up, and the star enters! Fashionably late, of course."

Avery jumped up, trying to see over the crowd of taller kids into the middle of the gym. "I don't know about you guys, but I don't want to be any kind of late! Let's get this dance thing going!"

Katani smiled at Avery. "That's right, girl!" Then she motioned to Reggie. "Want to dance?"

"You coming, Chels?" Avery asked as Katani and Reggie wove their way to a clear spot, followed by Charlotte, Nick, Maeve, and Dillon.

Chelsea clutched the wrapped-up frame she'd lugged all the way to the dance and looked around for Trevor one last time. *Why isn't he here?* Her spirits fell a little more every minute that passed. She'd worked on her surprise late into the night, hoping he'd be here to see it. "I'll meet you out there," she mumbled.

"No way!" Avery was not about to abandon a friend feeling down. "Aren't you just a little psyched to be here? I mean, look at all of this . . . hey, if you don't want to dance, let's go get some cupcakes." Avery pointed in the direction of the refreshment stand.

Chelsea shook her head. "You go, Avery. I have to put this down somewhere."

"Chelsea. We're here with all our friends . . . we're going to party all night, and have a great time . . . Trevor or no Trevor," she whispered.

Just then, the door swung open, letting in a blast of chilly air. A boy in a stocking cap stomped in, rubbing his hands together. "No one told me Boston was in the Arctic Circle." He took off his cap, and Chelsea almost fainted.

"Trevor!" she managed to squeak. He was wearing shorts and a Hawaiian shirt under his parka, and his hair was just as cute as ever, even all sticking up from his hat.

"Hey Chels, A-Train." He bumped fists with Avery, then pointed at Chelsea's bundle. "What's that?"

"She won't tell anyone—" Avery started, but Chelsea held up a hand. This was the perfect moment for the big reveal. Trevor was here.

"It's for everyone at this dance!" she explained. "Since the newspaper doesn't come out until next week."

Chelsea carefully unwrapped the package she had been hugging since she left home. A crowd of kids began to gather. When she finally took a large, framed piece of poster board out of its wrapping, everyone was really quiet.

Then came the *oohing* and *ahhing*. It was a collage—but what a collage! Chelsea had laid out all the photos from her "Love Is in the Air" project on a pink canvas covered with hearts of all colors and sizes. Some of the photos were blurry and dreamy looking while others were bold and graphic.

"Oh, my gosh," someone gushed. "This looks like something from a magazine."

A proud Chelsea beamed. Out of the corner of her eye she tried to read Trevor's expression as he stared at her presentation.

Kids clamored to see if their pictures were there. Avery found the Trentini twins posing by the lockers, Katani with a shirt she designed, Isabel with a painting, and a great picture of Maeve kicking in the final soccer goal . . . before her face-plant in the mud.

"Wow, Chels, you made this?" Trevor moved in closer to scan all the images. There was even one of him with a map of California.

"Nick wrote the captions," she explained, reddening with pride at Trevor's expression. "But I put it all together last night."

"We've *got* to hang that up where everyone can see!" Avery bounced closer to Trevor and Chelsea. Then she realized they weren't really paying any attention to her. Trevor said something about light depth, and now Chelsea was explaining exposure settings.

A rocking hip-hop beat blasted from the gym, calling Avery into the action. "See you photo dweebs later!" she yelled as the crowd erupted into a frenzy of shouts and jumps. Avery got right out there in the middle of it, flailing around and making everyone laugh with her latest dance moves.

Dance with Me

"Dude," Dillon said, and turned to Maeve. "Ave just totally broke out Kelley Washington's touchdown dance—check it out!"

"Kelley *who*?" Maeve racked her brain for recent reality TV stars, hip-hop stars, but she came up blank. Also, she couldn't believe Dillon had just called her *dude*. She was going to have to work on that.

"You know, the New England Patriots? Wide receiver?"

Maeve shook her head as she pulled off a perfect move she had learned from *Dancing with the Stars*. Dillon wasn't even watching. He was wielding his tie clip like a tiny football and making faces at Avery.

A slow song came on, and Maeve reached out one hand palm down, fingers extended, just like she'd seen in all the movies. "Dillon Johnson!" she gushed. "I'd love to dance!" He still hadn't asked, but Maeve couldn't wait any longer. This was the moment she'd been dreaming of!

Dillon reached his hand out so slowly, Maeve thought the song was going to be over before they even started dancing. Finally, he touched her fingertips, and she curtsied just like she imagined Princess Diana would have done.

As they danced Dillon stared squarely at the far wall while Maeve rested her palms lightly on Dillon's shoulders and swayed. If she closed her eyes, she could almost pretend he was pulling her in close, not locking his arms out straight and leaning back.

As the song crescendoed, Maeve got lost in her imaginary Hollywood rose garden, singing along, "Love comes walking in . . ." Suddenly, there were no shoulders under her hands. "I'm gonna get some cupcakes before they're gone, Maeve. I'll catch you later."

Before she could say anything, Dillon ran off toward the refreshment table.

"I'll catch you later!" Maeve fumed. Charlotte and Nick were off in their own little world, and Katani and Reggie had joined a group of science whizzes, so only Avery heard.

"What's up?" Avery asked, watching Dillon shuffle away.

"Everything!" Maeve dragged Avery out into the hall as the speakers started booming out YMCA. "First, he's wearing a T-shirt with his tie clip on the *sleeve*. Second, he won't even *look* at me. Third, all he wants to talk about is sports!"

"Uh, Maeve," Avery said, fidgeting, "that's what he *likes*."

"He likes sports more than *me*?!" Maeve ran her hands through her hair.

"Well . . . yeah, maybe," Avery said matter of factly. "You can't have Dillon magically become a copy of you that you can dress up and drag around."

"You get along with him," Maeve pleaded. "Can't you tell him to behave? I'm really not having any fun with him!"

"Geesh, Maeve!" Avery folded her arms. "Dillon's just being himself. Why can't you be happy? He asked you to the dance, didn't he?"

Maeve nodded. "But, Avery, he's acting like he didn't even want to come with me! I mean, why would he ask me if he didn't want to? Do you think he wanted to?"

Avery gulped. How could she say yes? That didn't feel like a white lie anymore. It just felt like a big fat fib. "Well"—Avery played with the sash on her dress again, tying and untying it—"maybe if you talked some sports with him . . . or something?"

"I hate sports!" Maeve whined.

"Then why did you want to go to the dance with him? Dillon loves sports." Avery raised her voice. Maeve was starting to get annoying, and she was beginning to feel bad for Dillon.

"Because he's cute, and he asked me, and I wanted to!" Her voice rose to meet Avery's.

"Well maybe he really didn't want to!" Avery shouted.

A passing group of ninth-grade girls on their way to the bathroom gave them a sidelong glance.

"Well, then," Maeve huffed. "He shouldn't have asked me, silly."

Avery felt her face redden. "I told him to ask you . . . 'cause, well, I thought it would make *you* happy, and now neither of you is happy!"

With that, Avery dashed back into the gym. *I hate secrets,* she fumed as she looked for Charlotte and Katani. They would know what to do.

Maeve Kaplan-Taylor stood absolutely still. She looked across the gym and saw Dillon fooling around with Billy and Josh and Chase. He looked happy with them.

"BIG problem," Avery gasped, grabbing Charlotte's arm. "Maeve knows about Dillon."

Tug of War

Chelsea felt a hand on her shoulder. She turned around and found herself looking into two sets of eyes lined with thick mascara. *Uh-oh . . . not the Queens of Mean again!* If anyone could ruin her good time, it was them.

"Hey, Anna, look at this!" Trevor held out the poster. Chelsea wanted to grab it from him. He hadn't been at AAJH long enough to realize the havoc Anna and Joline would wreak.

"Ooh, camera girl," Joline cooed. "Showing off your homework?"

Chelsea cringed. *How do they always manage to pull off just the right insult?* Now she felt like a complete fool. She did want to show off a little . . . for Trevor. She wanted him to think she was somebody. And now with a single comment Joline had reduced her to a loser.

"We wouldn't want to distract her from all her admir-ers," Anna said, smirking, "now *would* we, Trevor?" And she grabbed his hand. There were no admirers left now, only Trevor. Chelsea could feel her temper rising.

"What?" he looked at QOM#1. Chelsea realized that Trevor didn't quite get that Anna was insulting her. He obviously wasn't totally clued in to the whole mean-girl thing. But Chelsea was. She'd lived with their jabs her whole life.

"This is my song!" Anna flipped her hair. "Come on." Trevor gave Chelsea a quick backward glance as Anna dragged him toward the dance floor.

He really doesn't know any better, a tiny voice protested inside, but Chelsea still wanted to scream. *It's not fair!* There's no way a cute boy like Trevor would rather talk to her when he could dance with a gorgeous girl like Anna.

"That's such an . . . interesting dress you're wearing," Joline added before trailing her boy-kidnapping partner into the dance. "That color almost makes you almost look less . . . wide."

Chelsea froze. There was that word again. She wrapped her poster back up and set it against the wall by the drink-ing fountain. *Guys like Trevor don't want to hang out with a fat girl like me.*

Chelsea opened her camera case and settled into the soothing routine of selecting lenses and filters. *I should just fade into the background and take pictures, like I always do. At least I'm good at that!*

Chelsea took a deep breath and stepped into the gym, keeping her back to the wall. Right away, she saw a couple perfect shots: girls in sparkling dresses huddling together, a boy pulling off some serious break dancing, and a hundred colorful lights throwing pink shapes all over the crowd.

"What's up, Chelsea?" Nick asked, wandering over from the refreshments table.

"Where's Charlotte?" Chelsea wondered.

"She went to the bathroom with the other BSG." He laughed. "Why do you girls always have to go to the bathroom in packs, anyway?" Normally, Chelsea would have giggled, but she couldn't. Nick noticed, of course.

"Hey, what's wrong?" he asked, concerned.

Chelsea shrugged. "Oh, it's nothing. QOM on the loose."

"Okay." Nick suddenly understood. "I don't know what those two eat for breakfast, but the army ought to package it."

Chelsea knew he was just trying to make feel better, but for some reason, it only made her more miserable.

Nick looked uncomfortable for a moment. "Uh . . . would you like to dance?"

Chelsea nodded. *Maybe Anna and Trevor will see! Then they'll know I'm not a complete loser. . . .* The strains of *Titanic*'s theme song filled the gymnasium as Nick led Chelsea onto the floor. Feeling kind of weird, she put her hands on his shoulders. Nick reached out and held her waist, keeping plenty of space between them. *He's nice, like a brother,* Chelsea realized.

Chelsea nodded and hummed along with the music,

trying not to look at Trevor and Anna dancing together across the gym.

Loserville

"Will someone please explain why traitor Avery made me look a complete total, unbelievable, Valentine's Day loser?!?" Maeve plopped herself down in a folding chair someone had left in the bathroom.

Charlotte and Katani stood together, exchanging glances. Avery hung back, like she thought Maeve might leap up and attack.

"Well . . . ," Charlotte started.

"First of all . . . ," Katani said at the same time.

"Okay, I'll explain." Avery couldn't let her friends take the heat for her, so she ducked between them and put a hand on the back of Maeve's chair. "Look, I knew you wanted to go with Dillon more than anything, so I kind of asked him to ask you. Then everyone told me that wasn't cool. But it was too late and . . ."

Katani nodded. "We thought it would be easier if you just didn't know."

"We were wrong." Charlotte put an arm around Maeve's shoulders. "We all just wanted the dance to be perfect for you."

"You did?" She sighed.

Then Maeve surprised them all by jumping up and splashing her face with cold water from the sink. "So that's it?" she demanded.

"Well . . . yeah," Avery responded.

"All right then," Maeve said matter of factly. "If

Dillon really *doesn't* want to dance with me, it means =I can dance with anyone I want now, right? I can't let this night go to waste." And just like that, Maeve was back to her usual happy and vivacious self.

She got up and gave Avery a hug. "Don't do that again, okay? It's really kind of embarrassing for me."

"Cool." Avery nodded, stunned that she got off so easily. *But then again*, she thought, *that's Maeve . . . unpredictable . . . and forgiving.*

"Maeve!" Charlotte laughed as she stood in front of the mirror reapplying her lip gloss. "Who are you going to dance with?" She was glad her friend was back to her usual bubbly self.

"Hmmm . . . I'll get back to you!" Maeve ran through the list of seventh-grade boys in her mind, but couldn't think of a single one who actually knew how to dance like Fred Astaire.

"Speaking of boys, how is it going with Nick?" Katani joined Charlotte by the mirror and took out her own tiny makeup case.

"Nick is so sweet," Charlotte said. "I think I like him better than any boy I've ever met."

She wasn't sure how to explain to her friends their conversation on the phone the other night. In fact, she didn't really know how to explain it to herself, either. Nick was still just her friend, but in a way that meant they could share anything and not worry about what the other was thinking. "He's . . . well," she told her friends, "*special.*"

Maeve smoothed down her skirt and fluffed out her

hair. "You two make a cute couple. *Almost* as cute as me and Dillon were!"

Charlotte smiled, keeping her thoughts to herself, where she could treasure them. "Thanks."

When Katani finished her makeup, she grabbed Avery by the shoulder. "Your hair is going wild! What have you been doing? Hanging upside down?"

Avery crossed her arms and sighed. "I like to move around a lot when I'm dancing. I can't worry about hair-dos when I'm trying to break it down."

Katani rolled her eyes and got to work fixing Avery's hair with a hairbrush as slim and chic as a cell phone. "I should have brought some hairspray," she muttered.

Maeve grinned. "There's no hairspray in the world that could hold MKT's curls down!"

"Okay," Katani said. "Avery's hair is somewhat better. Ready to go back out there?"

Trouble on the Dance Floor

The gym looked even more crowded than when they had left. As Charlotte and her friends walked back onto the dance floor, she tried to pick out Nick from the horde of bodies. *Where is he?* she thought, her eyes scanning the faces around the room.

The first notes of the theme song from *Titanic* drifted through the air. Charlotte hummed along. She couldn't help it. Ever since she had first seen the movie with her dad when they were living in Paris, she had loved the way Céline Dion's voice rose and rose.

Katani made fun of her for listening to such old music,

but Maeve was totally into it too. Charlotte remembered watching the movie at one of their BSG sleepovers, singing along with Maeve at the top of her voice while Katani and Avery screamed at them and threw pillows until even Maeve couldn't sing anymore because she was laughing so hard. "Near, far, wherever you are . . ."

Charlotte anxiously searched for Nick. He would love to hear that story! And then they'd dance together again . . . maybe even holding hands. Charlotte closed her eyes for a moment, relishing a moment in the song that lifted her away from the dance, into a world of waves, disaster, lost love, and hope.

When she opened her eyes, one of the flashing colored bulbs in the ceiling cast a beam of harsh light on two dancing figures. They moved together, just a little closer than the other couples. *Nick and Chelsea!* At first Charlotte didn't believe it, but the light wouldn't move off of them, and the song wouldn't stop. Céline Dion's voice kept rising and bursting: "and you're here in my heart, and my heart will go on and on . . ." Charlotte stood there, frozen in place, trying to not to react. *It means nothing,* she told herself.

But why this song? Why tonight? Why couldn't Chelsea find someone else to dance with? *Has Nick been lying to me? They're dancing really close!* Charlotte couldn't believe that she was back to square one again.

"Hey, isn't that Nick . . . dancing with Chelsea?" Maeve pointed out.

Charlotte swallowed once, hard, then turned and walked out the door.

"Uh-oh," Katani said. "I'll be right back. YOU, go talk to Nick."

"Me?" Maeve stammered, but there was no time to argue. "Come on." She grabbed Avery's hand, and pushed through groups of dancers as Céline Dion's voice rose in a final, heart-wrenching crescendo.

"Nick!" Maeve announced. "What in the world are you doing?"

"Ummm, dancing?" he said. Chelsea let go of Nick and stepped back, cheeks flushed red. She hadn't meant to touch his hands, the song had just swept her up. She couldn't help it! She kept imagining that Nick was Trevor. . . .

"I think you better go find Charlotte," Maeve scolded.

"Yeah!" said Avery, though she really had no idea what the big deal was. They were all friends, what did it matter who danced together?

"I did, I mean, I will, I mean . . ." Nick looked around. "Oh no, Charlotte saw, didn't she?"

Maeve folded her arms and nodded. The look in her eyes could have drilled holes through metal.

"Where is she?!" Nick asked anxiously.

Maeve pointed toward the door, then bolted away, neatly swerving past the ninth-grade basketball team dancing in their own little circle beneath one of Isabel's giant painted hearts.

Nick stood in place, stunned. "Should I, um, go too? Or . . ."

Avery shrugged, and Chelsea shuffled from foot to foot. "It's my fault," she whispered to Avery, looking down at her feet. "I love that song, and well, Nick asked me to dance. . . . I didn't realize . . . I thought it would be okay. . . . I guess I'll go back to taking pictures."

"I should probably go," Nick decided, and with one quick apologetic smile to Chelsea, he made his way toward the door.

CHAPTER
18

A Winter Wonderland

A gust of wind swept through the courtyard as Nick called out, "Hey!" Charlotte looked up and then leaned against Katani, who was sitting next to her on a frozen picnic bench. Maeve had one hand on her shoulder and tightened her grip as Nick came up behind them.

"Do you want us to go, Char?" a hesitant Katani asked.

"No . . . yes . . . I don't know," Charlotte squeaked. Maeve thought her voice sounded a little like one of her guinea pigs.

Katani handed Charlotte a tissue. She sniffed and wiped her nose. *This is* great, she sighed. *Now my nose is all red and runny, and I look like Rudolph. What happened to my dream date?*

Seeing Nick standing there looking all sheepish, Charlotte simply couldn't understand why she felt so awful.

Nick already had explained that he and Chelsea were

just friends. And Nick had danced with her for at least ten songs, and they had been the greatest moments of her whole life. *It's just plain dumb to be jealous over one dance,* she scolded herself.

"It's okay. You two go ahead." Charlotte tapped Katani's hand and forced a smile at Maeve. "I'm fine."

"Are you sure?" Katani asked, her eyes narrowed at Nick.

"I'm sure."

Hearing her friend's voice return to normal, Katani stood up.

"Okay, then," Maeve said. "Come find us again as soon as possible!"

Katani brushed past Nick and walked back inside with Maeve. "There is just way too much drama going on around here!" she pronounced.

Charlotte watched her breath billow in and out in little clouds as Nick sat down on the bench. He stared at his hands while Charlotte sniffed up a drip.

"Have you been crying?" Nick asked

Charlotte shrugged, trying to keep her voice from sounding too pitiful. "I wouldn't exactly call it crying . . . it's more like snuffling."

Nick let out this huge whoosh like he had been holding his breath for an hour. "I tried to tell you before. Chelsea's just my friend."

"I know." Charlotte hugged her shoulders and listened to the drum beat coming from inside the gym. "I don't know why I freaked out."

"It's okay." He scooched over on the bench, so just

his shoulder touched hers. "This is weird, huh?"

"Yeah," Charlotte agreed. "It was kind of easier to just be friends."

"I guess." Nick sighed.

They sat quietly together for a minute as the snow drifted around them. Nick reached over and brushed off some flakes that had settled on Charlotte's nose and eyelashes. A light over the door to the gym illuminated the flakes as they began to twirl down, faster and faster. *It's like a beautiful ballet*, Charlotte thought, *put on just for me and Nick*.

Nick grinned. "Ready to head back in there?"

"Sure." Charlotte smiled, while secretly wishing they could stay out just a few minutes longer. Somehow she didn't feel mad at him anymore. She just felt confused.

Nick jumped up and brushed some snow off his shoulders. "You know, Chelsea was feeling really down after the QOM made a few of their *special* comments. That's why I asked her to dance."

"Let's go see if she's okay now." Charlotte reached out her hand to Nick. It was mind boggling to her how just a minute ago she was a wreck, and now everything was fine. She wondered whether the BSG should issue a *crush alert* should one of the them ever get bitten by the love bug again.

Food, Glorious Food!

Katani went off to dance with Reggie, so Maeve made her way over to Avery, who was standing next to a dejected Chelsea.

"Hey Chels, let's show Maeve your collage." Avery

suggested, remembering how proud she'd been when she showed it to her and Trevor.

So they walked out to the hall where Chelsea had left the large frame by the water fountain.

"Oh, Chelsea, this is *marvelous*!" Maeve pronounced. "You should sign it! Or," she joked, "I'll sign it seeing as I'm such a major soccer star."

"Woo-hoo, Maeve!" Avery hugged her friend.

Chelsea just shrugged. "It's not that big a deal." She looked over Maeve's shoulder to see if Trevor was nearby. She hadn't seen him since that glimpse before her dance with Nick. *Where did Anna take him? To a secret Queens of Mean hideout somewhere?*

"No, really, you deserve an award! AAJH photographer of the year!" Maeve continued.

"I'm the *only* photographer," Chelsea pointed out.

"I'm gonna get us some pizza," Avery suggested, feeling her stomach growl. "Be right back."

Dillon was guarding the refreshments table, snarfing down some chips and salsa, and another slow song was starting. *What's with all this slow stuff?*

Avery started to put her hands in her pockets until she realized her dress didn't have any. *Mental note*, she told herself, *Next time you buy a dress, get one with pockets.* How else were you supposed to stash stuff if you didn't have anywhere to put it?

"Don't even think about asking me to slow dance," Avery said to Dillon, hands on her hips instead.

Dillon laughed. "Are you crazy? I'd rather eat slugs on toast."

Avery sighed with relief. Maybe Dillon didn't like, LIKE her, after all. "That makes two of us, dude," she said, and she swiped a couple of brownies. The pizza boxes were all empty.

"Whoa, don't hog all of the food!" Dillon ordered.

Avery rolled her eyes. "First come, first served."

"Well, I was here first and the rest are for me." Dillon grabbed two brownies and stuffed them both in his mouth at once.

"I swear, Dillon, you are such a doofus!" Avery turned to walk away.

"Thank you so much," he said, wiping chocolate off his mouth with his sleeve. "So, what's up with Maeve? She was, like, dragging me everywhere and then you all disappeared!"

Avery turned around and lowered her voice. "I kind of told her about asking you to take her to the dance."

"So?" He looked baffled.

Avery sighed. "I know, dude. I don't really get it either. But I guess it really matters."

"Huh," Dillon grumbled. "Do I get to keep this cool pin?" He held up the tie clip.

"Who knows?" Avery laughed, and slipped off with her brownies.

But when she got back to the hallway, Maeve, Chelsea, and the framed collage were nowhere to be found.

Joline's Wide Retriever

"Maeve, come on," Chelsea insisted. She and Maeve had moved to the other side of the gym to get out of the way of a crowd of rowdy ninth graders, and now Chelsea could see Anna walking up, trailing Trevor. "Let's get out of here." But Maeve shook her head. She was tired of the QOM trying to ruin everyone's life.

"Where's *Dillon*?" Anna asked Maeve, with a queenly sneer.

"I think I saw him wolfing some brownies with Avery," Trevor started.

Joline interrupted. "What's it like having your date hang out with one of your best friends?"

Maeve shrugged. "He's not really my *date*, and Dillon is allowed to hang out with whoever he wants. We're not in prison here."

Joline smirked and pulled on the arm of a tall boy standing behind her, staring blankly at the ceiling. "This is Brandon. He's on the eighth-grade football team. He's the wide retriever."

Maeve cracked a smile. "Don't you mean . . . wide receiver? Like Kelley Washington?"

"Hey, this girl knows what's going on!" Brandon snapped to life suddenly.

"Ha-ha . . . wide retriever," Trevor laughed. "Is that, like, when you have a golden retriever on your team?"

Chelsea and Maeve laughed as Joline scowled. "That's *not* what I said. Whatever." Joline stormed off.

"Come on, Trevor," Anna went to follow, but Trevor hung back.

"I'm going to chill with these guys for a while." His eyes landed on Chelsea. "Hey, Chels, want to dance?"

"What?!" Anna's eyes flashed. "I give you a second

chance, spend my precious time introducing you to *every* cool person in this school, and you want to dance with *her*?!"

"Ahh, yeah, actually, I do," Trevor held out a hand to Chelsea, who suddenly felt like Sleeping Beauty awakening from her hundred years' sleep.

"Okay!?" Chelsea said with a surprised smile.

Trevor nodded. "Come on, this is a great song."

Maeve watched Trevor and Chelsea walk away, feeling a certain satisfaction at the furious look on Anna's face. She watched Anna stalk off in the other direction, then noticed Chelsea's collage forgotten against the wall.

Huh, she thought, *what am I supposed to do with that?* Not wanting Chelsea's work to get ruined, Maeve moved it back out into the hallway, out of the way behind the coats, just so no one would step on it or something.

Now, I'm going to dance! She ducked in the bathroom for a quick second to make sure her curls were all in place, then made her entrance onto the dance floor, just in time for her favorite song.

Dancing Queen

To her surprise, Chelsea didn't feel weird at all dancing beside Trevor. *Definitely not like dancing with my brother,* she sighed as Trevor held on to her hand. She remembered the dance with Nick; she was glad he'd asked her, but sorry she'd made Charlotte so upset. *I hope she's okay. . . .*

"I love your photos," Trevor said over the music. "Do you think you could teach me how to make collages like that? I take lots of pictures, but then I never know what to do with them."

Chelsea nodded. "Sure. It's not that hard to do. We should get together after school and work on something."

"That would be cool." Trevor moved in close as Chelsea spun around, her red dress billowing out around her legs. She felt like a queen—not a queen of mean, but a dancing queen.

"Hey, Chels!" Charlotte's voice broke into her thoughts. Chelsea and Trevor waved as Charlotte came running over, followed by Katani, Nick, and Reggie.

"You okay, Char?" Chelsea asked, holding out her arms to her good friend.

Charlotte hugged Chelsea. "Yeah, everything's fabuloso!" she said with a laugh, imitating Maeve. "How about you?"

Her friends were so cool. "Everything's great," Chelsea responded. "You should have seen Maeve take on the QOM!"

"Only Maeve!" Charlotte laughed as Chelsea told the story.

Then Katani waved her arms in the air. "Come on people, let's dance!"

Mustard Monkey Moves

I had no idea Riley was such a good dancer, Maeve thought. She'd walked over to hang out with his band members and a group of music kids because she couldn't find her friends anywhere. Of course, with so many faces, voices, the loud music, and so little light, she could have walked right by one of them and not noticed. She hoped Charlotte and Nick were okay. *Oh, well, we'll find each other eventually.*

Maeve turned her attention to Riley. All of a sudden she

noticed how cute he looked with his hair all gelled back.

Before Maeve could ask if he wanted to dance, Riley turned to her and said, "I can't believe they're playing this!" He grinned. "This band is *totally* the next big thing!"

"Really?" Maeve shouted over the ringing chords. She'd never heard it before.

Riley nodded. "People don't realize how hard it is to come up with great lyrics and a catchy melody. I write a lot of songs for Mustard Monkey and I can tell you that it's a lot of work."

Maeve leaned her face closer to his so she could talk in his ear. "I bet it is. It's really cool you compose your own stuff! When are you going to perform again?"

Riley paused as he bopped his head along with the song's beat. "Well, I've got one new song . . . I'm not sure if it's really ready to go yet, though. Want to give it a try sometime?"

Flattered, Maeve laughed. "Riley, I have a great idea!"

"Oh, yeah? What is it?"

She put her lips to his ear and whispered something that made his eyes light up with excitement.

"We should get some punch and discuss this," Riley suggested as Mustard Monkey's guitar player jumped straight up in the air, kicking his legs out to the sides.

"Sounds fantabulous," Maeve gushed, feeling a little flutter of excitement.

All Together Again

At the end of the next song, the BSG found Maeve and Riley deep in conversation at the refreshments table. A flurry of quick hugs, high-fives, and questions were interrupted by Avery, who came bouncing over, followed by Dillon.

"My feet are killing me!" Avery wailed, slipping off her right sandal and rubbing her toes.

"Yeah," Dillon joked. "And you almost gave Billy Trentini another nosebleed!"

"How do you always manage to knock into people when you dance?" Katani asked.

"It's a gift, I guess," Avery added with a proud smile.

"Avery, you should go with me to my hip hop class!" Maeve suggested, handing Avery a cup of punch. Then she glanced at Dillon. "Can I talk to you for a second?"

Dillon looked a little panicked.

"It's okay," Avery urged Dillon.

Maeve led him a little way away from the table. "Sorry," she whispered.

"Why?" Dillon looked confused.

Maeve threw up her hands. *Is Dillon as clueless as Avery?* she wondered. "'Cause you asked me to the dance then I didn't even really dance with you!"

He lightly punched her shoulder. "It's cool, Maeve. Forget about it. Can I keep the pin?" He pointed to the tie clip, which was fastened on his T-shirt sleeve.

"Yeah." Maeve grinned as Riley came up behind her.

"Ready?" he asked.

Ten minutes later, Maeve's voice rang through the gymnasium. She and Riley had hopped onstage and Maeve spoke into the mic.

"Attention! May I have your attention, please!" she

said, putting as much drama as she could into each word. "Riley Lee and Mustard Monkey, and me, Maeve Kaplan-Taylor, are here to rock the mic. But first, I'd like to thank Chelsea Briggs for making such an amazing tribute to every single student here at AAJH!"

Riley reached behind a speaker and pulled out Chelsea's project. Maeve flipped it around and placed in at the base of the stage with a flourish.

She didn't! Chelsea thought, but glowed inside.

"Way to go!" Trevor gave her a thumbs-up. "Everyone loves it!"

Sure enough, a crowd was forming around the poster.

"Yes, ladies and gentlemen," Maeve continued. "Love is in the air, so get ready to get your groove on to the new hit single 'You, You, You'!"

Riley pulled out his guitar and hit the first chord. The pure sound echoed through the gymnasium, capturing everyone's attention. And then Riley and Maeve launched into a cool duet:

> *"I never thought I'd ever want to sing,*
> *I never knew what the future would bring,*
> *It brought you, you, you . . .*
>
> *"I never knew my heart could feel this way*
> *I couldn't speak, didn't know what to say*
> *When I met you, you, you. . . ."*

The romantic fun song with the jazzy beat blew everyone away as Maeve and Riley blended their voices into a rich, harmonious sound. No one even minded when Maeve messed up on some of the lyrics.

"You know, Nick, one of our adventures might just be visiting Maeve and Riley in Hollywood some day," Charlotte whispered.

"I'm ready." He smiled and grabbed her waiting hand.

When the Music Ends

"Maeve, wait up," Riley called as she followed her friends outside. The dance was officially over, and everyone was leaving. Maeve turned around.

Riley thrust a CD in her hands. "Here."

Maeve ran her fingers along the side of the jewel case. "What's this?"

Riley grinned. "It's a mix CD of some songs I think you'll like. I meant to give it to you earlier, but I forgot."

Maeve flipped to the back of the case and quickly scanned some of the tracks. He was right. Some of her favorite songs were burned on the CD. It was as if he had crawled inside her head and learned exactly what type of music she liked.

"Oh, Riley!" she said, bouncing up and down. "That is so incredibly sweet of you! She squeezed his hand. "OMG. This totally reminds me of the Judy Garland movie where she and Mickey Rooney decide to put on a show and they sing that really cool duet together and—"

Riley's eyes widened. "You're so cool, Maeve. You're different from other girls. You, like, totally have this passion and just put it out there for everyone to see."

Maeve couldn't believe her ears. Riley thought she was interesting and different. Nobody had ever said that to her before. Usually people thought she was kind of silly for being so crazy about movies.

"Thanks," was all she could muster.

She and Riley walked through the snowy night, chatting excitedly about their duet and discussing ways they could improve it for the next time.

Charlotte stood by the curb, her heart as light as pink cotton candy. Could the night get any better?

"Are you ready to go home?" Nick asked, appearing at her side.

"Yeah, I'm tired." It had been a long night, and Charlotte felt as if she'd been dancing for days.

The evening was cool and quiet as they walked side by side. It was wonderful having Nick beside her as the snow fell through the night sky. She never thought she would love a place as much as she had loved Paris—but that's what happened. On this chilly winter night there was nowhere she'd rather be than right here in Brookline.

As they walked, Nick talked about a winter hiking trip he'd taken with his dad. They'd gone up to the White Mountains, hiked up to Franconia Notch, and skied down. Charlotte shared the time she tried to explain what snow felt like to her friends in Tanzania.

"There's a rainy season in that part of Africa," Charlotte explained. "But never any snow!"

The walk was over much too soon. When they reached the steps of the yellow Victorian, Charlotte turned to thank Nick.

"Thanks for walking me home, Nick. I really had a wonderful time." Charlotte hoped that they could put the whole misunderstanding of the past week behind them. She knew that she really liked Nick in a special way, but she'd had enough of crush craziness to last her at least a year.

Oh, no! Not again. Charlotte fell forward as she turned to go up the stairs.

Nick grabbed her arm and Charlotte righted herself quickly. "Uh . . . yeah. Guess I kinda missed a step."

"Yeah . . . kinda," said Nick, grinning. "So . . . do you think we could meet for breakfast at Montoya's on Monday?"

"Sure. I'd like that," she said, and stared down at her strappy sandals. Her toes were pink and frozen from the snow. She looked up with a mischievous grin. "Wait, are you actually going to show up this time?"

"I'll be there," Nick said.

Charlotte smiled and looked up at him. His eyes twinkled in the moonlight as he stared back into her eyes. She could have looked into those eyes forever, but finally she turned to go.

"Well, good night," she whispered as she turned to attempt to go up her steps once more.

"Charlotte . . . ?" she heard Nick say.

She turned around. What was he still doing here? She stood on the first step waiting for him to say something, but instead he was moving toward her. He put his hands on her shoulders and closed his eyes.

Her mind was racing and she felt as if a thousand

butterflies had flown into her stomach. Charlotte quickly shut her own eyes and before she could gain control of her thoughts she felt Nick's lips on hers, gentle and light as a snowflake! Her mind buzzed and she could feel every inch of her body beaming. Here she was on a beautiful, snowy night getting kissed by the nicest, cutest boy in the world!

"Good night," Nick said under his breath as he pulled away, and before she knew it, he had vanished down the street.

Charlotte ran up the porch steps, wrenched open the front door, and smiled radiantly as she slipped inside. She shut the door and leaned against it, trying to quiet her ragged breathing. As she blindly stumbled up the stairs, she heard her father call out, "How'd it go, sweetie?"

OMG! I can't talk to Dad! Not now, she thought.

"I had fun! Good night!"

Before he could ask her anything else, she flew up the stairs to her room. No way did she want to tell her dad about the kiss. Some things she just wasn't prepared to share with him. Kicking off her shoes, she picked up Marty and flopped down on her bed. The bedsprings squeaked in protest as she grabbed her pillow and hugged it close to her, Marty nestled by her side.

A *kiss. My FIRST KISS.* Staring up at the ceiling, she replayed every single moment on the walk home until she ended at the kiss. Then she started over again. Absently stroking Marty's fur, Charlotte opened her journal, staring at the blank page for a long time before beginning to write.

Charlotte's Journal
TOP SECRET

No one will ever read this, except maybe me when I'm older, but I have to write this down or I think I'll explode. Nick Montoya kissed me tonight. A real kiss! He said, "I'll be there," then just leaned in and kissed me. I can't believe it actually happened and with the cutest, nicest, handsomest boy in the whole world.

I feel like jumping up and dancing or burrowing under the covers and hiding all at the same time. What do I do now? Marty's giving me funny looks. I think he knows something's up. Can people go to sleep after their first kiss? Or do they stay up all night thinking about it over and over again?

CHAPTER

19

Pancakes in Paradise

It was close to eleven a.m. before a sleepy Charlotte opened her eyes. And that was only because her dad was cooking his world-famous pancakes, and the heavenly scent was wafting to her bedroom from the kitchen. But Charlotte wasn't quite ready to eat yet; her mind was still twirling from last night's adventure, and her feet . . . they were so sore. All that dancing in her fancy shoes and then the walk home through the snow had made her realize that fashion has its price.

Charlotte wiggled her toes and snuggled deeper into the covers. She smiled as she thought back to her final dance with Nick. The dance had been so dreamy. She'd almost felt like Cinderella at a modern day ball.

Suddenly she giggled as a vision of her first day disaster at AAJH popped in her mind. At the time, she was convinced that when she zipped the tablecloth into her pants and wiped out her whole lunch group in front of everyone in the cafeteria, that she, Charlotte Ramsey, would be forever labeled the biggest loser of all time.

And she almost was. But then the BSG happened, and she was happy to have the best friends in the world. And now there was Nick. Nick—who loved her stories about riding camels, crossing deserts, and watching stampeding antelopes. Nick—who she could talk to about her dreams of traveling the world. Nick—who really seemed to understand her. Nick—who had kissed her!

"Charlotte honey," her dad called out to her. "Your breakfast is ready."

"In a minute," she called as she threw back the covers and jumped out of bed.

First, she had to check her e-mail.

```
To: Charlotte
From: Sophie
Subject: crying


Is everything fine? For two days I
have only a message that you are
crying! Please write me soon, I must
know if ma meilleure amie Charlotte is
feeling better or no? I wish I could
come and see you this minute in Boston
and bring you many chocolates! My
feeling is that all will be well. But
let me know. Soon! I can not sleep!


Ton amie,
Sophie
```

"Oh, no!" Charlotte cried out loud to the empty room. "I never wrote back after Marty's walk."

At least this morning, she had good news to share.

```
From: Charlotte
To: Sophie
Subject: crying


I'm sorry I didn't write back before,
but life got really crazy. But you,
Sophie, can predict the future.
Everything between me and Nick was
one big fat misunderstanding, just
like your said. And now everything
is perfect . . . more than perfect.
And now . . . are you ready? Nick
kissed me. Yes, my first kiss. Is
it even possible? Everything is so
wonderful!!! I'm not sure I want to
tell anyone else yet about my first
kiss, but I know you will keep my
secret safe.

Au revoir,
Charlotte


P.S. I didn't get any sleep last
night!
P.P.S. You must write back . . . and
soon!
```

Charlotte sat for a minute, trying to recall exactly what the kiss had felt like. It was easier to remember the words Nick had said, and the way he blinked afterward, and stuck his hands deep in his pockets.

"You up there?" her dad's voice echoed up the stairs to the Tower where she sat at her computer.

"Yes," Charlotte answered, yawning, and stumbled down to the kitchen still dressed in her pj's.

"Good morning, Sleeping Beauty," Dad said, placing a steaming stack of pancakes on her plate. "Or should I say Cinderella? Cinderella's the one who danced the night away."

A knock on the door interrupted them. Mr. Ramsey walked down the winding staircase to answer it while Charlotte dribbled maple syrup over her pancakes.

"Maeve, Isabel! This is a pleasant surprise. Come and have some pancakes!" Charlotte heard them all pounding up the stairs, and then her friends burst into the kitchen, stomping the snow off their boots.

"Charlotte! You're awake! We just *have* to talk," Maeve gushed. "All of us! Wasn't that the most wonderful dance ever?" She threw up her arms and twirled around the kitchen next to a bemused Mr. Ramsey.

Then Maeve turned to Charlotte's dad. "Mr. Ramsey, we have to steal Charlotte and go to Montoya's. After all, it was the dance of the century, and all us girls have to debrief."

Charlotte tried not to smile too obviously. Maeve didn't even know half of what happened!

"But . . . I'm in my pj's, and . . ." Charlotte pointed at her breakfast with her fork.

Mr. Ramsey was at the stove again, pouring on more batter. "Girls! There's plenty for everyone."

"Oh, thank you so much Mr. Ramsey, but I absolutely *couldn't*." Maeve's eyes got all big and she sounded exactly like one of her favorite movie stars. "See, we're in *such* a hurry. Katani and Avery are already on their way to Montoya's! And we have to bring Charlotte—it wouldn't be right without her."

Charlotte nearly coughed up a bite of pancakes. Montoya's! *What if Nick thinks I'm following him around now?* It was unlikely, but still. He wouldn't say anything in front of her friends, would he?

"Well, I guess I'll just have to freeze my special pancakes," he said, patting his daughter on the back. "But, I am a little curious, girls. Didn't you all just see each other last night at the dance?" Her father looked at all of them quizzically.

"Well, I wasn't there—" Isabel started to explain.

"And there's so much to discuss!" Maeve interrupted. "The DJ, the refreshments, what everyone wore . . . think of it as super-important girl talk, Mr. Ramsey."

Mr. Ramsey went back to the stove and flipped some fresh pancakes onto a plate. "Well, in that case, Charlotte, I think you'd better get dressed," he said, smiling.

Charlotte looked down at her half-eaten breakfast. "Thanks, Dad. I should probably save some room if we're going to . . . the bakery." She hoped her friends wouldn't notice that she didn't say Montoya's. She was worried the name might make her voice go all funny like it had on the phone with Nick the other night.

Mr. Ramsey shrugged. "I'm sure Marty will enjoy the remains of your breakfast. Go have fun with your friends! The little dude's appetite seems to be back." He chuckled as Marty stood next to him looking up with a pleading expression.

Within five minutes the friends were walking down Beacon Street on their way to Montoya's. *What will Nick think?* Charlotte wondered nervously.

Hearts and Hummingbirds

Avery jumped up on her chair and waved when Maeve arrived at Montoya's with Charlotte and Isabel. The bakery was always crowded on Saturday mornings, and today was no exception. The girls had to squeeze their way through a line that reached from the cash register almost to the door just to get to the table. Charlotte sat down facing the counter, and kept an eye out for Nick's dark hair.

"What took you so long?" Katani asked, after hugging her friends. "People kept trying to take the chairs we saved for you!"

"Char was still in her pj's," Isabel explained.

"And Mr. Ramsey wanted to make us pancakes!" Maeve sniffed the air. "It was very gracious of him to offer, but we explained," she added with a flourish, "that this was an important BSG meeting. And I personally think we need Montoya's hot chocolate . . . agreed?"

As if answering her question, Nick appeared with a tray of five hot chocolates and a plate of fresh-baked muffins. Charlotte avoided his eyes, but watched him pass the drinks around and lay the plate of muffins on the table.

She tried to keep her breath steady but couldn't, partially because Maeve kept looking over at her with sparkling eyes.

Really, she felt ready to explode inside. It was a strange feeling, partly anticipation, like opening a birthday present, and partly feeling like you were hiding under the covers.

"Hey, Char," he said quietly, holding out the plate. "What's up, BSG?" He nodded at the other girls.

"Busy place this morning," Katani commented.

Nick nodded. "Yeah, everybody's coming in today. My parents had to drag me out of bed to help. I saw you guys sitting here, and well . . . I figured I'd grab you some fresh pastries 'cause the line is so long you might not get any."

Charlotte thought Nick was rambling a bit. *Maybe he's a little nervous too,* she figured as she twisted a strand of her hair.

"Thanks, dude!" Avery grabbed a warm muffin. "If any more people come in, you'll have to get some of those swingy things like they have for lines at the airport."

"Swingy things?" Maeve laughed.

"*What?* Do *you* know what they're called?" Avery challenged.

"Charlotte?" Katani asked. "You're the resident expert on words *and* airports!"

"Umm . . ." Charlotte couldn't think of anything at all with Nick standing right there.

Nick answered instead. "I think you just call them ropes, Ave . . . I have to get back to work," he said quickly. "Wish I could hang out, but . . ." He gestured at the line.

"No problem," Isabel assured him. "Good luck!"

"Thanks for the muffins," Charlotte blurted out, and he gave her a little wave as he disappeared back behind the counter.

"You guys are sooo adorable!" Maeve exclaimed, all talk of airports and lines forgotten. "So tell me everything! What did he say to you out in the falling snow? I bet it was romantic! Did he kiss the back of your hand and apologize?"

"Maeve!" Katani scolded, seeing Charlotte's pale expression. "Maybe she doesn't want to talk about it."

"It . . . it's okay," Charlotte said quietly. "I mean, things are actually great! We had the best time together after I stopped acting all weird!"

"I know what you mean!" Isabel agreed. "I thought it would be terrible to miss the dance, but you know what? I had a great time at Jeri's Place." She lifted up an old shopping bag she'd been carrying. "I even had time to make something for each of you."

"You didn't?!" Maeve stared at the bag, eyes sparkling. She just loved gifts!

Isabel unwrapped a ceramic heart magnet about the size of her palm. Painted in the middle was a beautiful pink hummingbird. "This one's for you, Maeve, because you are so sweet and friendly."

Maeve clutched her magnet and crooned. "It's beautiful! I'm going to keep it in my locker."

Isabel gave Charlotte a crane, for world travel and good luck, Avery a bluebird for happiness, and Katani an elegant swan.

"What about you, Izzy?" Charlotte asked.

"Well . . ." Izzy reached into the bag and pulled out a green-and-pink egg-shaped magnet. "Kevin made this one for me," she confessed. "It's an Easter Egg."

"What?!" All her friends said at once.

Isabel laughed. "You had to be there!"

Confessions of a Single Dad

Charlotte arrived home again two hours later. After Isabel's gifts, they'd started discussing the girls' dresses, then they went on to the best dance moves, and everyone agreed that Riley and Maeve's performance was awesome.

And just when they were ready to leave, Chelsea showed up with Trevor, Dillon, and Henry Yurt. She'd run into the boys while printing out her favorite pictures from the dance at the automatic photo machine in the pharmacy. They all laughed at a shot of Yurt doing a spectacular jump move, and Maeve fell in love with an adorable picture of all the BSG holding the hearts they'd helped hang all over the gym.

Charlotte's dad was washing dishes at the sink when she walked in. "So?" he asked. "Are ever going to fill me in on this dance?"

Charlotte had enjoyed herself so much, she'd barely had time to think about what to tell her dad. She picked up a towel and started drying the dishes. *I can't tell him everything . . . not yet, at least.*

"It was fun, Dad." She leaned down to put the frying pan away. "The music was fantastic."

"I'm glad you had a nice time," her dad said. "So . . . you and Nick . . ."

How does he always know what I'm thinking? Charlotte

was glad she had her head in a cabinet so her dad couldn't see her blush.

"Yeah?" She stood up and calmly took a plate from the drying rack.

"You really like him, huh?"

Charlotte shrugged. "Well, he's . . . really nice . . . and he wants to travel, too."

Mr. Ramsey nodded. "It's okay, you don't have to tell me everything, but you know you can . . . if you want."

Charlotte put the plate away and they worked in silence for a few moments.

When Mr. Ramsey finally spoke again, he looked wistful. "I can still remember my first date with your mom. She looked so lovely that day with her long hair hanging down—looking like someone out of a Renaissance painting. And I still remember what she was wearing—a simple pair of blue jeans and a red sweater." Dad shook his head and laughed. "We went to the Beacon Street Movie House. I remember we saw the movie *Casablanca*, a great Humphrey Bogart flick." Her dad stood quietly for a minute, letting the water run into the sink.

An echoing sadness filled Charlotte's heart. Maybe, if her mom were still alive, she'd be able to tell her about last night and her very first kiss. That was what moms were for. Charlotte sighed and tried to focus her mind on something else, but thinking about moms made her remember Mrs. Madden and the voice mail she'd overheard.

Charlotte put the last dish away and sat down at the table. "Dad, I need to ask you something," she said.

Mr. Ramsey sat down on the chair next to her

and folded his hands. "Ask away, sweetie."

Charlotte took a deep breath. No use dancing around the issue. *I'm just going to blurt it out,* she thought. "Dad . . . how did your date go with Avery's mom?"

Her dad jerked back so suddenly, he almost fell off his chair. At first Charlotte thought he was choking, but then she realized he was totally blown away by her question.

He took a napkin and dabbed at his watering eyes as Charlotte went back to her seat. "Okay. Wow. I wasn't prepared for that one." He laughed.

"Dad!" Charlotte couldn't believe it. It felt like he was the kid and she was the grownup! "This isn't funny. I heard the message she left you. You went to that French restaurant last night."

Mr. Ramsey smiled at his daughter. "Oh, Charlotte! I'm so sorry, I should have explained, but you were so busy getting ready for the dance . . . I didn't want to bother you!"

"Well, next time you decide to date my friend's mom, maybe you could let me know?" She was still a little annoyed, but something about the look in her dad's eyes made her think she was missing something.

"It wasn't a date, Charlotte! We went with a whole group of people. A friend of mine at the university had the idea. Why don't a bunch of single parents get together so we don't have to spend Valentine's Day alone? I invited Bif because I thought she might be interested . . . now, we all had such a great time, the group is thinking of getting together once a month, maybe."

Charlotte laughed with relief. "You're not dating?"

Her dad shook his head, then reached over and patted

Charlotte's shoulder. "No, honey . . . I . . . there's no one right now. But, I do get lonely sometimes, so this group could be a really nice way to meet new people."

My dad lonely! Charlotte felt terrible. She never thought of her dad being lonely. He was so busy at school, he had his articles to write, and he had her and Marty. Suddenly, she realized she wasn't the only one to miss her mom.

When her dad saw the look on her face he sighed deeply. "You know, Charlotte, when you lose someone you love, it sometimes takes quite a while to imagine another person in your life."

Charlotte ran and hugged her dad. The two of them stood together comforting each other until Marty started jumping on both of them.

"I think he wants in on the hug too," Charlotte laughed.

The Truth and Nothing but the Truth

After eating more than her fair share of muffins at Montoya's, Avery lay curled up on the couch, watching Boston College basketball. Scott was sprawled in the arm chair across the room. It was their favorite local team.

"When's Red Sox opening day again?" Avery asked. Soccer and basketball were her favorite sports to play, but baseball had to be her favorite to watch. She couldn't stand waiting all winter for her favorite team's first game.

"Not 'til April," Scott yawned.

A commercial came on, and a singing cat tap-danced across the screen, waiting for its owner to fill its food bowl. Mrs. Madden stuck her head in the room. "Are you two going to peel yourselves away from that screen anytime soon?"

"Mom, we deserve a break . . . ," Avery started.

"Well, I need some help here some time today. This room is a *mess*!" Their mom gestured around at what, to Avery and Scott, seemed to be a pristine and dustless living room.

"Sit down and relax, Mom," Scott pointed to the couch. To Avery's surprise, she actually sat, perching with her hands clasped.

"Did you have fun last night?" she asked Avery.

"Sure, Mom." Avery shrugged, then blurted out before thinking, "What about you? How was your date?"

Scott gave her a look. "Come on, Ave, don't bug her."

"Oh!" Their mom looked confused. "I had a wonderful time. But it wasn't a *date*! Whatever gave you that idea?"

Scott glared at Avery, who jumped up and stared like an undercover detective. "You're not dating Mr. Ramsey?"

"Mr. Ramsey!" Avery's mom burst out laughing. "Oh, oh, dear!"

"What?" Avery insisted, standing in front of her mother with her arms crossed.

Mrs. Madden gathered Avery in her arms. "We went out as a big group of single parents. Mr. Ramsey was there, but so were about ten new friends of ours!"

"Really, Mom?" Avery asked, comfortable inside her mom's hug.

"Really, sweetheart. I would tell you if I had a date." She kissed the top of Avery's head.

Scott stood up and stretched. "Cool. I'm meeting some friends. Tell me how the game ends, Ave?"

When her brother left the room, Avery pulled away from her mom.

"I . . . I wanted to talk to you about something else, Mom."

"Go ahead, my love."

And then Avery told her everything—about Dillon asking her to the dance and her turning him down because Maeve wanted him to ask *her*.

"But everything worked out," Avery finished up, "Because Maeve decided she has way more in common with this dude named Riley—which is totally true because both of them are crazy about music and performing."

"But here's the thing," she tried to explain. "I still feel kind of weird about the whole Dillon situation. I mean, he asked me to the dance so I think he might kinda sorta like me or something, and . . ."

The basketball game ended in a cascade of cheers. Avery stared at the screen for a minute.

Mrs. Madden nodded encouragingly. "And?"

"How can I play soccer and stuff with him now? Won't it be weird?"

Mrs. Madden's lips twitched. "Honey, it's perfectly normal and fine to be *just friends* with boys. Dillon's one of your best buddies, and that hasn't changed. He'll probably be relieved if you just go back to that," she said as she ruffled her daughter's hair.

"You'll know," she added, "when you start seeing boys a new way. And there's no need to be in a big hurry to get there! Someday you'll find a guy with the perfect sense of humor, intelligence, and . . ."

"And crazy skill at sports, right?" Avery piped in.

"You got it, kiddo!" Her mom laughed.

Avery smiled. Her mom might get on her nerves a lot, but she always knew the right thing to say to make Avery feel better.

She gave her mom a quick hug. "Okay. I'll help you clean up after I get some homework done."

Before taking out her English book, Avery signed onto IM. None of her BSG friends were on, but another name caught her attention. SnwbrdrJ. *Jason.* Compared to Dillon and all the boys at AAJH, he was a totally different kind of dude.

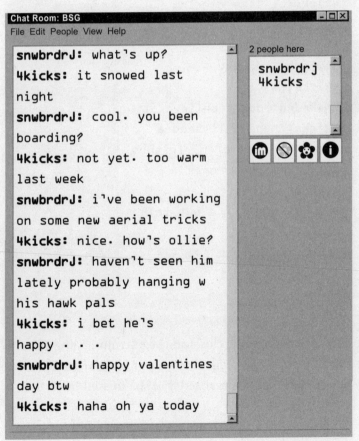

Chat Room: BSG

File Edit People View Help

snwbrdrJ: what's up?
4kicks: it snowed last night
snwbrdrJ: cool. you been boarding?
4kicks: not yet. too warm last week
snwbrdrJ: i've been working on some new aerial tricks
4kicks: nice. how's ollie?
snwbrdrJ: haven't seen him lately probably hanging w his hawk pals
4kicks: i bet he's happy . . .
snwbrdrJ: happy valentines day btw
4kicks: haha oh ya today

2 people here

snwbrdrj
4kicks

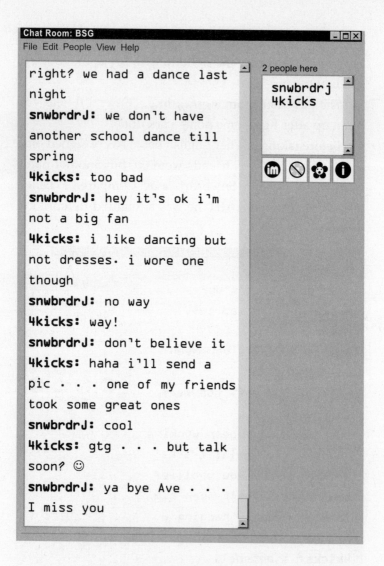

right? we had a dance last
night
snwbrdrJ: we don't have
another school dance till
spring
4kicks: too bad
snwbrdrJ: hey it's ok i'm
not a big fan
4kicks: i like dancing but
not dresses. i wore one
though
snwbrdrJ: no way
4kicks: way!
snwbrdrJ: don't believe it
4kicks: haha i'll send a
pic . . . one of my friends
took some great ones
snwbrdrJ: cool
4kicks: gtg . . . but talk
soon? ☺
snwbrdrJ: ya bye Ave . . .
I miss you

2 people here

snwbrdrj
4kicks

Avery went to her closet and began rummaging through
her backpack. *Jason misses me.* An unfamiliar feeling crept
up on her when she realized that she missed Jason too.

CHAPTER

20

Love Is in the Air

Outside, the sun shone off drifts of freshly fallen snow. Marty trudged along beside Avery and Charlotte, his stubby tail drooping, as the girls walked toward Amory Park.

"Poor Marty," Avery said, stooping down to pet the little doggy. "We've got to figure out how to snap you out of your doggy funk."

Charlotte sidestepped a kid on a skateboard as he zoomed past. "I don't know what we can do. It's as if he's determined to stay miserable—no matter what."

Avery bent down, grabbed a handful of snow and threw it in the air. "Hey, Marty—want to chase some snowflakes?"

"So I asked my dad about the date," Charlotte admitted, to get her mind off down-in-the-dumps Marty, who ignored the snowflakes fluttering before him.

"I asked my mom too!" Avery grinned. "So it was

nothing after all." Avery pulled a pack of gum out of her pocket and offered Charlotte a stick.

"Yes, they were just a group of single parents trying to have a happy Valentine's Day!" Charlotte said as she unwrapped her gum and stuck it in her mouth. "Oh, well. I guess we won't be sisters."

"Well, I'm kind of glad they're just friends, but maybe I can adopt you as a sister, anyway. That would be totally cool!" Avery cracked her gum and grinned at Charlotte.

Avery was adopted, and sometimes she wondered if she had other brothers or sisters out there. If she did, she hoped they were happy, but she also couldn't imagine any family other than the one she had . . . except maybe a new sister . . . a sister like Charlotte.

"I'd like that too!" Charlotte smiled at Avery. She often wished her BSG friends were her sisters, so if she ever had to move again, they'd come with her. If she had sisters, there would always be someone to talk to any time of night . . . someone to share secrets with, someone for the good times and the bad.

"What do you think, Marty man?" Avery asked the dog. He sat down in the middle of the sidewalk, nose up and ears pricked.

"He thinks *something* . . . but what? That is the question," Charlotte said, gently nudging Marty with her shoe so he would keep walking.

"What's up, little guy?" Avery asked, noticing that Marty was sniffing in a particular direction.

Charlotte crinkled her forehead and bent down to pet him. Just then, Marty jumped up, yanking Charlotte's arm so hard she almost fell on the sidewalk. "Ow!"

"Come on!" Avery shouted as Marty led them running over the packed-down snow to a familiar pink overhang. Today, it was covered with hearts and streamers.

"Think Pink!" Charlotte exclaimed. "That's it! He wants to see his girlfriend, La Fanny!"

"That's not La Fanny!" Avery pointed down the sidewalk. Coming from the other direction was Ms. Pink's boyfriend, Zak, with his dog. The rottweiler's brown-and-black coat gleamed in the afternoon sunshine as he pawed at the ground, his tail wagging like a windshield wiper. But when he saw Marty, he let out a low growl and bared his teeth.

Avery and Charlotte backed away from the larger dog, their eyes widening. The huge dog was definitely someone they didn't want to tangle with.

"Brady," the man chided, gripping the leash tighter, "where *are* your manners?"

Charlotte gasped as Marty's fur bristled. Suddenly, the little dude's loud barking rang across the street as he stamped his paws and bared his teeth at Brady.

Avery and Charlotte couldn't help themselves. They started laughing, and so did Zak.

"What in the world is going on out here?" Ms. Pink appeared in the doorway of her shop with La Fanny peering out from behind.

"Hi, Razzberry," Zak said, keeping a firm grip on Brady's leash.

"Marty's acting like he's King Kong!" Avery exclaimed. The tiny dog's fur bristled with fury as he growled and snarled at the big rottweiler. It was like a canine confrontation between David and Goliath! It was all Charlotte could do to keep a grip on Marty's leash. The rottweiler wasn't sure what to do with the little bundle of Marty attitude either. He kept cocking his head from side to side.

But then La Fanny let out a delicate yelp, and Marty jumped straight up in the air. Brady was so freaked out by Marty's gymnastics that he let out this huge whine and cowered behind Zak, trying to make himself as small as possible.

Ms. Pink's lips twitched with amusement. "My, my, what a brave little man you are, Marty!"

"Way to go, Marty!" Avery yelled, gazing with admiration at the little dude. "That dog is five times your size and you're still ready to take him on!"

Charlotte laughed and reached down to calm her pup. "No way is he going to let Brady take away his pink poodle sweetheart!"

Zak scratched Duke behind the ears. "Cheer up, Brady. We'll find you another girlfriend. Don't worry."

Marty stood next to La Fanny as she bent her nose down in a doggy greeting.

"Charlotte!" Avery gasped. "I know why Marty was depressed. The poor little guy was lovesick. Just look at him."

"You're right, Avery," Charlotte exclaimed as she watched Marty jump all over La Fanny. "He thought Brady had stolen her from him."

Marty did a flip in the air, and they all laughed.

"He's his old self again!" Charlotte cheered. She bent

down and hugged Marty so tight, he yipped. "I'm so glad."

"Now that you're all here," Ms. Pink announced. "You just *have* to see what I've done with the store!" And they all trooped inside with the dogs.

"Happy Valentine's Day!" announced the eccentric young shop owner.

Avery definitely didn't care for the color pink as much as Maeve, but she had to admit, Ms. Razzberry Pink had done an amazing job decorating for her favorite holiday. The ceiling inside the store was strung with strands of metallic hearts and lights blinking on and off. Romantic music played quietly while helium heart balloons spun around in the air over a display of Valentine's cards, fresh roses, and chocolates.

"Wow!" Charlotte declared. "Amazing!"

Zak took off his coat to reveal a hot pink T-shirt, then put on a cowboy hat from a stand near the register. "How do I look?" he asked Avery and Charlotte.

"Um, pink?" Charlotte giggled.

"Good!" He produced a box of chocolates from behind his back. "These are for you." He leaned forward and gave Ms. Pink a peck on the cheek.

Meanwhile, Marty and La Fanny were dancing around the display of roses, woofing and nuzzling.

"Why don't we take these crazy dogs out to the park?" Ms. Pink suggested. "I'll just go talk to one of my assistants. I think we all need some fresh air!"

On the way to the park, Zak talked sports with Avery while Brady, named after the famous football player, it turned out, trailed behind. La Fanny and Marty danced ahead of the group, tangling their leashes together at least every five minutes.

Charlotte stared at the box of chocolates Ms. Pink was carrying tucked inside her jacket, and remembered the way Zak had kissed her cheek. *Now I know what it feels like to be kissed!* The thought buzzed inside of her like a bumblebee.

Sharing Secrets

After watching the canine sweethearts chase each other through the snow for fifteen minutes, Ms. Pink and her boyfriend said their good-byes.

"I can't leave the shop for too long on such an important day," Ms. Pink said as she walked away with La Fanny.

Marty tried to follow, but Avery and Charlotte distracted him with some heart-shaped dog treats Ms. Pink had shared.

As the little dude chowed down, tail wagging and eyes bright, Charlotte cleared the snow off a nearby swing set and sat down. Avery plopped down on the swing next to her and pumped her feet back and forth, rising up into the air. "Whee!" she shouted.

"Ms. Pink and her boyfriend are so cute together," Charlotte commented, dragging her feet through the powdery snow.

Avery slowed down a bit. "He's cool, but it's weird he wears pink."

"I know, it's a little matchy-matchy." Charlotte smiled. "But they're perfect for each other . . . besides, he probably just put on the shirt for Valentine's Day."

"Hey, Char." Avery said, suddenly serious, "are you really going to be my adopted sister?"

"Of course!"

"There's something I've been thinking about for a while now . . . it's kind of private."

Charlotte was surprised. Usually, her energetic friend always told everyone exactly what she felt.

"Remember Jason, my friend from Colorado?" Avery leaned off her swing to pack some snow into a ball.

"Yeah," Charlotte wondered where this was going.

Avery threw the snowball as hard as she could, and Marty went barreling after it. "We talked on IM today, and I kind of miss him. Is that weird?"

"That's okay," Charlotte said. "I mean, I miss Nick, and I just saw him this morning!"

Avery laughed. "Really?"

"Oh, yeah." Charlotte sighed. Their kiss was so precious and special and important. *Would it spoil the whole feeling to tell Avery?* But Avery, one of her closest friends, had just shared her feelings, and some part of Charlotte was bursting inside to let hers out as well.

Marty came running back and Charlotte reached down to scratch him behind the ears. *If she really were my sister, I'd tell her.*

"Nick kissed me," she whispered, so quietly Avery had to reach over and pull their swings close together. "He kissed me," she repeated.

"Where?" Avery asked, leaning her head in close to her friend's forehead.

Charlotte pointed to her lips and held her breath, worried that Avery might laugh or say something to make her even more embarrassed. But that didn't happen.

Avery just smiled at her. "Wow, Charlotte! I'm happy for you."

Charlotte's eyes widened. "That's it? I expected you to tease me at least a little bit."

Avery shook her head. "I don't tease about important stuff! Have you told the rest of the BSG?"

"No. You're the only one I've told," Charlotte confessed.

Avery nodded, her expression suddenly serious. "Well, your story is safe with me. I'll take it with me to the grave."

Charlotte giggled. "I don't think you need to do that. Just keep it quiet until I'm ready to share with everyone."

"Sure thing." Avery hopped off her swing and threw another snowball for Marty. But he ran off in the opposite direction.

"What now?" Charlotte shouted, racing after him.

Love Birds?

Marty came to a stop beside a bench. Miss Pierce and Yuri were sharing a steaming cup of tea. Miss Pierce leaned over and patted the little dog's head, then waved to the girls.

"Look at that," Avery whispered to Charlotte. "Are they drinking from the same cup?" The two adults sat close together, and even from where Charlotte stood, she could see the happiness on Miss Pierce's face. And the usually grouchy Yuri was actually smiling. That's something you didn't see every day—a smiling Yuri.

Charlotte just had to know. The mystery had gone on long enough. She wanted to find out what was really going on with her landlady and the owner of Yuri's Fruit Stand.

"I'm going over to say hi," Charlotte said.

"Okay . . ." Avery danced from one foot to the other. "I think I'll head back home. My mom needs my help, and I've got a ton of homework. . . ."

"You still think they're too old, don't you?" Charlotte joked under her breath.

Avery giggled, then scampered off, waving to the adults on the bench. "Bye, Marty!" she shouted. The little dude raced in a circle around Yuri and Miss Pierce, barking happily. It was final: The little dude was 100 percent back to normal!

"Glad to see Marty got his spark back," Yuri pronounced in his funny accent when Charlotte came over to the bench. "See you ladies later? I have fruit to sell," the grocer said, a big smile still creasing his round face.

Charlotte watched him go, confused. "I'm sorry, Miss Pierce. I didn't mean to scare Yuri away."

But Miss Pierce merely patted the bench next to her. "Don't be silly, Charlotte, dear. I'm always happy to see you . . . and you didn't run Yuri off. He has fruit to sell," she said, and laughed.

Charlotte wasn't sure if Miss Pierce was being honest or just trying to make her feel better. The older woman always seemed to be concerned about making the people around her feel comfortable and safe.

Charlotte thought back to the early days when she and her father had moved into an apartment within Miss Pierce's Victorian house. At first, she had been a little afraid of the reclusive landlady, especially when the BSG broke her rules by exploring the Tower and letting Marty stay there. But Miss Pierce didn't get angry. Instead, she allowed the girls to turn the beautiful Tower into their club headquarters. That's just the type of person Miss Pierce was—incredibly kind and welcoming.

Charlotte brushed her concerns aside and sat down on the bench.

"Okay, Miss Pierce. Is there something going on with you and Yuri? Are you two, like, crushing on each other or something?"

Miss Pierce chuckled. "Well, Charlotte, I'm not sure if I would call it *crushing*, but I'll say this: I enjoy Yuri's company very much. He is a kind and gentle man, with a keen intellect and a fascinating personality.

"You know," she whispered conspiratorially. "In Russia, Yuri was a teacher of Russian literature. He knows everything about Tolstoy and all the great Russian writers."

Charlotte wasn't sure who Tolstoy was, but one thing was for sure. Miss Pierce was glowing, and she looked beautiful for an older lady.

But Charlotte still had one question to ask. "Miss Pierce, do you mind that Yuri gets a little grouchy sometimes?"

Miss Pierce stroked Charlotte's hair away from her forehead. "Not at all. Did you know that Yuri loves poetry?

Why, he can recite some of Pushkin from heart!"

"Pushkin?" Charlotte rested her head on Miss Pierce's shoulder.

"A famous Russian poet, my dear. Listen: 'The wondrous moment of our meeting / I well remember you appear / Before me like a vision fleeting / A beauty's angel pure and clear.'"

"Wow." Charlotte breathed in and out, watching her breath cloud in the frost air.

"How do you know if you're in love, Miss Pierce?" she asked suddenly.

It was a question meant to be asked in the middle of the night right before bed, when Mom comes in to tuck you in and plant a comforting kiss on your forehead. *Miss Pierce will just have to do,* Charlotte realized as she inhaled Miss Pierce's perfume, which smelled of green tea and flowers.

Miss Pierce smiled and thought for a while before answering. "I'm not a poet, but I think . . . Pushkin was on the right track, for the most part. Love is in the wondrous moment of meeting and recognizing yourself in someone else."

"What about beauty's angel?" Charlotte asked.

"Well, love goes beyond physical appearance . . . what's most important is the person within: the beauty of the heart. People grow old. Hair fades to gray. We get wrinkles." Miss Pierce pointed to some of the lines on her own face.

"I don't really notice those, Miss Pierce!" Charlotte blurted out.

"Charlotte," Miss Pierce said with a nod, "that's because you already care about me. We always think the people we love are beautiful. But the people you think are beautiful do not always love *you*. It can get very confusing. But that's love."

Charlotte thought of Nick, his smile, the way his eyes lit up when he talked about sports or a new book he was reading. The way he looked at her. The special kiss they had shared after the dance. She thought about the misunderstandings and the confusion, the tears she had cried when she thought he didn't like her anymore. And she knew that whatever there was between Nick and her—it was something she would always keep close to her heart.

One thing was for sure, if astronomers could fall in love with fruit sellers and mutts could fall in love with pink poodles, then she could find someone to love and who would love her back, and so could Katani, Avery, Maeve, and Isabel.

That evening, Charlotte logged on to her computer and found an e-mail from Sophie waiting in her inbox.

```
To: Charlotte
From: Sophie
Subject: Bonjour!


Charlotte, ma cherie, you are the
most fortunate girl! I knew Nick was
honorable boy. I will give you a rose
to celebrate. @}~~~~ (Do you like it?)
I can't believe he kissed you! I only
```

kissed a boy on the cheek once. Do not
worry, your secret is safe with me,
but you can talk to your BSG friends!
They will keep your secret too.
I miss you, Charlotte. Never forget
me.

Bisous,
Sophie

To: Sophie
From: Charlotte
Subject: *Bonjour, Mon Amie!*
Dear Sophie,
I really miss you, too. I wish you
could meet Nick, and all my new
friends. I told Avery about the kiss,
and I felt a little better. Less
crazy, but I am still walking on
air!!!! And Marty is all better too.
He was lovesick over a pink poodle
named La Fanny. They are such a cute
couple!
If you see Orangina, tell him I'm
writing a story about his travels.

Au revoir!
Charlotte

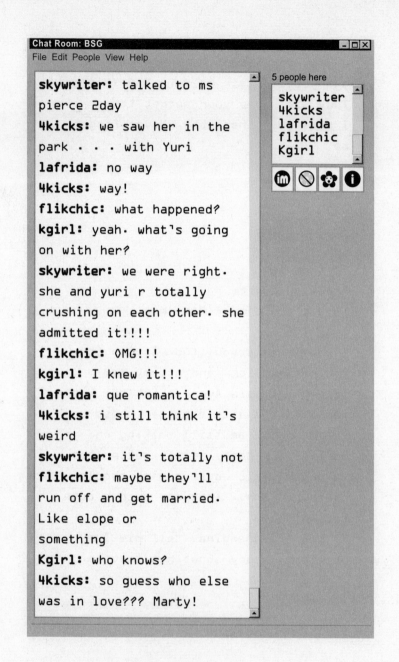

File Edit People View Help

5 people here

skywriter
4kicks
lafrida
flikchic
Kgirl

skywriter: talked to ms pierce 2day

4kicks: we saw her in the park . . . with Yuri

lafrida: no way

4kicks: way!

flikchic: what happened?

kgirl: yeah. what's going on with her?

skywriter: we were right. she and yuri r totally crushing on each other. she admitted it!!!!

flikchic: OMG!!!

kgirl: I knew it!!!

lafrida: que romantica!

4kicks: i still think it's weird

skywriter: it's totally not

flikchic: maybe they'll run off and get married. Like elope or something

Kgirl: who knows?

4kicks: so guess who else was in love??? Marty!

5 people here

skywriter
4kicks
lafrida
flikchic
Kgirl

Kgirl: dogs don't fall in love

skywriter: marty did! he totally stood up to Brady, ms pink's boyfriend's dog

4kicks: ya and brady is the size of a horse with huge teeth and stuff but marty would NOT back down!

kgirl: R U kidding me?

lfrida: i saw that rott-weiler he's giant . . .

4kicks: ya. marty is 1 tough little dude. brady got really scared and hid!

flikchic: OMG!!! I would have loved 2 C that

lafrida: me 2

Kgirl: wtg, marty!!

skywriter: well marty's back 2 his old self. right now he's attacking happy lucky thingy

lafrida: thank goodness

flikchic: im glad hes ok and he wasnt sick

```
┌─────────────────────────────────────────────────────────────┐
│ Chat Room: BSG                                    [_][□][X]   │
│ File  Edit  People  View  Help                                │
│ ┌───────────────────────────────────┬──┐  5 people here       │
│ │ 4kicks: yeah. the poor        │▲│  ┌─────────────────┐      │
│ │ doggy was only lovesick       │ │  │ skywriter     ▲ │      │
│ │ haha                          │ │  │ 4kicks          │      │
│ │ skywriter: ok, gtg            │ │  │ lafrida         │      │
│ │ Kgirl: me 2                   │ │  │ flikchic        │      │
│ │ lafrida: bye every1 this      │ │  │ Kgirl         ▼ │      │
│ │ was a great week              │ │  └─────────────────┘      │
│ │ 4kicks: sure was              │ │  ┌───┬───┬───┬───┐        │
│ │ flikchic: happy valentines    │ │  │🏠│🚫│✿│ⓘ│        │
│ │ day all! <3<3<3               │▼│  └───┴───┴───┴───┘        │
│ └───────────────────────────────────┴──┘                      │
└─────────────────────────────────────────────────────────────┘
```

To be continued . . .

Crush Alert

BOOK EXTRAS

 Love Potion #9 Recipe

 Trivialicious Trivia

 Charlotte's Word Nerd Dictionary

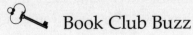 Book Club Buzz

Love Potion #9 Recipe

*Remember to ask for an adult's help and
permission before trying this at home!*

Ingredients:

1 head of red cabbage
1 knife (or blender, or grater)
1 pitcher
1 coffee filter
Several clear plastic cups (or beakers)
Hot tap water
Baking soda (sodium bicarbonate, $NaHCO_3$)
Vinegar (acetic acid, CH_3COOH)

Extra credit:

Antacids, lemon juice, seltzer water, household ammonia . . .
and anything else you want to try!

Directions:

1. Ask an adult for help to chop, grate, or blend the
    cabbage into very small pieces.
2. Place the cut up pieces in a pitcher and cover just
    to the top of the cabbage with very hot tap water.
3. Wait at least fifteen minutes for the water to turn
    pinkish purple. (The longer you wait, the stronger
    your cabbage juice will be.)

4. Pour some of the juice through the coffee filter into a plastic cup (or beaker).
5. Add a teaspoon of baking soda . . . then watch what happens!
6. Next, add some vinegar. Can you turn the juice pink again?
7. Get out some more plastic cups and experiment with the rest of the juice and any "extra credit" ingredients you have at home. How many different colors can you make?
8. Clean up!

The Facts:

Red cabbage juice contains *flavin*, a special kind of pigment molecule that changes color depending on the pH of the liquid. Vinegar is acidic, and baking soda is the opposite: a base. You can actually use cabbage juice to measure the pH of different chemicals using a color scale like this:

Color	pH	
Red	2	acid
Purple	4	
Violet	6	
Blue-Violet	7	neutral
Blue	8	
Blue-Green	10	
Greenish-Yellow	12	base

Crush Alert trivialicious trivia

1. Where is the new boy Trevor from?
   A. Hawaii
   B. California
   C. Florida
   D. Texas

2. What kind of snack does Charlotte knock over at the newspaper meeting?
   A. Cheese Doodles
   B. Pretzels
   C. Chex Mix
   D. Barbecue potato chips

3. What footwear does Maeve ruin in the soccer game?
   A. Pink boots with sparkly fur
   B. High-heeled black boots
   C. Pink-and-white-checked rain boots
   D. Soft pink leather loafers

4. When Charlotte first discovers Marty's illness, where does she find him?
   A. Out on her balcony
   B. In the bathroom
   C. Under her dad's desk
   D. In Ms. Pierce's apartment

5. When Charlotte talks to her Dad about Nick, what show are they watching?
   A. A special about the Serengeti
   B. A documentary about Renaissance France
   C. A romantic comedy
   D. A discovery show about exploring the Great Barrier Reef

6. What do you add to cabbage juice to make it froth with pink foam?
   A. Diet Coke
   B. Baking soda
   C. Vinegar
   D. Tums

7. Which is NOT the title of a song that Riley writes in this book?
   A. "Furniture Boy"
   B. "Valentine Song"
   C. "You, You, You"
   D. "My Girl, My Star"

8. What Valentine's Day craft do Isabel and Kevin teach the kids at the homeless shelter?
   A. Crepe-paper flowers
   B. Pop-up Valentine's Day cards
   C. Painted heart magnets
   D. Heart stamps cut out of potatoes

9. What is the name of Ms. Pink's boyfriend's dog?
   A. Duke
   B. Brady
   C. Washington
   D. Rex

10. What color dress does Charlotte wear to the dance?
    A. Light green
    B. Lilac purple
    C. Periwinkle blue
    D. Rose pink

ANSWERS: 1. B. California **2. D.** Barbecue potato chips **3. A.** Pink boots with sparkly fur **4. C.** Under her dad's desk **5. A.** A special about the Serengeti **6. C.** Vinegar **7. D.** "My Girl, My Star" **8. C.** Painted heart magnets **9. B.** Brady **10. B.** Lilac purple

Book Club Buzz

10 Questions for You and Your Friends to Chat About

1. Maeve pretends to be interested in sports to impress Dillon. Is it a good idea to change who you are just to get someone to like you? What should Maeve have done instead?

2. Marty has to go to the vet because he's "lovesick." Have you ever accompanied a favorite pet to the vet? What happened there? Did your pet get better?

3. Charlotte makes a top-ten list of things to do alone on Valentine's Day. What would your list look like?

4. Maeve makes a winning goal for her soccer team, but falls facefirst in the

mud! How would you feel in her place? What was your most embarrassing sports moment ever?

5. Charlotte finds Riley's personal notebook full of lyrics he wrote. She decides not to read them, and gives it back without telling her friends. Was this a good decision? Have you ever discovered a secret you weren't meant to know? Did you tell anyone or keep it to yourself?

6. Katani asks Reggie to the dance, then talks Charlotte into asking Nick. The plan backfires, but what do you think of Katani's reasons? Would you rather ask a boy to go to a dance with you or wait for him to ask you? Why?

7. Isabel chooses to keep her promise to help out at a homeless shelter instead of going to the dance. Have you ever had to choose between two events happening at the same time? How did you make your decision?

8. The Queens of Mean give Chelsea a hard time at the dance, but both Maeve and Trevor stand up to them. How does it make you feel if someone is picking on one of

your friends? What if the victim is not
a friend, just someone you know? Would
you respond differently?

9. Sophie assures Charlotte that it's okay
   to tell to her friends about her first
   kiss. Do you think a moment like Nick and
   Charlotte's is meant to be kept secret or
   shared with best friends?

10. Charlotte and Avery both confide in their
    parents about boys. Have you ever talked
    to anyone in your family about a crush?
    What happened? How much do your parents
    or siblings know about who you like?

Charlotte's Word Nerd Dictionary

BSG Words

ginormous (p. 133) adjective—*gigantic and humongous*
fantabulous (p. 137) adjective—*fantastic and fabulous combined*
beauteous (p. 160) adjective—*beautiful and gorgeous combined*
awesomest (p. 166) adjective—*most awesome*
fabulosity (p. 170) noun—*fabulousness*
fabuloso (p. 68) adjective—*fabulous*

Spanish Words & Phrases

maravilloso (p. 3)—*marvelous*
abuelita (p. 108)—*grandmother*
chica (p. 145)—*girl*
muy bonita (p. 148)—*very pretty*
mi hermana (p. 149)—*my sister*

mi hija (p. 158)—*my daughter*

que romantica! (p. 250)—*how romantic!*

French Words & Phrases

ma chere (p. 63)—*my dear*

au revoir (p. 64)—*good-bye*

bonjour (p. 67)—*hello*

très magnifique (p. 67)—*very wonderful*

mon amie (p. 67)—*my friend*

bisous (p. 131)—*kisses*

beaucoup de bisous (p. 131)—*many kisses*

ma meilleure amie (p. 222)—*my best friend*

ton amie (p. 222)—*your friend*

Other Cool Words . . .

commiserated (p. 9) verb—*discussed and offered sympathy*

hypocritical (p. 30) adjective—*supporting something one doesn't really believe*

intimidating (p. 32) adjective—*causing fear or a lack of courage*

sepia (p. 35) adjective—*reddish-brown color*

emphasis (p. 38) noun—*added importance*

feistiness (p. 51) noun—*energy or spirit*

lethargic (p. 53) adjective—*having slow and sleepy behavior*

reminisced (p. 61) verb—*remembered*

figment (p. 82) noun—*little piece*

sophisticated (p. 88) adjective—*cultured, grown-up*

pact (p. 93) noun—*promise*

phenomenon (p. 97) noun—*an unusual or extraordinary event*

subtleties (p. 117) noun—*fine differences that are hard to see*

pulverize (p. 125) verb—*to pound into dust*

terrarium (p. 130) noun—*a glass cage for keeping small animals*

nonchalant (p. 186) adjective—*unconcerned*

jubilant (p. 190) adjective—*joyful*

vivacious (p. 200) adjective—*full of life*

pristine (p. 233) adjective—*perfectly neat and clean*

reclusive (p. 246) adjective—*shy*

conspiratorially (p. 246) adverb—*as if planning something together*

Here's an excerpt from the

next adventure,
The Great Scavenger Hunt

*C*harlotte was having a difficult time focusing in Ms. O'Reilly's first period social studies class. She had to keep pretending there was a big red sign in front of her blinking PAY ATTENTION! This was unusual for her, because social studies involved her favorite topic—the adventures of famous people in history!

Charlotte thought whoever had come up with the idea of teaching about such a thing should get a prize or something. But how on earth was she supposed to pay attention to Ms. O'Reilly when her mind was on a different kind of adventure—the surprise adventure that she, Nick, and Chelsea had been planning for weeks. The adventure she was supposed to announce to everyone in five minutes!

Today Ms. O'Reilly was introducing an important research project—the type of thing that would have normally set Charlotte's mind whirring in anticipation, an oral report on a historical figure who was a Massachusetts native.

"I don't want this to be just another research paper," Ms. O'Reilly explained to the class. "I want you to pick a person who means something to you and write about how he or she has left their mark on history."

Charlotte wasn't quite sure who to pick. She loved to write, so perhaps someone like Louisa May Alcott or Henry David Thoreau. Thoreau was one of the first environmentalists, and he wrote about the beauty of nature at Walden Pond, one of her favorite places to go swimming with the Beacon Street Girls. And *An Old-Fashioned Girl* by Louisa May Alcott was one of her favorite books.

Or just maybe she'd pick Benjamin Franklin. He was born in Boston, but then ran off to Philadelphia where he became a statesman, inventor, publisher, and one of the signers of the Declaration of Independence. He also thought the national bird should be a turkey! That was such a hoot. Charlotte really hoped they'd see some wild turkeys on the adventure she had planned. Those big, goofy-looking birds travel in flocks and look like they aren't afraid of anything!

Charlotte glanced over at Maeve, who seemed transfixed by something on her computer screen. Charlotte had to bite her lip to keep from laughing out loud. The sparkly redhead had typed her name followed by a selection of names from the Hollywood yellow pages—Maeve Kaplan-Taylor Jett, Maeve Plume, Mrs. Ontario Plume . . . Jett and Plume were the biggest names in film right now, with their award-winning series of pirate movies.

Charlotte restrained a giggle and turned around, expecting Avery to be staring longingly out the window at the lively eighth-graders having recess outside. But to Charlotte's surprise, Avery's hand was waving in the air and she was pleading, "Ooh! Ooh! Ms. O'Reilly! Right here!"

Ms. O'Reilly smiled. "Yes, Avery?"

"Can I do Tom Brady?"

Isabel, sitting in the desk next to Charlotte, gave her a sly grin and mouthed, *Big surprise!*

Ms. O'Reilly looked pained. "Well, the assignment is to select historical figures from Massachusetts. . . . I am just not sure the Patriots' star quarterback is exactly . . ."

Quick-as-a-whip Avery smartly replied, "Well Tom Brady *will* go down in *sports* history as being the quarterback responsible for two Patriots Super Bowl victories. He's history in the making. Am I right here, people?" Dillon Johnson and some of the boys gave Avery approving cheers and high-fives.

"I'll tell you what, Avery. If you can come up with a compelling argument, then we will see," Ms. O'Reilly offered. "Does anyone else have any suggestions?"

Of course Betsy Fitzgerald's hand shot into the air. Charlotte and Isabel had to stare ahead to keep from from rolling their eyes at each other. Betsy's knack for sounding like a complete know-it-all every time she opened her mouth in class was hard to take seriously.

"I think Paul Revere would be an *exemplary* figure to do a report on, Ms. O'Reilly," Betsy said in her super-confident voice. "My father is a historical re-enactor who plays Paul Revere. Did you know that if it weren't for Paul Revere, there might not even *be* an America? In fact, Paul

Revere was famous in his own right for his silver work *before* his midnight ride. And did you know—"

"Thank you, Betsy," Ms. O'Reilly interjected. "It sounds like you will have ample material for your report."

Charlotte saw a few other kids stifle their giggles. Betsy was smart, all right, and she was famous at Abigail Adams Junior High . . . not so much for silver work or saving America from the British as for her long-winded, show-offy comments in class; the ones that annoyed everyone.

Poor Betsy. Charlotte sighed. She just couldn't help herself. Her brother went to Harvard and Betsy lived in fear of not being able to go there too. The fact that she was only in seventh grade didn't appear to slow Betsy's drive down at all.

Not wanting to be outdone, Danny Pellegrino, also a major fact-chaser, stretched his hand up.

"I have a figure who is just as historical but not as well known as Paul Revere," he announced. "Ms. O'Reilly, you might not have heard of 'Black Sam' Bellamy, but he was a famous pirate whose ship, the *Whydah*, was discovered off the coast of Cape Cod."

Charlotte almost gasped. She totally couldn't believe Danny. He was actually trying to outsmart the teacher!

"Thank you, Danny. And yes, I am familiar with Sam Bellamy. And I think he would be a great figure to research," Ms. O'Reilly agreed patiently.

"Yes, Henry?"

Henry Yurt, aka the Yurtmeister, was class president *and* class clown rolled into a short ball of wit and fuzzy hair. All the Beacon Street Girls, even serious Katani, enjoyed the Yurt's antics. Charlotte couldn't wait to hear what historical figure Henry wanted to choose—probably someone like Bozo the Clown.

Henry coughed loudly and importantly before asking in a serious voice, "Might I do JFK, Ms. O'Reilly?"

Charlotte almost fell off her chair. Henry Yurt, serious? Even Ms. O'Reilly looked surprised. But she smiled broadly. "Why, yes, Henry. President Kennedy would be an excellent person to research. What made you think of him?"

Yurt sat up as tall as he possibly could, leaned forward on his desk, clasped his hands, and explained. "Well isn't it obvious? JFK and I are both super-popular presidents!"

At this, everyone in the class, including Ms. O'Reilly and Betsy Fitzgerald, hooted with laughter. The only one who didn't crack a smile was Anna McMasters, Queen of Mean #1, who used to be Henry's main crush. Anna was still mad at Henry because he dumped her for Betsy Fitzgerald, who dumped *him* a week after the Valentines' Day Dance because she felt the Yurtmeister wasn't dedicated enough to his studies, and Betsy was afraid he might distract her from hers.

"A tragic romance destined for the history books," Yurt had moaned to Charlotte when it happened.

Anna obviously did not find Henry's comment hilarious at all. Instead, she tossed her sunshine-colored hair over her shoulder and primly raised her hand.

Dabbing her eyes, Ms. O'Reilly managed to get out, "Yes, Anna?"

"I call Ben Affleck," Anna stated, seeming extremely proud of herself. "He's from Cambridge, Massachusetts, he's made Oscar-nominated movies set in Massachusetts, *and* I got to meet him at Kiki's house once."

"Try to focus on historical figures please, Anna," Ms. O'Reilly instructed as she raised her eyebrows at Avery, who had burst out laughing.

A movie star? Avery mouthed to Charlotte. Meanwhile, Maeve was scanning her list of movie-star last names, trying to remember if any of *them* were from Massachusetts, too.

As Anna began to object that Ben Affleck *was* histori-cal, Charlotte felt something being crushed into her left hand. It was a note from Isabel. Charlotte, using her best secrecy skills, silently unfolded the note under her desk.

AHHH! How can U stand it? Isn't the big announcement 2day?

Charlotte flipped the scrap of paper over and wrote back:

Yes! Any second now! I just hope everyone likes the idea and signs up. So, so nervous . . .

Iz ripped off another piece of paper, scribbled some-thing, and sent it back to Charlotte.

Chill! Nick Montoya will get the guys to come and you and Chelsea will get the girls. I think this will be the most fun in the history of seventh grade! Maybe I'll even write my research paper on you. ☺ Ha!

Charlotte gave her friend a grateful smile. Isabel was such a sweetheart—she had a real knack for making her friends feel better, no matter how awful the situation. Charlotte was happy to be a part of the Beacon Street Girls. Since she had joined forces with Maeve, Avery, Katani, and Isabel back in the beginning of seventh grade, life had been a blast, and when it wasn't, they were always there for each other "through thick and thin," as her dad always said.

"Charlotte, is there something you'd care to share with the class?" Ms. O'Reilly's voice boomed. "Please come to the front of the room."

Charlotte felt her stomach do a somersault. Oh, no! It was bad enough that she'd been caught passing notes, but now she was going to be humiliated by sharing the note with the whole class. *Well this figures,* Charlotte thought. She should be used to public humiliation by now, considering that she was the class klutz. But she wasn't. Embarrassment was embarrassment no matter how many times it happened!

Face flushed, Charlotte reluctantly made her way to the front of the room with the speed of a hermit crab slowly shrugging out of its shell, and started to unfold the crumpled note.

"Ummm . . ." she started, then noticed the doorknob turning.

"If it isn't the co-captain of the Outdoor Adventure Club herself!" Mr. Moore, their goofy science teacher, strode into the room, a tie full of tiny cows bouncing over his bright purple shirt. "As club adviser, I couldn't be late for the big announcement! Please, Charlotte . . . proceed."

Charlotte gulped back a sigh of partial relief. She wasn't going to be totally humiliated, but she still had to talk in front of everyone. Mr. Moore had helped her, Nick Montoya, and Chelsea Briggs organize the super surprise adventure, so it was nice to have his support.

Suddenly, Charlotte shot Isabel a panicked look.

Luckily, her friend understood, and passed the rolled up poster beside Charlotte's desk up to the front of the room. Charlotte, Nick, and Chelsea had slaved over the poster last weekend.

As Mr. Moore helped her pin the poster up to the front of the room, Charlotte felt her heartbeat slowing at the sound of her classmates' *Cools* and *Wows*. And she hadn't even explained anything yet!

"A treasure map! Cool!" murmured Dillon.

Unlike Maeve, the actress extraordinaire of the BSG, Charlotte was distinctly uncomfortable in the spotlight. *Why did I let Nick and Chelsea talk me into this?* she groaned inwardly as her hands began to tremble.

But then she saw Katani and Isabel nodding encouragingly, Maeve giving her two thumbs up, and Avery looking like she was about to jump out of her seat and start cheering. Her confidence returned.

Charlotte took a deep breath and began her prepared speech. Unfortunately, just as she opened her mouth, she hiccupped . . . loudly . . . *very* loudly.

"Nice one, Char." Yurt clapped as the class began to giggle. Charlotte wanted to slink out of the room. Instead, she looked over at the one person who might rescue her. Maeve sat tall at her desk, then leaned forward in a bowing motion. Charlotte got it. Maeve always said, "Join the laugh! It puts the audience on your side. Even if you've messed up."

So Charlotte, mimicking her friend, grinned, bowed, and started over again. This time . . . no hiccup.

"Next weekend the Outdoor Adventure Club will

have its first official field trip. The club leaders—myself, Nick, and Chelsea—have organized a scavenger hunt."

She paused for applause, but the class was still waiting to hear more. *Have I just bombed?* Worried, Charlotte added in a rush, "It's on Cape Cod, there will be three teams, and the winners will receive an incredible prize!"

"Cape Cod? Awesome!" Dillon called out. "I love the Cape!"

"What's the prize?" shouted Henry.

"Um . . . the prize?" Charlotte glanced nervously at Mr. Moore. The prize part was something she'd just made up on the spot to get people excited. The truth was, she had no idea what the prize would be. For Charlotte, just going on the adventure was prize enough.

"It's a surprise, Henry," Mr. Moore answered quickly. "To be announced at the prize ceremony." Charlotte gave the cow man a grateful smile. She would have to thank him later for coming to her rescue.

"You forgot the best part!" Avery blurted, then clasped her hands over her mouth remembering that this was supposed to be Charlotte's big announcement—not hers.

"Oh yeah!" Charlotte remembered. She couldn't believe she'd forgotten. "The trip is a *two-day* hunt. Which means . . . we'll be spending an overnight someplace cool . . . by the beach!"

There it was—finally, the cheers and clapping. Of *course* people would be excited about a big beachside overnight on the Cape.

Spending a night somewhere other than your normal, old, safe bed is so thrilling, thought Charlotte. And she loved everything about Cape Cod—the beautiful sandy beaches, saltwater taffy, and digging for clams. Before she and her dad moved to Tanzania (then Australia and Paris), they had spent several precious weeks on the Cape. Of all the marvelous places she'd been in the world, the Cape was one that she knew she had to return to. And now she was!

Kids were talking so loudly they could just barely hear the bell for last period ringing. Charlotte felt as though she were walking on air as she packed up her bag.

"Dude! Where do we sign up?" Dillon shouted to Yurt across the room.

"We must approach the captain of adventure!" Henry Yurt held out his arms like a game show host as he trotted up to Charlotte. "Team Yurtmeister is ready to win the jackpot!"

Charlotte pulled out the sheet. "You better sign up sooner rather than later," she warned everyone. "The trip is on a first-come-first-served basis. And you have to bring back a signed permission slip by Wednesday! We are only taking three cars down, driven by teacher chaperones, and space is limited."

That announcement set off a mad scramble as kids tried to be the first to get their name on the list.

"Do we pick our own teams?" Riley Lee asked as he signed his name.

"No, Mr. Moore is organzing them."

"Should we bring history books?" Betsy Fitzgerald asked, just as Danny bumped in front of her. "Who's fact-checking the clues?" he interrupted. "I could help."

Charlotte tried her best to answer all the questions, and she was relieved when Joline and Anna haughtily marched out of the room *without* making any comments *or* signing up. But she really wasn't surprised—nature and the Queens of Mean was not a good mix. Besides, the QOM paid way more attention to their eye makeup than they did to getting their homework in on time. Mr. Moore said that you had to have all your work completed to go on the trip. It was kind of a reward.

As kids continued jostling around the desk, Charlotte noticed Kiki Underwood sprint into the room. *Uh-oh,* she thought. The QOM were out of the picture, but Kiki was a totally different kind of royalty.

"Mr. Moore!" she squealed. "Oh, thank goodness I caught up with you. Listen, it's about that detention you gave me this morning . . ."

Collect all the BSG books today!

#11 Ghost Town
The BSG's fun-filled week at a Montana dude ranch includes skiing, snow boarding, cowboys, and celebrity twins—plus a ghost town full of secrets.

☐ **READ IT!**

#12 Time's Up
Katani knows she can win the business contest. But with school and friends and family taking up all her time, has she gotten in over her head?

☐ **READ IT!**

#13 Green Algae and Bubble Gum Wars
Inspired by the Sally Ride Science Fair, the BSG go green, but getting stuck slimed by some gooey supergum proves to be a major annoyance!

☐ **READ IT!**

#14 Crush Alert
Romantic triangles and confusion abound as the BSG look forward to the Abigail Adams Junior High Valentine's Day dance.

☐ **READ IT!**

Also . . . Our Special Adventure Series:

Charlotte in Paris
Something mysterious happens when Charlotte returns to Paris to search for her long-lost cat and to visit her best Parisian friend, Sophie.

☐ **READ IT!**

Maeve on the Red Carpet
A cool film camp at the Movie House is a chance for Maeve to become a star, but newfound fame has a downside for the perky redhead.

☐ **READ IT!**

Freestyle with Avery
Avery Madden can't wait to go to Telluride, Colorado, to visit her dad! But there's one surprise that Avery's definitely not expecting.

☐ **READ IT!**

Katani's Jamaican Holiday
A lost necklace and a plot to sabotage her family's business threaten to turn Katani's dream beach vacation in Jamaica into stormy weather.

☐ **READ IT!**

Isabel's Texas Two-Step
A disastrous accident with a valuable work of art and a sister with a diva attitude give Isabel a bad case of the ups and downs on a special family trip.

☐ **READ IT!**

FREE Club for you and your BFFs on BeaconStreetGirls.com!

If you loved this book, you'll love hanging out with the **Beacon Street Girls** (BSG)! **Join the BSG** (and their dog Marty) for virtual sleepovers, fashion tips, celeb interviews, games and more!

And with **Marty's secret code** (below), start getting **totally free stuff right away!**

BEACON STREET GIRLS

MARTY $ MONEY™
VIRTUAL RESERVE NOTE

CLUB

BSG®

SECRET CODE
CRU128145

MARTY $ MONEY is **not** legal tender.
MARTY $ MONEY can only be used on
www.BeaconStreetGirls.com to purchase
virtual gifts online for your Club BSG friends
and **cannot** be used to purchase "real world"
gifts at the BSGshop.

MARTY
FIVE DOLLARS

BEACONSTREETGIRLS.COM

To get **$5** in **MARTY $ MONEY** (one per person) go to **www.BeaconStreetGirls.com/redeem** and follow the instructions, while supplies last.